Taken by Nightfall

Mikaela Bell

Contents

Chapter One

"Aria, can you come down here, please?" My guardian, Killian, calls from downstairs.

I put the book I was reading down and hop off the bed before hurrying down the stairs of our farmhouse. My fuzzy socks cause me to slide a little as I stop abruptly. Sitting on the couch in the living room are two strangers. Killian stands off to the side with his brows lowered.

Something tells me I know why they're here.

I don't say anything. I cross my arms and stare at them, waiting for one of them to start explaining.

After a minute, the male, who looks to be in his early forties- although it was hard to tell since fae age slower than humans- stands. He's built like a linebacker with short sandy blonde hair and deep brown eyes.

"Hello, Aria. My name is Ajax, and this is Isabelle." Ajax introduces himself and the female with him.

My eyes move to Isabelle. She looks younger than Ajax, with long chocolate brown hair pulled in a bun and emerald green eyes. Her smile is warm when she looks at me.

"Aria, they are from Nightfall Academy," Killian says gently, moving over to where I stand. I whip my head back and forth; this is not happening.

"No." I grit out.

Ajax raises his eyebrow at me. "No is not an option. Especially not for you."

The back of my neck feels slick with sweat, and my hands tremble as fear rolls through me.

Located in Oxynmire, the capital of Noctem, Nightfall Academy is where the most magically gifted fae are sent to learn magic. I always knew there was a chance I'd have to go, but I had hoped that when I didn't respond to their acceptance letter and didn't show up three weeks ago when the year started, they'd forget about me.

But I guess that's not the case.

It's not that I didn't want to attend Nightfall. I've heard it's the best academy out there to learn magic. But I ignored the letter simply because of Nightfall's location.

"Please, don't make me go there. I would rather have my magic bound."

One of the laws in Noctem is that everyone must attend an academy. It doesn't matter if it's Nightfall they go to. It just has to be somewhere they can be taught how to control their magic. But if a person refuses to attend an academy for whatever reason, they will be forced to have their magic bound.

The process of binding magic is quite simple. Noctem's first king and queen created cuffs out of iron that snap around a person's wrists, effectively cutting the wearer off from their magic.

The thing that makes the cuffs work is the iron in them. Iron is deadly against the fae. It takes our ability to use our magic away, can cause immense pain, and is the only thing that can leave scars on us.

Isabelle stifles a gasp with her hand. Her eyes are wide with horror. "My dear, you know what that means, right? If we bind your magic, we will be sentencing you to a life of servitude."

Oh, that's the other thing about wanting my magic bound. With their magic bound, fae are required to become servants for the wealthy. I don't understand why that is, but it's one of the old laws we still follow.

I know all this, yet I'm willing to pay the price. If it means I don't have to attend Nightfall Academy, then I will choose to be potentially treated no better than the dirt beneath a shoe, beaten every day, and have no magic.

"Why are you so against going to Nightfall Academy?" Ajax asks me. He sits back down on the couch, studying me.

I'm petite, with waist-length wavy blonde hair so pale it's white, wide lavender eyes, alabaster skin, and slightly pointed ears that mark me as fae. The first thing people notice when they meet me are my unusual colored eyes. I have never met another fae with the same eye color as me. Most fae have earth tones for their eye color.

"I don't want to be in the capital, and I don't need to learn my magic," I say.

"Your reasons don't make sense," Ajax argues. I can tell he's getting annoyed with me because his jaw is clenched tight. Tough for him, he annoyed me the moment I saw him in my sitting room.

Killian clears his throat, "I'm sure you know what happened to Aria when she was little. I think that is a good enough reason for not wanting to be in Oxynmire."

"I understand you lost your parents and were kidnapped," Ajax starts. I flinch at the reminder. "But you need to learn your magic. You are an extremely powerful fae."

I don't know the whole story of why my parents were killed. I don't even know who they were. All I know is that someone killed them and then took me. I was missing from six months old to the age of five. I never asked for more details. To me, life started when I came to live with Killian just after turning five. After twelve years, I'm not about to start asking those questions.

I shake my head, "I'm not powerful." I've only felt a spark of magic once since I turned seventeen and gained access to my magic.

A spell is placed at birth to prevent us from using our magic before our seventeenth birthday. It's another law made up by the first king that was never reversed.

Ajax snorts. "You know that's not true. We have the report of what happened a couple of weeks ago."

Ah, that explains why they are here. I had a minor incident two weeks ago, or at least that's what I call it. I was out one night when Felix, a guy I had repeatedly told to leave me alone, hit on me. I had gotten a tad angry when he wouldn't go away. So, when he tried to get handsy with me, I heated my skin, so he burnt his hands when he grabbed me and his chest when I shoved him off. Of course, Felix didn't like this and reported it to the authorities. Such a baby. Anyway, they let me off with a warning this time.

"It was only a little burn, nothing major." I shrug.

"Only a little burn? You gave the male third-degree burns on his hands, arms, and chest!" Ajax explodes. So, maybe it was more than a little burn. But what can I say? I don't like being touched by sleazy guys. "You showed extraordinary magic without being trained."

"What do you mean?" Killian asks. I still remember the smile on Killian's face when I told him what I did to Felix and how he couldn't stop telling me how proud he was of me.

"Aria managed to heat only her skin. She didn't damage her clothes or catch fire in the process. Something like that can take ordinary fae years to master." Isabelle explains.

Huh. I didn't know that.

"When you were born, they tested your power levels before the lock on your magic took hold." Isabelle goes on. I've never heard of them doing a test on me. "The test ranked you higher than the king."

My jaw drops. More powerful than the king? That must be a joke. "That's impossible. No one is more powerful than the king. That's why he is the king!" King Baston's bloodline has always been the most powerful; it's how they became the rulers of Noctem.

"That is usually the case. However, you are an exception. You had two powerful parents. They were second in command to the king for a reason." Isabelle explains.

"Second in command to the king? What are you talking about?" I sputter. No one has ever told me that before.

5

The pair share a look before Ajax speaks. "Aria, what do you know of your situation?"

I shrug again. "Not much. Just that I went missing from six months old to five, and then somehow, I found myself standing with the king on Killian's front steps. He asked Killian to hide me."

"Do you know why the king asked Killian to hide you?" Isabelle asks.

"I figured it was because I was kidnapped," I answer. As far as I know, the person who took me is still out there.

"As we said, they were the king's second in command. Until you were born, that is." Isabelle starts in a soft tone. "Once you were born, a prophecy was told about you. Your parents and King Baston decided it would be best for them to leave their positions as second in command and take you to their summer home in the Bellvista mountains. To protect you."

I sag against the staircase railing. I always assumed I was the reason my parents were dead. But having it confirmed cracks my heart open. I bite my cheek to stop myself from breaking down in front of these people. I will not show them weakness.

One question keeps popping up in my head: What prophecy?

"Someone on the council betrayed them, though." Ajax continues, oblivious to my internal struggle. "The king never found out who. But whoever it was knew you and your parents were at your summer home. The king covered it up, saying that you and your parents died from a demon attack. It wasn't until you were five that he found you again."

"How do you know all this? Why wasn't I told this when Baston brought her to me?" Killian demands. His jaw is clenched tight. He doesn't like to be kept in the dark about things.

I place my hand on his arm to offer him silent comfort. He sighs and wraps his much larger hand around mine.

"We were only given this information before we left. I cannot answer why the king did not inform you." Isabelle answers.

"What does the prophecy say?" I ask the question I've wanted to know since they first brought it up.

Ajax shakes his head. "Only the king and the council know what the prophecy says."

I tuck the new information away for now. I'll deal with it later.

"Wouldn't I be a risk to the king if I study my magic?" I bring the conversation back to the reason they are here. I'll take any reason not to attend Nightfall.

Ajax and Isabelle laugh softly. "No, you won't. The king's son has stronger magic. King Baston is only sitting on the throne until his son finishes his schooling and can assume the role of king." Ajax says.

I'm honestly shocked. It's unheard of for a king to step down when their heir comes of age. Typically, the king will rule until they no longer can.

"What about going to an academy here?" I plead with them.

Ajax shakes his head. "That's not an option for you."

My heart sinks. "I still won't go." I shake my head. "Bind my magic if you must."

I know that I'm being stubborn. I know I don't have a say in the matter, but something about going to Nightfall doesn't sit right with me.

Without a word, I turn, leaving out the back door.

Chapter Two

I sit on the cold, damp earth underneath a large oak tree in the forest that butts up against our house, breathing in the fresh air.

The forest is where I get my best thinking done, where I can relax and let my worries wash away.

I sit alone for almost half an hour, contemplating everything I've learned and what I want to do.

I could suck it up and attend Nightfall Academy or I could work harder to convince them to bind my magic. I even contemplate just running away, but that will only hurt Killian in the long run.

"I think you're making a mistake," Killian says from behind me. I jolt at the sound of his voice. I'd been so lost in my thoughts that I didn't hear him coming up behind me. He joins me on the ground, stretching his long legs out in front of him.

I glance over at the only parent I've known. Killian is tall, with shoulder-length auburn hair he keeps tied back and deep blue eyes. Years of training have kept his muscular form in top shape.

"What makes you say that?" I want to know what he thinks of me attending Nightfall Academy.

"Because I know you. If you had your magic bound, you'd regret it for the rest of your life," Killian says. "You always love learning new things. So why are you letting the fact that Nightfall is in the capital stop you?"

I sit in silence for a minute, contemplating how to respond. "I'm scared," I whisper. I don't like to admit that, even to Killian. "What if they find out I'm there and come back for me? And this news about a prophecy? What am I supposed to do about that?" I worry my lip between my teeth.

"Aria, no one knows who you are now. You don't look anything like you did when you came to me." Killian says gently.

I don't remember anything from the time before Killian. It's like there is a stone wall hiding those memories from me. I don't even know how King Baston found me. My first memory is standing beside the king on Killian's front steps.

I do, however, know what Killian is talking about. When I first came to live with him, I was bone thin. It took months for me even to speak to him. And that's not mentioning the haunted look that was in my eyes. One that spoke of horrors that I can't remember.

Killian was patient with me, taking the time to fatten me up before working on getting me to speak. He never forced me to talk or pushed me to do anything I wasn't comfortable with. Killian is why the haunted look slowly left my eyes, why I have curves in the right places and muscles everywhere else, and why I smile.

"What if someone recognizes my eyes, and it gets back to the council, and they figure out who I am?" My eyes would be the only recognizable thing at this point.

"That's a possibility," Killian agrees. "But don't you want to learn your magic?"

I sigh, tipping my head back to look at the fluffy white clouds rolling by. "Of course I do. I would love nothing more than to use my magic."

"I think it is time to stop hiding. Besides, I'm not sure you have a choice in going." Killian muses, wrapping his arm around my shoulder. I let my head rest against his shoulder. "Also, if you have your magic bound and they find you, you'd never be able to fight them off. I know I've trained you in self-defense for years, but against magic, you're helpless."

I know if I walk into the house and try to tell Ajax and Isabelle to bind my magic again, they won't listen. Instead, they will drag me to Nightfall Academy, kicking and screaming the whole way. It's just that I have this feeling in the pit of my stomach that going to the academy is a bad idea. I felt it when the letter arrived and felt it again today.

But maybe Killian's right. Maybe it's time to stop hiding. Maybe that gut feeling is just nerves.

"Okay. I'll at least hear them out. I'm not promising I won't still fight them, though."

"I only ever want you to be happy." Killian stands, stretching his hand out to help me stand.

I throw my arms around him, holding him close. "Thank you," I mumble into his chest.

Ajax is tapping his foot from impatience when Killian and I return. I don't care how annoyed Ajax is; I want some questions answered first.

"What can you tell me about Nightfall Academy?" I ask when I sit down in front of them in one of the matching oversized navy couches. Killian takes the open spot beside me.

The living room is cozy, with warm wood floors, cream walls, and two oversized couches in front of a large fireplace. Bookshelves are built into the wall, framing the fireplace and adding to the cozy feeling.

Isabelle beams, clearly pleased with my question. "You will learn to control each element: earth, air, water, and fire. You will also learn basic healing, potion-making, history, and beginner magic. There are other specialty classes as well. Such as defensive magic, combat, art, politics, advanced healing, and etiquette. Along with options to learn any specialty powers."

"Specialty powers?" I question.

"If you can read emotions, speak with animals, or have shape-shifting abilities, for example. We have staff who can train you." Ajax looks at me like he expects me to tell him I have one of these specialty powers. I don't say anything, knowing none of those apply to me. I'm nothing special.

"What if I don't hold all the elements?" I ask them. Not all fae have the ability to weld all four elements. Many can only control one or two. And there are some who have all the elements, but their magic isn't strong.

I've only ever felt my fire magic that one time. Maybe that's all I have.

"My dear, as we said, you are an extraordinarily gifted fae. You hold all the elements." Isabelle tells me. "That's another reason you have a spot at Nightfall Academy. Only the strongest, most magically gifted, attend.

11

Everyone else will attend other academies spread throughout the kingdom."

Well, there goes my excuse about not being strong enough.

I take a minute to ponder everything they've said. The pros are that it's the best academy out there and they offer a good range of classes. I'll be able to keep up my combat skills while learning defensive magic to go with it. The cons are that I'll be leaving the only home I've ever known and living in Oxynmire, the one place I'd rather never set foot in.

"Can I think about it?" I finally ask them.

"No, I'm sorry. But you must decide today." Isabelle's eyes are full of pity. At least she has the decency to feel bad, unlike Ajax, who glares at me.

"Is it safe for Aria to go to Nightfall Academy? You just said that it was someone on the council that kidnapped her. What makes the capital a safe place for her?" Killian asks. Even though he thinks it's time for me to stop hiding, his protective instincts are kicking in, needing to ensure it's safe for me.

"Aria shouldn't encounter any council members if she stays on the academy grounds. They would be the only ones to recognize her." Ajax explains.

I look at Killian, silently asking him what to do. I know they are sugarcoating everything. Making me believe I have a choice in the matter. But I know they don't plan to leave without me. Killian dips his head in response, telling me I should do it.

"Okay, I'll go. On one condition. I want to know about my parents."

I've never asked questions about my parents, and I was content not to open that wound. But now that I've learned something about them today, it's created this desire to learn everything I can about them.

"That's not possible." Ajax shakes his head.

"What about at least their names?" I plead with them.

"I'm sorry, but we don't know their names," Isabelle tells me gently. "Only the king and the council would know."

"How can you not know their names?" I run my hand through my hair in frustration. Killian reaches over and squeezes my shoulder in comfort.

"The king removed all records of your parents and you when they were killed. On paper, you and your parents don't exist." Ajax explains. His voice has lost some of its edge, coming out softer.

Tears pool in my eyes, threatening to spill over. All I want is their names, to have one small piece of them. But I can't even have that.

"So, will you come with us?" Ajax asks. The willingly goes unsaid, but I hear it all the same.

I nibble on my lip, thinking everything through again. "Fine." I finally say after a few minutes. "I'll go."

Chapter Three

I stand in front of the only home I have ever known with my bags packed at my feet. Turning, I watch Killian walk out of the house to meet me at the bottom of the steps.

A chill races down my spine as deja vu overwhelms me.

Twelve years ago, we stood in this exact spot. Back then, King Baston begged Killian to take me in, protect me, and hide me from the realm. Now, Killian is here to say goodbye, not greet me.

"This isn't goodbye." Killian tries to smile, but it comes out sad. "I'll see you every winter and summer break, and when I visit the capital on business. We can talk on the phone whenever you want."

We have phones, cars, and planes, all the same technology the human realm uses. But unlike theirs, ours runs on magic. The crystals used are infused with magic, giving our technology power. Even our electricity is a form of magic.

Killian doesn't have to travel too often for his job since he trains soldiers and makes weapons for Noctem. He's earned the title of weapons master for producing the highest quality weapons and the most well-trained soldiers.

We have a mini version of the castle barracks beside the farmhouse, where Killian works. The soldiers he trains stay in there as well, rather than stay in the house with us. Killian only has to travel when he delivers weapons to different army outposts.

This will be our first time apart for more than a day.

"I know." I sigh as I shift on my feet. "It's just this all feels unreal. Like I am going to wake up any moment and find out it was some bad dream." I sniffle, trying to keep the tears in for a little longer.

I don't often cry anymore, but today has taken a toll on my emotions. Leaving Killian is proving to be one of the hardest things I have ever had to do.

I glance over to where Ajax and the driver, Hale, are loading my bags into the back of the SUV. Isabelle stands off to the side, trying to give me privacy to say my goodbyes.

"Come here," Killian pulls me into one of his bone-crushing hugs. I sag into his warmth. "Always remember how much I love you and how proud I am of the young lady you have become. You will excel at this, just like everything else you put that stubborn mind to." A few tears escape, sliding down my face. My chest aches the longer he holds me.

Gods, why does this hurt so much? Why is it so hard to leave him? It's not like I'm never going to see him again.

"You were the one bright spot in my life when things got dark for me," Killian whispers into my hair.

Killian's life has been full of tragedy. But the worst part for him was when he lost his wife and unborn child in a demon attack.

Demons, nasty creatures with bat-like wings and claw-tipped hands, are barbaric. They slip into our realm through rifts, wreaking havoc everywhere they go. The rifts they use to enter our realm are simply doorways they create with magic. We can create them, too, but we tend to stick to our own realm.

We never know when a rift will open or where. But when they do, hordes of demons come through.

The attack happened out of the blue one evening when Killian and his wife were walking home from the village. They were nearly home when a rift opened in front of them. Never without a sword, Killian was ready when the first demon ran at him. He fought hard to keep them back, but there were too many of them for just one person to take on. Killian shoved his wife behind him, worried for their unborn child, and told her to run home and get the soldiers. He was already getting weak from fighting them off for so long. But before she could run, one of the Demons slipped past him and drove its talons through his wife's heart, killing her and his unborn child instantly.

Killian said he felt the blow as if the demon had stabbed him through his own heart. The Demons took advantage of his pain. They beat him and sliced their talons. They toyed with him, bringing him to the brink of death but not killing him. Killian only survived because the soldiers he was training at the time heard the commotion and came running to help.

It took months for Killian to heal. And even then, it took him a lot longer to recover mentally. He blamed himself for a long time, thinking there was something he could have done differently.

Killian had just been released from the healing center when King Baston asked him to care for me. At first, Killian said no, too lost in his grief to imagine taking care of a child. But King Baston wouldn't take no for an answer, knowing that Killian needed me as much as I needed him. So, when Baston showed up with me beside him, Killian said it took one look in my lavender eyes to know he couldn't refuse. It was like he was being given a second chance at happiness.

"Thank you for everything you have done for me," I say around the lump in my throat. "I'll text and call as often as possible, and I expect to see you the next time you are in Oxynmire." I force myself to let go of Killian.

"I love you," I tell. My feet drag as I walk away from my home and enter my next adventure. An adventure I'm not sure I want to take.

The journey from Lockwood, where I grew up, to Oxynmire, is a week by car. There are no planes from Lockwood to Oxynmire. The town closest to us, Listra, has one, but flying is very expensive. As much as Nightfall Academy wants me to attend, they aren't willing to pay for a plane ticket to get me there.

When I asked Isabelle why we weren't portaling to the academy, she told me neither she nor Ajax had the ability.

Portaling is a rare ability that only a few fae have mastered. When someone can create a portal, they have the ability to travel from wherever they are to any destination of their choosing. They only have to look at a map to be able to select where they would like to go. However, it takes an extraordinary amount of magic to do, and it can potentially drain the person creating the portal.

Since neither can make a portal and we aren't taking a plane, I'm stuck in a car for a week with three strangers.

We've been traveling during the day and staying at small hotels at night. Luckily, we're on the last stretch of the trip. I am looking forward to getting out of this car more than arriving at the academy. I have to sit in the back with Isabelle, who constantly talks, while Ajax sits up front with Hale. Occasionally, he switches places with Hale to give him a break.

I study Hale, who is currently driving. He looks around the same age as Ajax, with close-cropped chestnut hair, deep brown eyes, and stubble coating his jaw. Hale only speaks when spoken to, and even then, he doesn't respond with more than a few words. He is currently my favorite person in the car.

"We should be arriving around dusk. Do you have any questions about the academy?" Isabelle asks.

She has been trying to talk to me for a while now. But I really don't want to talk. I don't particularly like talking to people on a good day, especially when they are strangers. I prefer to be left alone, content to not let anyone get close to me. Killian is the only person who managed to get past my defenses.

I've always had the feeling that if I let people in, it will only lead to heartbreak. I don't know if that comes from something that happened while I was missing or some other reason. Either way, I stick by it.

"Not really." I decide to reply. Knowing that if I don't, she will continue to try and talk to me anyway. "I know I'm here to learn to control my magic. What else is there to know?"

"It may seem as if you are only there to learn about controlling your magic, but there is more to it. You have other classes besides magic that are just as important. The first year is about control. After that, it is about honing and expanding those skills."

"Are you saying I only need to attend the academy for a year, then I can go home?" I ask. Excitement thrums through me. I can't believe it. Instead of the four years I've been dreading, I'll only have to stay for one. I can handle one year.

"Now, don't get too far ahead of yourself," Isabelle chuckles. "The law states that you must attend for all four years."

"Oh." The excitement I felt only a moment ago drains in a flash.

Turning away to watch the scenery go by, I slide my headphones in and block everyone out for the rest of the drive.

Chapter Four

As we enter the city limits, the setting sun bathes Oxynmire in a golden glow.

Having never been to the capital, I didn't know what to expect. But it wasn't this.

Nestled between two mountains, Oxynmire is spread throughout the valley, with the castle at the peak, overlooking the city. The houses are painted in bright colors, giving the city a cheery feel.

The castle, made from black stone so shiny it looks like glass, is much more imposing than I had expected. It's enormous, spanning the entire width between the two mountains and reaching so high into the sky the turrets disappear into the clouds. It would be ominous if not for the large windows everywhere. The windows soften the castle's look and make it seem more open. Finishing it off is a curtain wall surrounding the castle, adding a layer of protection for the royal family.

Hale turns the car left, leading us away from the city and further into the mountains. He drives through the dense forest for a few minutes before the trees thin out, and Nightfall Academy comes into view.

I sit forward, pressing my body between the two front seats for a better look.

Like the rest of Oxynmire, Nightfall is nothing like what I thought it'd be.

Nightfall Academy is an exact replica of the castle. The only difference is it's about half the size. Its structure is made from the same dark, glittering stone, with four towers and ivy climbing up the sides. A flag flies from the top of the towers with the academy's logo: a mountain with a symbol representing each element above it. The grounds are fenced in, with a large lake to the right.

Nerves make my stomach roll and my heart race. I try to breathe, but it's like my lungs have stopped working properly. No air wants to enter.

What was I thinking? I can't do this. I can't attend Nightfall and be in the Oxynmire.

I feel like I'm going to be sick. "I've changed my mind." I blurt out as we drive through the gates.

Ajax turns around in his seat, giving me a stern look. "You don't have a choice. We were trying to be polite earlier, but you were always going to be attending Nightfall Academy."

I stare at him with my mouth slightly open. I hadn't been expecting him to tell the truth. I thought maybe they would at least try to make me feel better. Not tell me, too bad, you are attending whether you want to or not. At least, that's how I interpret Ajax's words.

"No, take me home," I say once I regain my composure. I cross my arms over my chest, giving Ajax my best glare. The one that Killian usually knows, I mean business.

"Aria, I'm sorry, but we have our orders. We were told not to leave without you. You must attend Nightfall Academy. The king has ordered it." Isabelle says, placing her hand on my shoulder.

I shrug her off. I don't want her comfort. I just want to go home. "This is bullshit."

The nauseous feeling has spread since I left Lockwood. Now my skin feels itchy, and my head pounds too. Everything in me screams to leave and run away while I still have a chance. Something about being at Nightfall doesn't sit right with me. A feeling I wish I had listened to more before getting in the car.

Hale drives around the bend, stopping in front of the large steps leading inside Nightfall. Everyone steps out of the car, but I don't move, half hoping they won't make me go if I don't get out.

Isabelle ducks her head back into the car. "I understand you are upset. But you need to be here."

I want to demand they take me home. But they haven't listened so far, and I doubt they'll start now. I'll have to think of a plan to leave the academy on my own. Because there is no way I'll be staying here. Not when everything in me is telling me to leave.

With a sigh, I slide out of the car as a young male comes bounding down the front steps.

As the male comes up to greet me, I can't help but notice how handsome he is. With copper hair that falls into deep blue eyes, his face is soft and boyish, making me think he's probably my age or a year older.

"Welcome to Nightfall Academy." His lean frame towers over me. But the broad smile on his face makes him less intimidating. "My name is Nox, and I am here to help show you to your accommodations."

I have to tilt my head up to look him in the eyes. Although that isn't uncommon for me, I am unusually short. Most fae are gifted with long, beautiful legs; I somehow missed that gene.

"Thank you. My name is Aria," I reply softly. Just because I'm upset about being here doesn't mean I won't be polite to him. Killian taught me better manners than that.

"Right this way." He says with a flourish of his arm, directing me up the steps. "The dorms are located on the west side of the building. Hale will follow along behind us with your belongings."

I don't bother waving goodbye to Ajax and Isabelle.

"Once I show you to your rooms, I'll escort you to the headmaster's office. He'll explain how the academy works and determine your class schedule and books." Nox explains as he pushes open the grand oak doors.

My jaw drops.

The inside is nothing like I was expecting. In my mind, it was going to be all stone and cold feeling. Instead, it has high ceilings, deep forest green walls, dark wood floors with rich brown rugs, and large glass chandeliers. The interior gives off the feeling of walking in a forest.

I scramble to catch up to Nox, already walking up the stairs. The stairs go up four flights, but Nox stops on the first-floor landing and turns left. I look around to see a little sign above the archway, marking it as the west wing. The deep colors continue on the second floor, with the same deep wood floors, brown rugs, and navy-painted walls. Portraits of previous headmasters hang throughout the hall.

"Your rooms are the second to last one on the left of this hall, number 105," Nox says.

"You keep saying rooms, as in multiple," I comment.

"Every student gets a bedroom, a bathroom, and a small sitting room."

"That seems a little excessive." I muse.

"I guess it would be if you are not used to it." Nox agrees with a chuckle. "This was the first king and queen's castle before the Blackwell line took the throne and decided they wanted to be closer to their citizens. King Alexander Blackwell was the one who converted it into an academy. He left the rooms set up the same way since the school is reserved for the most magically gifted fae."

Well, I guess that explains why it reminded me of the castle and the name. Noctem is another word for Nightfall. It only seems fitting that they named the academy after the kingdom.

I don't get to comment because we've arrived at room 105. Nox unlocks the door and steps aside, letting me enter first.

I take a hesitant step inside.

The sitting room is cozy, with its walls painted sapphire and fluffy cream rugs covering the wood floors. In the center of the opposite wall is a marble fireplace with floor-to-ceiling windows overlooking the mountains on either side. A butter-soft cream leather couch faces the fireplace, with two matching chairs on either end and an oak coffee table in the middle.

I walk over to the only other door in the room. Pushing it open, I find the bedroom. The room holds a four-poster bed big enough to fit multiple people, two oak nightstands, and the same rugs covering the floors. The walls are painted a soft gray, with the wall behind the bed depicting the night sky. The wall on the right-hand side of the bed is made up of floor-to-ceiling glass doors that lead out to a small balcony with the same view of the mountains.

Turning left, I find the huge bathroom. A freestanding copper tub sits beside the large glass shower, with a marble vanity across from it. The cream walls and black tile floors add to the luxuriousness of the room.

At the end of the bathroom is a walk-in closet the size of my room at home.

I shake my head at how ridiculous this place is.

I didn't live in a cupboard at Killian's, but my room at home was nothing like this. This is too much.

I leave the bathroom, heading to the glass doors. The mountains go on for miles, with a waterfall in the distance.

At least while I'm stuck here, I'll still be surrounded by nature.

"If you would like a minute to settle in before I show you to the headmaster, please say so," Nox says from behind me.

I startle. I'd forgotten he was even here.

"That obvious?" I try to joke. However, the laugh that accompanies it feels brittle.

"Not to everyone, but I have the gift of reading people's emotions, and I can sense that this is very overwhelming for you." He tells me gently.

So, Nox is one of those faes that Isabelle mentioned as having special abilities. I don't know how I feel about someone reading my emotions without my knowing.

"If it will make you feel better, I don't go around reading people's emotions. I only know how you are feeling now because you are projecting it. When a person feels a strong emotion, it is harder to conceal. Meaning I will sometimes pick up on it without meaning to." Nox explains.

Knowing he isn't doing it on purpose does make me feel better.

"I don't know your story, but the academy is truly a good place. I'm in my second year, and I was terrified my first few days here, but once I settled in, this place became my home. It will get better." Nox moves to stand beside me.

I get a good feeling from Nox. It's the same feeling I get when I'm around Killian. "I don't want to be here," His calm presence makes me decide to be honest with him.

Nox cocks his head to the side. "Why not?"

I continue to look out the glass doors, not meeting his eye. "I don't like the capital."

In the reflection, I watch Nox furrow his brows in confusion.

"Why didn't you attend an academy from where you are from?" He asks.

I sigh, "Because I wasn't given a choice. The options I had were to come here or have my magic bound. Even then, those choices were an illusion."

Nox inhales a sharp breath. "That doesn't sound right. Ask headmaster Nickolas when I take you to him. I'm sure there is some mistake."

"There is no mistake." I turn to look at him. "The king gave the order."

Nox is speechless. He keeps opening and closing his mouth, trying to think of something to say to me. "I-"

"Please don't." I hold up my hand. I know he is going to apologize, and I don't want to hear it. I need to get this day over with and get some sleep. Hopefully, in the morning, I can figure out a way out of here. "I am ready to go see the headmaster now."

Chapter Five

Nox leads me back down the stairs and turns right. He stops at the end of the hall in front of a wooden door with a glass window that reads "Headmaster."

He raps his knuckles on the door before opening it without waiting for a reply.

"Sir, I have the new student here to see you," Nox says into the room.

"Send her in. Thank you, Nox." A deep voice answers.

Nox steps back, leaving the door for me to enter. But I can't get my feet to move. My muscles have locked up, refusing to respond to my commands as panic threatens to overwhelm me.

Why am I so scared? It's just the headmaster.

I have nothing to fear from him. I don't even know him. But it doesn't stop the panic running through my veins, making my hands shake and sweat trickle down my spine.

Nox gives me a little push on the center of my back to get me moving. His calm demeanor makes my feet move.

The headmaster's office looks more like a library than an office. One wall is lined with bookshelves, with books spilling out and onto the floor. The other wall has more bookshelves but is broken up by a fireplace. Two chairs in chocolate brown face the fireplace with a low table between them. In the center of the room is a large mahogany desk with paperwork neatly stacked to one side.

"Good evening, Aria, and welcome to Nightfall Academy. I am head-master Nickolas." The male behind the desk snaps me out of my perusal of the office. His warm smile matches the warmth in his brown eyes. "Please have a seat." He pointed to the chairs in front of his desk.

I cross my arms over my chest and scowl at Nickolas as I sit. I can't help it. When I agreed to attend the academy, I didn't think being in Oyxnmire would bother me so much. But boy, was I wrong.

Nickolas sighs, running his hand across his short chestnut hair. "I spoke with Ajax and Isabelle, and they made me aware that you do not wish to be here."

"I don't," I bite out. "I would rather have my magic bound at this point. I shouldn't be here." I try to hold my anger in. It's not his fault I'm being forced to attend. That's on the king.

"I'm sorry to hear that. But you must learn your magic."

I throw my hands up in the air. I am tired of only getting half the answers from everyone. "Why is it so important for me to learn my magic?"

"Because of the prophecy," Nickolas says quietly like he is afraid of someone overhearing him.

I suck in a sharp breath. "You know about that?" I whisper. "Do you know what it says?"

Nickolas shakes his head. "I was only told you must be taught how to control your magic." He tells me. "I understand that being in the capital would be hard for you. But there's nowhere else you can learn your magic." His eyes are full of pity.

I don't want pity; I want answers.

I sigh. "I just want to get this over with. Learn my magic and leave."

Nickolas nods his head in understanding. "Let's discuss your classes then." He says, moving forward with the meeting. "You are automatically enrolled in all four elemental magic classes, potion making, basic magic, history, and healing. Are there any other courses you think you would like to take?"

"Isabelle mentioned defensive magic. Is that a possibility? Or combat classes?"

"I don't see why that would be an issue." Nickolas flashes me that same warm smile. "You can take defensive magic with Ajax, and I will have you enrolled in combat training as well. Will you need the basic course, or has Killian been teaching you a few things?" He asks with a knowing glint in his eyes.

"No, the basics will not be necessary." A slight grin works its way past my anger.

"Very well. Everything is in order for you to begin classes in the morning. There are uniforms in your closet, along with clothes for combat class. In addition, your books, class schedule, and a grounds map will be in your sitting room when you return. Breakfast begins at six and ends at seven forty-five, with classes beginning at eight." Nickolas explains.

"Now we only have one rule here that is very important." I sit up straighter at the stern tone of his voice. "Under no circumstances should you use magic on a fellow student outside the classroom. Anyone found doing so will be expelled."

"I understand," I respond. I kept that bit of information in mind. Just in case I need to find another way to leave.

Nickolas stands from his chair. "That is all for tonight. Nox will show you back to your room. Have a good night, and good luck on your first day."

I dip my head in response as I stand from my chair. Exhaustion has set in, making my body feel heavy. I haven't slept well since leaving home.

"Oh, one other thing. I suggest you don't mention who you are."

"Sir?" I stop and turn back to face Nickolas. His mouth is turned down slightly and his warm eyes look sad.

"It's just that it would be wise if everyone only knew you as Aria Umbra. It may not end well if word gets back to anyone on the council that you are here."

"You don't have to worry, sir. I don't know my original last name. I have only ever known it as Umbra." I say with a small smile. I don't mind; I like being an Umbra. However, knowing my parents' last names would be nice. Just add that to the long list of things I don't know.

Nickolas gives me a sad smile. "Maybe someday I will be able to tell you."

With that parting note, I leave the office to find Nox waiting for me to escort me back to my rooms.

Chapter Six

As I gather my books for my classes the following day, there is a knock on the door.

"Good morning, Aria," Nox says with a bright smile as I open the door.

Nox is also in uniform, wearing a white button-up shirt–the school logo on the breast pocket–untucked, black pants, and a black tie. The only difference between us is I'm wearing a mini straight plaid black skirt with knee-high socks and my combat boots. There were heels, flats, and loafers in the closet, but I opted for the comfort of my own shoes.

"Good morning. Are you always this cheery in the morning?" I ask with a slight laugh, unable to help myself. Nox is charming and knows how to make me smile. Something that only Killian is usually able to do.

"Only when I look at a pretty face first thing." He says with a wink. I give him a slight shove as I step out to lock my door.

"I thought since it is your first day, I would walk you to breakfast and show you where your first class is." He tells me as we head down to the grand hall where they serve meals.

"Thank you. I'd appreciate the help." I reviewed my class list and map last night when I returned to my rooms. However, I still feel like I'm going to get lost.

Nox explains the ins and outs of Nightfall Academy as we walk the short distance from my room to the grand hall. I'm grateful to have Nox helping me out.

I decided last night to give the academy a few days before deciding what to do. My best options for leaving are either getting kicked out or running away. But I promised Killian I would try. And I'm not someone who breaks my promises.

I'm pulled out of my thoughts as we walk through the archway leading to the grand hall. My mouth parts slightly. The ceiling draws my attention right away. It is painted like the night sky, with four massive chandeliers making the stars on the ceiling appear to glow.

Nox continues to lead me to the buffet set up along the room's border. There is every type of breakfast food imaginable spread out in the stations.

"They serve the best food here," Nox tells me as he hands a tray to me. I pick eggs, toast, sausages, to pile onto my tray, before grabbing a coffee.

After we have our food, Nox leads me to an open table further toward the back.

As I sit down, I feel a tugging sensation in the center of my chest. Frowning, I rub the spot. It feels like my soul is trying to lead me somewhere.

Odd, I've never felt anything like this before. I shrug off the feeling. It's probably nothing, anyway.

As soon as I dismiss the feeling, someone else's power dances along my skin. It feels like the sun beating down on me during a hot summer's day.

My head snaps up, seeking out the power, when I see one of the most gorgeous males I've ever laid eyes on walk in. My mouth goes dry, and my heart skips a beat.

He's tall, even for fae standards, with hair so black it shines blue in the light, a sharp jaw, and coils of muscles. But it's his eyes that pull me in. They're like two pools of liquid gold. I've never seen eyes like that before.

The power I felt dance along my skin is unmistakably his. It pours off him in waves. That tug in my chest grows frantic.

The male stops abruptly by the breakfast bar, whipping his head around the room. He searches wildly for something.

He freezes when his eyes land on my lavender ones. His expression is unreadable, but he doesn't look away from me. Just like I don't look away from him, his golden gaze holds me captive.

Another male comes up behind him, shoving him in the arm and breaking the spell between us. The first male's eyes turn cold before he shakes his head and marches over to get breakfast.

Everyone instantly jumps out of his way, almost like they are scared of him.

I have to shake my head to clear it. What the hell was that?

Nox glances in the same direction, finding what caught my attention. "Ah, I see you have spotted the prince," Nox chuckles.

"Prince?" I choke out. That would explain the power I felt coming from him. I turn my wide-eyed stare back to Nox.

"Yes, that is Prince Jace Blackwell."

We never had a TV in our house, and I wasn't allowed to use social media for safety reasons. So, I didn't know what the prince looked like before today. He's more handsome than I imagined him to be.

"Why does the prince go here? Shouldn't he have private tutors or something?" I rub my sweaty hands along my skirt.

I wasn't expecting to attend the academy along with the prince.

"The law states that everyone must attend an academy when they turn seventeen. That includes the prince." As Nox explains, the prince and three other guys walk over to where we are sitting. My heart beats faster, and the tugging feeling returns.

Jace is even more attractive up close. I can see now that his eyes are pure gold. There's not a speck of any other color in them. His nose is perfectly straight, and his thick, dark brows are pulled together as he stares at me. It's the only emotion on his otherwise expressionless face.

My mouth feels like the desert.

I can't be sitting with a prince. I'm trying to avoid attention, not get more of it. It's too late now, though, because they've already reached us.

"Morning, Nox. Who is your new friend?" One of the prince's friends asks as they take the open seats at the table. The prince keeps his eyes on me as he settles in.

"Morning Theon. This is Aria Umbra. She is starting the academy to-day." Nox tells Theon. "Aria, this is Theon, Chase and Carter-who are twin's if you couldn't tell-and, of course, our prince, Jace." Nox introduces the guys to me.

Theon has short, warm brown hair with deep emerald eyes. Meanwhile, the twins have longer golden blonde hair and sea-blue eyes.

"Nice to meet you," I say, trying to be polite. But I really just want to run away from them. They all exude power. None more than Prince Jace, though. His power has moved from dancing around me to coiling tight against my skin. I have no idea if he is doing it on purpose or if he has any idea it is happening.

"Umbra?" Prince Jace's voice is like music to my ears. It is low and gruff while still being smooth. I have the urge to listen to him talk for hours. "Any relation to Killian Umbra?"

His question snaps me back into the conversation.

"Oh, um, yes. Killian is my guardian." I say quietly without meeting his eyes.

"No way, Killian is a legend!" Carter exclaims.

"What was it like growing up with him? Did you get to go with him when he traveled?" His twin, Chase, butts in. They both lean across the table from their spots beside Jace. Excitement lighting their eyes.

I fidget in my seat from the attention. "I never went with him. But he would always bring a little trinket back for me."

For the rest of breakfast, the guys pepper me with questions about Killian, wanting to know everything about the notorious weapons master.

Jace stays silent, keeping his golden eyes locked on me instead. His attention sends an unexpected warmth to spread through me.

But it doesn't matter how he makes me feel warm or how my heart flutters in his presence. Because he's the prince, the one person I should do my best to avoid during my time at Nightfall.

Chapter Seven

I stand outside in the gardens, away from the others, waiting for earth elemental class to begin.

I've been the subject of conversation since Nox left me to go to his class. The other students have a lot to say about me behind their hands but nothing to say to me. I'd try to go and talk to them or smile to seem more friendly, but I'd rather it be this way.

Even though I had no problem talking to Nox and his friends at breakfast, I don't typically do well in social situations. I find my anxiety always rises, and that old fear of trusting people resurfaces.

"Good morning, class!" Says a petite lady with light brown hair pulled into a tight bun and soft green eyes. According to my class information, her name is Candice.

"Today, we are going to work on growing individual flowers. First, I want you to kneel and press your palms to the damp earth. From there, I want you to picture a flower and infuse your magic to make it grow." Candice explains.

She makes it sound so easy. But since I haven't felt any earth magic since my seventeenth birthday, I doubt it will be.

"I know you are a month behind, Aria, but give this exercise a try, and if you can't do it, we will go back to the basics," Candice says as she passes by.

Willing to at least give it a go, I kneel on the ground with the rest of the students. Resting my palm against the damp soil, I close my eyes and think of a single red rose.

A warm tingle starts at my palm before spreading up my arm.

A gasp beside me has my eyes flying open.

Over a dozen red roses sprout from the ground in front of me. Each one is perfect, with their petals open wide and their scent permeating the air.

Instead of feeling joy that I was able to use my magic, I felt panic. I was supposed to only create one rose, not a dozen. What will Candice say when she sees I didn't follow her instructions?

I want to rip out the extra roses. But it's too late.

"Well done, dear. It is rare for someone to be able to grow more than one flower on their first try." Candice says as she inspects the roses I grew.

"I'm not in trouble?" I ask hesitantly.

"Trouble? Oh, no, Aria. We always encourage our students to grow past the boundaries we set. I only instructed a single flower since it is easier only to grow one first." Candice says with a kind smile. Her smile has my shoulders dropping and the panic loosening. "Could you try again? But this time, try growing two different types of flowers."

I nod and close my eyes again. This time, I picture a white lily and a soft pink rose. I feel the same tingle in my palm again with the use of my magic.

"Truly impressive, Aria." Candice praises. When I open my eyes this time, I find closer to twenty flowers, with a mix of lilies and roses. "I think this task may be too simple for you. Hold on while I get the rest of the class going, and I'll come back with something harder."

Candice turns away to instruct the rest of the class on what to do. However, no one is paying attention to her. Instead, they are staring at me again. Shifting, I cast my eyes down, uncomfortable with the attention.

The rest of the class is a blur. First, Candice had me grow a few more flowers. Then she had me move on to growing trees.

"Very well done," Candice says after I grow a five-foot apple tree. "I think I'll recommend a more advanced class for you to the headmaster. You are clearly at a skill that does not require my help."

"Thank you, Candice, but I'm happy to stay in your class." I don't want any more attention than I'm already receiving.

"I understand that you wish to stay here, but I'm afraid I won't be able to give you the attention you need to learn your magic. You need a more advanced class, and I must focus on my other students." Candice explains.

"Okay," I mumble, knowing I won't be able to change Candice's mind. I secretly hope the rest of my classes will not be the same.

I was foolish to hope my other classes would turn out differently than my earth class.

In my fire elemental class, I created birds that flew around me while everyone else struggled to keep a simple shape in their hands. And for my air elemental class, I was the only one able to create a shield.

By the time lunch rolls around, I'm barely coherent, completely exhausted.

"You look like a feather could blow you over," Nox comments as he approaches me in the lunch line. I grunt in response. Even talking takes too much energy at this point. Nox just laughs at me. "Go take a seat. I'll get you something to eat and a coffee; it'll help."

I take him up on his offer and walk over to the same table we had breakfast at. I slump down, deciding to lay my head on the table while I wait for Nox.

I hadn't realized I had fallen asleep until Nox gently pushed my shoulder. I yawn and stretch out my muscles.

"Rough morning?" He asks.

I take a bite of the sandwich that he brought me before answering. I moan in pure bliss from how good it tastes. Nox chuckles at my reaction to the food.

"I guess you could say that." I finally say after eating half my sandwich.

I feel the tugging return in my chest moments before I feel his power. I look up and find Jace standing just inside the grand hall, talking to Carter. He laughs at something Carter says, but the moment his eyes find mine, the smile drops, and a hard look enters his eyes. Carter tries to keep their conversation going, but Jace ignores him. His jaw is clenched tight as he storms off to the buffet.

What the hell? What happened between breakfast and now to make him look pissed to see me?

Oh well, maybe it's better this way. Perhaps now I'll be able to avoid him more easily.

Theon and the twins join us, interrupting my musing.

"I heard a little rumor about our newest student," Theon says with a wink in my direction.

"Oh?" Nox asks. "Please do tell."

"It seems our little Aria here is very good at first-year elemental magic," Theon says. The guys turn to me for an explanation.

I wipe my mouth with a napkin before answering. "I don't know what you mean."

"So, are you saying you didn't grow an apple tree and make animals out of fire magic on your first day?" Theon asks.

"Um, yes, I did. But it's not a big deal. I mean, nothing was perfect by any means." I try to justify.

However, it falls on deaf ears. The guys start to ask questions at once. I want to curl up in a little ball and disappear. I expected everyone else to look at me differently. But, for some reason, it bothers me more than I like that the guys do too.

"Enough," Jace cuts in gruffly, taking the open seat beside me. Wait, why is he sitting beside me? I thought he didn't want anything to do with me. He was supposed to make it easy to ignore him, not harder.

"Leave her alone." The table falls silent at Jace's command.

"Thank you," I whisper low enough for only him to hear. I don't want to talk to him. I want to go with my plan and avoid him. But I owe him my gratitude.

"Well, no wonder you were so tired when you got here. You must have used an extraordinary amount of magic." Nox says, trying to diffuse the tension Jace had created. "Food always helps. We burn calories when we use our magic in high quantities. So, you won't be as tired after a few days of practicing your magic."

"Yeah, it's like working a muscle. The more you work it, the easier it becomes." Chase chimes in.

I can feel Jace's eyes burning a hole in the side of my head. I want to pretend he doesn't exist, but the intensity of his stare is too hard to ignore.

"Yes?" I raise my eyebrow at him.

"Who are your parents?" He asks me.

I flinch. The question hurts more than I expected. "I don't know." I drop my head, hiding behind a curtain of hair. I can't look at him when I say the next part. "They are dead."

"I'm sorry." His gruff voice whispers. I look up to tell him I don't need his pity, but the words never leave my mouth. Jace isn't looking at me with pity. Instead, his gold eyes hold an unexpected warmth to them.

Jace is an enigma.

"Thanks." I break his stare. I push my food away, suddenly no longer hungry.

Carter clears his throat. "Is that why Killian is your guardian?"

Jace lets out a growl beside me. The sound is animalistic and full of warning, causing my head to snap up. He glares at Carter, with his jaw clenched tight and displeasure evident in his eyes.

Why would Carter's question bother Jace? Why does he care? I think I might get whiplash from Jace's emotions. No one comments on Jace's outburst. Carter just raises his hands in surrender.

"It's okay." I smile sadly at Carter. "Yes, that's the reason. He took me in when I was five."

I can see the questions on the tip of Theon's tongue.

What happened? Was that when your parents were killed? Why didn't you go live with other family members?

All questions that I don't have the answers to. So, I changed the subject before he could ask.

"How were your classes?" I ask them.

Nox must be able to tell that I am building a wall inside me from that question because he jumps on the topic change.

The guys talk about their morning classes for the rest of lunch. The whole time, I could feel Jace watching me, studying me. Even with the mixed emotions I'm getting from Jace, his presence brings me comfort.

Comfort I can't let myself afford to feel.

I've always lived by the rule of not letting people in, and I'm not going to start now.

After today, no more spending time with these guys. It's too dangerous with Jace being a prince. There's too much risk getting close to him, too much of a chance the council will find out about me.

Chapter Eight

My last two classes of the day are combat and defensive magic. They are taught in the large glass building, a short walk from the academy's main castle. They're the only classes offered as a combined year course since fewer students take them.

I change into the black combat-style pants, a tight black top, and light-weight sneakers provided for class in the female changing rooms. The outfit surprisingly fits me perfectly, showing off my curves. I braid my hair into two braids to keep it out of the way.

I've always loved training with a sword, so the fact that I'll be able to keep it up while at Nightfall has excitement pumping through my blood and a bounce to my step.

But that excitement quickly dwindles when the door to the training room slams closed behind me—leaving me in a room with none other than Nox, Theon, Chase, Carter, and, of course, Jace. They all wear the same black cargo pants and tight black shirts.

I was too excited about training to notice the tugging in my chest that I feel when Jace is around.

"Well, well, look who we have here." Nox comes up and puts his arm around me. "You look hot." He says with a wink.

Jace scowls at Nox's arm around me. I feel an unwanted, unexpected thrill at seeing him angry with Nox for being so friendly to me. However, at the same time, I don't understand why he would. Jace has said a total of three sentences to me since I met him this morning. It's not like he knows me.

I shove Nox off me. "You're such a shameless flirt." I can't help but laugh at him. I don't want to like these guys as much as I do. The fact that I just laughed at Nox's flirting should show how fast he got past my defenses. I hardly ever laugh or smile. And yet, this is not the first time it has happened today.

I'm completely screwed when it comes to these guys.

"What are you doing in this class?" Jace asks through his teeth. He looks furious at me for being here. Too bad for him; I don't care.

"I requested it," I simply reply.

Jace doesn't like that answer if the narrowing of his eyes is any indication. I narrow my eyes back at him. Neither one of us is willing to break eye contact—a silent battle of wills. I can feel his magic dance around me. This time, I know he is doing it on purpose. We're still staring at each other when the teacher comes in.

"All right, everyone, it's time to begin today's class." The teacher, Emmett, says. I finally break Jace's eye contact, but not before seeing the smirk on his face.

Emmett is exactly what I was expecting for a combat teacher. He's a giant with pounds of muscles, a shaved head, and tattoos running down both arms.

"I need everyone to pair up. We'll be starting with some sparring." He tells us.

"Partner?" Nox asks me. I nod my head in response.

The guys are the only ones in the class I recognize. There are no other first-years, not that they would want to partner with me anyway. They didn't like me after my display in earth class, which only grew to hatred after my other morning classes.

Nox grabs the practice swords from the racks lining one wall and hands me one. The edges are dulled, so the blades can't cause too much damage. You can still hurt someone with them, but it's much more challenging.

"Do you need help with how to hold your sword properly?" Nox teases me as I take up position across from him, keeping my sword pointed down.

He doesn't waste any time after that.

He comes at me fast, but I'm faster. I bring my sword up with perfect timing to deflect the blow he was trying to deliver before quickly darting out of the way.

I switch from defensive to offensive. I slam the flat side of my blade against his left side, the side he left wide open. Nox grunts as his eyebrows shoot up. He probably didn't expect me to get a hit in so fast, or maybe he didn't expect it at all.

Not waiting for him to have time to respond, I dart behind him, kicking his knees out from under him. As Nox goes down, I knock his sword from his hand and bring mine up, pointing it directly at his heart. The match is over in just under three minutes.

Nox is out of breath, whereas I am hardly winded. "I'm sorry," I say coyly. "Did I forget to mention that Killian has been training me with a sword since I was six?" I bat my eyes at him sweetly.

Nox's laugh fills the training area.

"Well, you've just proved I should never underestimate you again," Nox replies as I help him up.

Looking around, I see that Jace has been watching the whole encounter. I drop my head, feeling my cheeks turn red from embarrassment.

I understand why Jace is staring at me. It's because it's uncommon for females to be proficient in combat. Not that we aren't allowed. It's just that most females prefer not to do it. I never understood why, either. Why would you not want to defend yourself?

"Again?" I ask Nox.

The rest of our sparring time follows much of the same. Nox was able to get a few blows in but was only able to disarm me a few times.

"That's enough sparring for today. I would like you to practice throwing knives now." Emmett gathers our attention.

I place the practice sword back on the rack and grab a belt loaded with throwing knives before finding an empty target.

I stand around ten feet from the target, with my feet planted wide– one back further than the other–and my knees bent. I draw a throwing knife, and on my exhale, I throw it. The knife hits the target with a thump.

A bullseye.

"How did you do that?" Theon's eyes are wide. "I've been practicing for a year now, and I still can't hit the center of the target."

"Can I see how you are doing it?" I ask as I step back to watch.

I see his problem right away. Theon stands with his feet too close together and his knees not bent. When he brings up the knife, he doesn't exhale when he throws it and snaps his wrist too soon. The knife lands on the outer ring.

"I see the problem. First, you need to stand like this." I show him the proper stance. "Then you need to exhale when you throw it. Also, you need to snap your wrist further back." Theon does as I instruct and lands the knife in the inner ring this time. It's not a bullseye, but it's very close.

"Thank you! Thank you! Thank you!" Theon says while picking me up and spinning me around. I wasn't expecting him to pick me up. But once I overcome my shock, I laugh along with him.

"Try again," I say once he finally puts me down.

By the end of the class, Theon can hit the bullseye.

Chapter Nine

I stand with the guys, waiting for the day's last class to start, defensive magic.

Ajax walks in and gives me a nod in greeting before addressing the class. "Good afternoon, everyone. Today, we are going to be working on breaking through shields. Since most fae with a moderate amount of magic can shield, this is an important lesson." Ajax explains. "Now, I want you to find a partner, and then I'll explain what I want you to do."

I turn to Chase beside me, silently asking him to be my partner this time. He nods with a smile for an answer.

"Now that you have someone to work with, I would like you to face each other and stand a couple of feet apart," Ajax says. Everyone gets into position. "I want one person to build a shield, and the other attempt to break it, then switch. I want you to use whatever magic you wish to break the other's shield. Whether that be fire, ice, or earth. The thicker the shield, the harder it is to break. Give it a go."

"Would you like to try first?" I offer Chase.

"Sure," he replies.

We get into position. I build an air shield while Chase gathers his magic to try and break it. It takes me a couple of tries to get the magic to hold since this morning was the first time I made one.

Once I'm ready, Chase throws a series of daggers made from ice at the shield. But each one bounces off, not leaving a mark behind. He switches to his fire magic, creating balls of fire to throw, but the shield still holds.

After a few minutes of trying, he curses under his breath. "I can't get it." He says, hanging his head now.

"Here, try again. Maybe you need to infuse more magic than you originally thought." I say with an encouraging smile.

"Maybe your shield is just too strong. You try," Chase says instead of trying.

I drop my shield while Chase raises his. Where my shield shimmered iridescent purple in the light, Chase's is a soft blue.

With Chase's shield in place, I gather my earth magic, forming a pile of stone daggers. I throw each dagger the same way I'd throw a blade, trying to hit the shield in the same spot.

I throw dagger after dagger, but none break the shield. I grab my last dagger, giving it one more go.

The dagger goes sailing through the air, hitting the tiny hole I created and shattering the shield into a million pieces.

"Shit," he whispers. His wide eyes match my own. I didn't think it would work.

"Why don't you try again? You'll be able to get it this time." I suggest. Chase nods his head in agreement. I raise my shield again but try not to make it as thick this time, hoping it will help.

Chase mirrors my idea but uses ice daggers instead of stone ones. When his eighth dagger slams into my shield, it shatters. Tiny particles of hard air float around me, dissolving before hitting the ground.

"Yes!" Chase punches the air in his excitement. I just shake my head at his enthusiasm.

"Once you've broken a shield, I want you to change partners," Ajax interrupts the class. "Since shields are unique to the person, it is important to practice breaking other's shields."

I move from classmate to classmate, pairing up with Jace last.

"Let's see how good you really are, Sweetheart," Jace said with a smirk and cold eyes. It's not a friendly smirk. He always seems slightly angry when he looks at me. I have yet to see him actually smile.

Sweetheart?

I scowl at the nickname. Who does he think he is calling me sweetheart?

The shield Jace forms around himself is as thick as the one I had made previously and is almost crystal clear, only catching a slight blue tint when the light hits it just right.

Look at it, I know his shield is too thick to break the way I broke the others. So, I try to hit it with brute force.

Lifting my hands, I try to hit the shield with a ton of fire magic, which, surprisingly, does not work. So, I try again. But this time, I try to build the magic I'm pouring into it, bringing it to the same level as before but at a slower rate. Which still doesn't work.

I let my magic dissolve and take a minute to figure out another plan.

"Having a hard time?" Jace taunts. That stupid smirk is back.

I glare at him, not bothering to respond. He knows that he made it harder for me than for anyone else. I've seen other people break his shield relatively easily. Taking a deep breath, I try again.

When I raise my hands to break it this time, I feel for any cracks with my magic first, any areas weaker than the whole shield. I close my eyes to concentrate.

There! Jace left a little hole in his shield in the bottom right corner. I open my eyes, zone it on that spot, and use my air magic to expand the hole.

Instantly, Jace's shield shatters, causing us to fly apart. I land a few feet away with an "oomph." There's no air in my lungs, and my head spins.

Theon and Nox are by my side in an instant.

"Are you okay?" Nox asks.

"Can't... Breathe..." I get out in between gasps of air.

"Deep breath in through your nose," Theon instructs. I listen to him and try to pull a breath in through my nose. "That's it. Now hold for a second, then let it out through your mouth. Just keep doing that slowly."

It takes a few minutes, but eventually, my breathing evens out, and I can sit up.

"Is Jace okay?" I ask, trying to look around the guys to see him.

"I'm fine," Jace replies as the other students jump out of the way for him to reach my side.

Jace is looking at me with an unreadable expression on his face. I want to say he almost looks concerned, not mad like I'd expected. But that can't be right.

"I think that's enough for today's class," Ajax announces. "You're all dismissed."

I start to shuffle out of the class with everyone else, but Ajax stops me with a hand on my arm. Jace stays behind as well.

"How the hell did you break that shield? No one has ever broken one of my shields when it is that thick!" Jace explodes once everyone else is out of the room. His stance is wide, arms crossed over his chest, eyes narrowed, and jaw locked tight. Looks like I was wrong about him not being mad.

"I... I looked for holes in the shield." I start hesitantly. Ajax nods for me to go on. "I found one in the bottom right corner, so I poured air magic into it to make it bigger."

I wring my hands, nervous I'm going to be in trouble for being able to break a prince's shield. Maybe I should have pretended that I couldn't do it. But it is too late now.

Jace has yet to say anything after his outburst. I glance at him and see he's staring at me with no emotion now. He doesn't even look mad anymore. It's unnerving how quickly he can go from spitting mad to nothing in seconds.

"Would you do something for me, Aria?" Ajax asks, bringing my attention back to the matter at hand. I nod in response. "I want you to make your shield as thick as possible, and Jace, I would like you to try to break it. Try to use fire, water, or earth magic first."

We turn to face each other again while Ajax takes a few steps back. I build my shield as thick as I can make it. Jace spreads his feet apart and raises his hands, concentrating on breaking the shield.

He tries to throw earth daggers at the shield in rapid succession. But they bounce off. He tries again, doing what I did earlier, by throwing a ton of fire magic at the shield. It doesn't break, but I can feel the heat of his fire magic brush against me.

After a minute, Jace shakes his head. "Her shield is as strong as mine. I can't break it the way I would normally." He looks at Ajax. From how Jace clenches and unclenches his hands, I can tell this fact annoys him. I'm surprised; I didn't think my shield was as strong as the prince's.

"Try to break it the way Aria explained how she broke yours," Ajax instructs. Jace nods and turns his focus back to me.

Without warning, my shield shatters, and I am flung back again.

I land a few feet away, smashing my head off the hard floor as I do.

I groan as I roll over. Trying to will the world to stop spinning.

Ajax crouches down in front of me. "Aria?" He asks. "Are you alright?" I want to nod yes, but I am afraid that any sudden movement will cause me to be sick.

"I'm okay. I think I need a minute, though." I finally reply. I lift my head enough to find Jace crouched beside Ajax. This time, there's no mistaking the concern on his face.

"How did you not get hurt?" I grumble at him.

That smirk of his is back. "Because I know how to shield my fall, Sweetheart."

I scowl at that stupid nickname. That's the second time in the last hour he has said it. He won't give me a genuine smile, show any emotion, or have a normal conversation with me, but he will give me a nickname? I don't understand him.

"Why does it affect us so much when we break a shield that way?" I ask as I slowly sit up.

"I think it has to do with the way it is breaking. Your shield is connected to you. So, when you are breaking it by looking for holes, it causes it to break faster and harder compared to traditional methods. I have never thought of using air magic to break an air shield. I want to investigate it more." Ajax helps me stand once I feel the room stop spinning. "I think that is enough for now. Go enjoy your dinner."

With one last look at Ajax and Jace, I stroll out of the room to get changed and cleaned up for dinner.

Chapter Ten

The whispers and stares start as soon as I enter the grand hall for supper.

"Did you hear what she did in earth class?" One girl whispers to another as I walk past them. Their heads are bent low, but their eyes follow me.

"What about how she took down Nox in combat class?" The second girl responds. I glance over to see more have joined the first two girls. But I drop my head when I meet their hard stares.

"That's nothing! Listen to what I heard she did in defensive magic class." One of the new girls chimes in, not bothering to keep her voice down, knowing I'm listening to them anyway.

I hasten my steps, keeping my head down to avoid hearing any more of their conversation. I don't want to listen to their judgments or see the look of hatred in their eyes. It was bad enough being the new kid, starting the year late, but now I have gained their attention, it's worse.

When I arrived at the academy last night, I didn't believe I was powerful like everyone kept telling me. But after today, I fear I am more powerful than they let on.

I don't want to be powerful. I just want to keep my head down, learn my magic, and get out of here. But instead, on my first day, I attracted more attention than I thought possible.

With a plate full of pasta, I look around the grand hall for the guys. But I don't stop them.

Maybe this is my opportunity to start putting some distance between us.

I make my way through the crowd, choosing an empty table in the back corner. It's dark back here, so the chances of the guys noticing me are slim.

"Excuse me?"

I look up from my supper to find a tall female with long, straight honey-gold hair and deep-sea blue eyes. Her shirt is unbuttoned enough that anyone can see her boobs if she moves slightly, and her skirt is too tight and short. This female knows she's good-looking and enjoys flaunting it.

"Yes?" I respond, wondering why she's talking to me.

"I was wondering if the rumors are true. You know, the ones about you attacking the prince?" The female asks.

My eyebrows shoot up.

Attacking the prince? How did what happened become so twisted?

"I'm sorry, but I don't know what you are talking about. I never attacked the prince." I try to explain. The female just scoffs at me.

"Well, of course, you did. Did you not break his shield and throw him across the room?" The female says with a flip of her hair.

"Yes, I broke his shield, but I didn't throw him across the room. That only happened as a result of his shield breaking." I don't like this female. She's twisting everything that happened.

"Sure, that's what happened." The female says with a mocking laugh.

I don't have a chance to respond. The female's expression changes in a blink when her attention shifts to someone behind me. Her face softens, and her smile changes from mocking to sweet.

I know why when I feel the tugging sensation a moment too late.

"What are you doing, Nova?" Jace takes the seat to my left while Nox takes the one on my other side. The rest sit across the table from us.

So much for them not seeing me.

"I heard about what happened in defensive magic class. Are you okay?" Nova says in a sickly sweet voice, completely ignoring his question.

"Nothing happened in defensive magic class." Jace's tone suggests that she drop it. However, Nova doesn't take the hint.

"Oh, but I heard this one attacked you during class!" Nova points an accusing finger in my direction. "You don't have to take pity and sit with her. Please come sit with me at my table, your highness." Nova all but purrs the last words. She twirls her hair and leans over the table so the prince gets an eyeful of her cleavage.

For some reason, Nova's words cut deep, leaving me angry and embarrassed. I drop my gaze, trying to hide behind a curtain of my hair; she can't see the effect her words have.

"She has a name, and it's Aria," Jace says coldly. My mouth pops open with surprise; the prince is defending me. I whip my head up to find him staring at Nova with his jaw clenched. He looks angry, but I don't know why he would be. "I am good here."

"But, Your Highness," Nova starts.

Theon interrupts before she can say anything else. "The prince does not wish to sit with you. Please kindly remove yourself from our presence."

Nova huffs. Flicking her hair over her shoulder, she throws a glare in my direction before leaving.

The guys all sigh in relief as soon as she is gone.

"I apologize for her behavior. I heard what she said before she noticed us, and I'll make sure all rumors are put to rest as soon as possible." Jace says to me.

I look up into his gold eyes and smile. "Thank you."

That unreadable expression crosses Jace's face once he sees my smile. I'm starting to think he shows that expression when he doesn't want someone to know his feelings.

"Anyway, who is she?" I turn back to the others.

"She is councilman Victor's daughter. Nasty thing, always trying to get Jace's attention by any means necessary." Carter says.

"Very fake, too. Can never take what she says to be true," Chase adds.

My blood turns to ice—a councilman's daughter. I have caught the attention of a councilman's daughter.

Oh gods, this is bad.

"Aria, are you okay?" Nox asks, but his voice sounds like it's underwater.

I can't get my mouth to respond.

I should have fought harder for the academy to make an exception and let me stay with Killian and attend the academy in my village. I should have begged them to bind my magic. I was so dumb today. I should have never shown off in class. I should have acted like I barely had any magic.

My heart is racing, and my head is pounding with the growing panic. I start to shake slightly. I can't be here. I can't do this. I have to find a way out of here. Whether that be convincing Nickolas or running away. It's not safe for me here.

I abruptly stand. My chair legs squeal against the floor with the sudden movement.

"I need to go," I mumble to the guys. I probably seem a little crazy to them right now, but I'm not thinking straight. If I don't get out of here in the next couple of minutes, I'll start hyperventilating. And that's not something I want anyone to see.

"Aria, wait! What's wrong?" Nox asks me.

I shake my head, not meeting his eyes. "Nothing. I'll see you later." I turn and walk as quickly as I can out of the grand hall without attracting more attention. I can feel the guy's eyes on my back. But I'm too scared to care what they think right now.

The distance between the grand hall and my room seems farther away than it did this morning. But, I make it there without incident.

I stumble into my room, falling to the floor once I am safely inside.

That's when the panic takes over.

I tuck my body into a tight ball, trying to hold myself together. But it doesn't work.

Air won't move past the lump in my throat, and my vision starts to blacken around the edges, warning me I'm going pass out soon if I don't breathe.

It's been a while since I had a panic attack like this. I used to get them all the time when I first started living with Killian. I would be fine one minute and the next a mess, just like I am now. Over the years, Killian found ways to help me.

I try to think of some of those techniques now, like concentrating on what I can feel.

I dig my fingers into the rug, using the soft texture to bring me back. I count backward from one hundred at the same time.

After what feels too long, my breath stops coming in short pants, and my vision clears. I sit up and wipe the tears from my face.

"I'm not staying here," I say aloud. With determined steps, I head to the closet to pack my bags.

A plan starts to form as I pull my things out.

I'll wait until late tonight, so there are fewer chances of someone seeing me. Then, I'll use the emergency credit card Killian gave me. I don't know if it is safe for me to fly to Listra and have Killian meet me there and take me home or if the academy will just drag me back. But I'll call Killian and ask him when I'm out of the academy. He'll know what to do.

Once my bags are packed, I start pacing, wearing a path at the foot of my bed.

All I can think about is the council finding out I'm alive and the one who kidnapped me coming back to take me again. I still don't understand why they would want me anyway. Nothing is special about me. I guess besides the prophecy. But even then, I don't know what it says.

All these thoughts are swirling around in my head when someone knocks on my door. I don't want to answer it, worried it might be one of the guys, but I open it anyway.

It's not one of the guys on the other side, but Isabelle.

My shoulders relax slightly, knowing I don't have to answer the questions I'm sure they have.

"Good evening, Aria. Could you please come with me? The headmaster would like to see you," Isabelle says with an encouraging smile.

I can't leave until nightfall anyway. So, I might as well see what the headmaster wants.

"Um, sure."

Chapter Eleven

"Please take a seat." Nickolas gestures for me to join him in the seating area by the fire. "I wanted to see how your first day went."

"It was alright," I answer as I take the open chair. I would have enjoyed it if it weren't for everyone staring and whispering about me. Oh, and the nasty surprise about attending school with a council member's child. It occurs to me now that I don't know if it's only Nova or if more go here.

"Only alright?" Nickolas asks me with a raised brow. I have a feeling he has already heard the rumors.

"I'm honestly still not sure I should be here. Why didn't you tell me that a council member's child goes here? Or better yet, the prince?" My nostrils flare. I fist my hands in my lap. I can feel my magic simmering under my skin. I hadn't realized how angry I was with him until now.

Nickolas gave me a peculiar look. "I apologize for not telling you last night. I should have been more considerate and warned you." He at least had the decency to look guilty.

My anger dissipates some. But not fully.

"Now that we are talking about it, how many council members' kids attend here?"

"Well, they are all in their second year. But there are five in total. Nova, Chase, Carter, Theon, and Nox."

I want to hit myself in the face. Of course, Nox, the twins, and Theon are council members' children. No one else would be as close to the prince as they are. The rest of my anger disappears as the panic comes back, along with sadness. Even though I wanted to avoid getting close to them, I already saw us becoming friends.

But now that I know who they are, that can't happen.

I guess it doesn't matter since I'm not staying.

Nickolas' head is cocked to the side as he studies me.

"What?" I ask him after a minute of him staring at me like I'm a puzzle.

"Have you ever been told that your eyes turn deep violet, almost black, from your normal lavender when you're upset?"

I nod my head. "It used to happen all the time when I was younger. It only happens now when I get angry." I can feel it when the shift happens. I usually duck my head to avoid anyone seeing my eyes. But I forgot this time. "Killian always used to joke and say it was the demon in me coming out."

I smile at the memory. I would lose my temper at the littlest things when I was younger. Killian would always tease me about being a part demon, making me laugh and causing me to lose my anger.

Thinking about it now, it is surprising that Killian could joke about me being a part demon.

"Curious." Nickolas shakes his head, dispelling the thought he had. "I had Candice Speak with me about the display of magic you showed today.

She believes you should be placed in second-year courses, not first. I wanted to know what you thought about that."

"You want to know my opinion on it?" I ask, surprised. I figured when Candice said she was going to talk to Nickolas about placing me in second-level courses, I would have no say in the matter.

"Of course I do. It's your life, not mine. You should make the final choice."

It's interesting I get a say in my future now.

I don't say that, though. Instead, I turn my attention to the flames in the fireplace, watching them dance as I think about what I want.

Sure, I'd love nothing more than to advance my magic. But the fear of being found by the council member who betrayed my parents still outweighs the desire for magic.

"I think a better idea is letting me go home and attend the academy there." I finally say.

"You know that is not an option," Nickolas replies softly.

"Why not? Why do I have to attend this academy? Why can't I just learn my magic elsewhere?" I snap. Anger has my eyes changing back to their deep violet color and my hands shaking.

I'm tired of only getting cryptic answers.

"Aria, I'm sorry. But as you showed today, you have an extraordinary level of magic. Unfortunately, not just anyone can teach you how to harness it. The only people who could are here at this academy." Nickolas says. "And don't forget the king ordered you to attend this academy."

I blow out a breath. I understand what Nickolas is trying to say, but I'm not happy about it. The only way out of this place is to run away. Which I still plan to do tonight. I thought I would at least try to convince Nickolas to let me leave since I'm with him. But I know he is not going to budge on the matter. Not when the order came from the king.

"Can I take some time and think about it?" I ask once I regain my composure. "Maybe stay in the first-year classes for a couple of weeks and then decide? I want to do the second-year classes, but I'm worried about the council finding out and the one who killed my parents discovering I'm alive."

Nickolas rubs his chin, lost in thought. "I'm fine with that." He finally says. "I agree there is a risk in you taking second-year classes. However, I think it's more important for you to learn your magic."

"I understand that, truly I do. I'm simply scared. I don't think it is safe for me here. Not with the council member's children enrolled here." I tell him my fears.

Nickolas smiles at me sadly. "I know you are. Anyone in your situation would be. But the better you are with your magic, the stronger you'll be if anyone does come after you. You would have a chance of fighting them off." He tells me. "I understand you don't feel safe here, but you are. No harm will befall you while you are at the academy."

That makes me pause. Killian said something similar when Ajax and Isabelle came to get me. Maybe running away wouldn't be the best option after all. Maybe I should learn everything I can and then disappear. I made the choice to run away tonight in panic. Maybe I should wait and figure out if that is the smart thing to do.

"I know I would be safer if I had my magic." I sigh. "Can I please take the next couple of weeks to decide?"

Those two weeks will also help me figure out if I should be running away or sticking it out.

"Of course, as I said earlier, it's your choice. We'll meet again in a few weeks once you are more settled. I know this last week has been very hard on you."

"Thank you." I get up to leave. Walking to the door, I think of something I had meant to ask last night. I stop and turn back to Nickolas. "Sir, did you know my parents?"

"I did very well, actually. They were some of my closest friends." A flash of pain crosses his face.

"What were they like?" I ask desperately.

Nickolas' eyes take on a faraway look like he's lost in a memory.

"Your mother was funny, strong, independent, and the most stubborn person I knew, but always kind. Nothing would get in her way when she set her mind to something." There's so much warmth in his voice as he talks. "Your father, on the other hand, was serious, a little rough around the edges, but fiercely protective over those he loved. I have never seen anyone love each other more than your parents did. They would do anything for each other and you when you came around."

My eyes well up with tears. They sound like amazing people.

Nickolas stands and walks over to me. He wraps his arms around me, engulfing me in his warmth. The hug was unexpected, but I let myself sink into it.

"Were they fated mates?" I sniffle into his button-up shirt. I have heard of fated mates, but they are rare now.

"They were. Their love story is one full of trials. I know I'm not allowed to tell you anything more about them. But someday, I will. You were their proudest achievement." Nickolas says as he holds me. "I'm sorry you lost them. I wish you could have known them as I did. But just know they would be proud of the young lady you have become."

Nickolas's words warm my heart. I can't run away if I want to continue to make my parents proud. I need to face this challenge head-on. I have been hiding almost my entire life. It was like Killian said: it's time to stop.

I pull back, wiping my face from tears. "Thank you for telling me what you could about them."

"You're welcome." He smiles at me. "Now get some rest. You need to recover from today's classes. Sleep and food are the best ways to replenish your magic."

"Then it looks like I will be spending all my time eating and sleeping." I open the door and turn back to him. "Goodnight, Nickolas."

"Goodnight, Aria."

Chapter Twelve

The following day, I have my first water elemental class.

The first-year class takes place outside by the lake. It isn't until the end of the first year that we learn how to call on our water magic from thin air. We first must learn how to use it by pulling from water sources around us. The other elements are easier to control, so we don't need a source to learn how to use the magic.

I stand apart from the rest of the class in the standard one-piece bathing suit the academy gave me and a robe to fight off the chill. The other students are ignoring me today. I suppose that's better than them all staring and whispering about me. Although it still makes for a lonely day.

I can't help but admit that I'm impressed with how quickly the prince convinced everyone to stop talking about me. I don't want to appreciate it, but I do.

I was able to avoid the prince and the others at breakfast by not going. I know it will be harder at lunch since I can't skip two meals in a row. But I'll figure out what to do when the time comes.

"Everyone in the lake." Lucas, our teacher, orders, pulling me from my thoughts.

According to Nox, Lucas is the youngest teacher at Nightfall, but everyone's favorite.

Lucas is on the shorter side with curly blonde hair and striking green eyes. An easy smile sits on his face as he waits for us to get into the lake.

I remove my robe, shivering in the chilly air without it. Dipping my toe in the lake, I'm pleasantly surprised to find it warm.

I should have known the academy would keep the lake warm with magic.

I join the others in the lake, stopping when I'm waist-deep.

"Today, I want you to work on creating a dome around you. It'll be like when you build a shield with air magic but with water instead." Lucas explains from his stop in the water. "Pull up the water with your hands and then guide the water into a dome shape around yourself."

I move away from everyone to give myself space as I pull from the water around me. The water follows my command and rises above my head, encasing me in a dome shape.

I hold the shape for a minute before dropping my hold.

The water comes crashing down around me, soaking me in the process. Sputtering, I shove the wet strands of my hair away from my face.

That may not be the best way to let go of the magic.

"Excellent, Aria," Lucas says when I can see him again. "Keep practicing while the others try to get it. Also, try and see how long you can hold it."

I repeat the process a few more times, learning how to bring the dome down without soaking myself.

Lucas swims back to me after I've made a dome for the fifth time.

"It looks like it might take the entire time for the others to get it. Would you like me to show you what to do next so you can work on that?" Lucas asks.

"Please, sir," I respond. As much fun as it is to make domes, it's getting a bit boring after so many times.

"I want you to freeze the dome once you form it around you," Lucas tells me. "The trick is to only let your magic freeze the dome, not everything in the lake."

I grew up watching Killian form his water magic into ice daggers and build walls of ice when he was training with the soldiers. But I never asked him how he did it. I was more focused on watching the soldiers train with their weapons. I didn't think it was necessary to ask questions about magic, but now I wish I had Killian tell me everything about magic.

"How do I do that?" I question with a tilt of my head.

Lucas rubs his jaw, thinking of a way to explain. "Think of your magic as a living, breathing thing inside of you. It knows your intentions. It knows your desires. All you have to do is think about those intentions. Tell it that you want the water to freeze."

I nod my head before making another dome. This time, I think about solidifying the water. My magic responds to my command. The ice starts at the base, slowly crawling up to encase me in a solid dome.

I can only hold the shape for a minute before my arms shake and fatigue sets in. I let my hold on the magic go, turning the water into liquid and dropping the dome.

"Very well done," Lucas praises. "This time, I want you to hold it while I try to break it."

"Okay."

I'm tired, but I do as he asks and make another frozen dome. I nod to Lucas through the ice when I'm ready.

Lucas punches the dome, but nothing happens. He tries a few more times before encasing his fist in fire.

The dome shutters when he hits it this time. I pour more magic into it, trying to maintain the dome shape. But I can't stop the hole his fire magic leaves behind.

"You can lower the dome now," Lucas tells me. "That was impressive. Most first-years forget to reinforce the dome, causing it to shatter with one punch."

"Thank you, sir," I say as I drop the dome.

Sweat slides down my spine and pools around my neck from using so much magic at once.

"I would like you to get out of the water and try to call on your magic. Just create any shape in your hand. I know we don't teach this until the end of the first year, but I feel you might be able to do it."

I don't share his confidence in my ability.

"Okay, I'll try."

I get out of the water, towel off, throw my robe on, and walk far enough away that I won't pull from the lake.

I lift my hand out in front of me and think of creating a block of water. Then, taking a deep breath, I close my eyes to concentrate—my palm tingles from the magic forming.

When I open my eyes, I find a perfect block of water hovering over my palm. My mouth parts in surprise. I hadn't expected to be able to do it. I look at Lucas and see his expression of awe.

"Very well done, Aria." Lucas clapped his hands. I blush at his praise.

"That, class, is what you will be able to do by the end of the year." Lucas brings everyone's attention to me. I quickly look away from them once I see the open looks of hatred across most of my classmates' faces.

"That is all for today. You are dismissed." Lucas ends the class.

I head to the healing wing for my first healing class with Isabelle.

The room is already full, but there's one empty table left in the middle. I drop into the seat, setting my bag at my feet.

The healing wing is appropriately named since it takes up a whole wing of the academy. Large windows run down the entire length of one wall, with beds for patients under them. On the other side, where the class is held, tables are set up with neat stacks of supplies on each.

"Good morning, class," Isabelle greets as she heads to the front of the room. "Today, we are going to work on healing minor cuts. It's important to note that if you are going to heal a cut, it must first be cleaned to prevent infection. Just because we heal faster and have healing magic doesn't mean we can't get infections. Another thing to note is that if you go into advanced healing later, you will learn how to clean a cut with magic.

"For today, I want you to slice your palm with the knife provided. Then, you will clean the cut in a bowl of soapy water. After it's clean, you need to hold your other hand over the cut palm and pull your raw magic to your hand. You must infuse the magic slowly. If done too fast, the underneath won't heal. Instead, you will heal only the top layer of skin, which can lead to problems later."

Picking up the knife, I run it across my palm in one quick movement. A hiss slips out from the sting the blade causes.

I dunk my hand in the soapy water, cleaning the area and removing the excess blood. Once it's clean, I place my uninjured hand over the one I cut and close my eyes, picturing the well of magic inside me.

My well of magic is so deep that I can't picture the bottom of it. I don't know where it ends inside me, only that it does. It's not a bottomless thing. There is an end to it.

The well inside me is split into sections. There's the cool spray of my water magic, contrasting the blazing inferno of my fire magic. There's the gritty feeling my earth magic has and the chilly breeze that comes with my air magic. But I ignore all those and reach for my raw magic. The magic that feels electric and colder than the pits of hell.

As I pull on my raw magic, my body chills, and the hair on my arms stands up from the electric, icy feeling. The only warmth I feel comes from my hands as the skin on my injured palm knits back together.

I open my eyes and find my palms surrounded in the same glowing, golden light Isabelle's were. The icy feeling slowly leaves as my raw magic finishes knitting the skin back together.

I pull my hands apart, checking if it worked, to find my palm completely healed, with no mark in sight.

Holy shit, I did it! I healed myself!

I keep looking at my hand, expecting to see a scar or something to show a cut there only a moment ago. Of course, Killian has done it for me over the years when I got hurt. But it still amazes me that I can do it myself.

"You did a good job. Healing comes naturally to you." Isabelle compliments me as she passes by on her way to help other students.

The female beside me scoffs. "Of course, you are good at healing. You are good at everything else. Why wouldn't you be good at this, too?"

I look over at the female. She is slim, with mousy brown hair and brown eyes to match. "Excuse me?"

"What? Do you want to rub it in that you are better than everyone else in the first year?" The female asks, looking at me with pure hatred.

I flinch at her words. It's not my fault magic comes naturally to me. But it seems everyone has already made up their minds about me. Choosing to hate me simply for something I have no control over.

I bow my head and don't respond.

For the rest of the class, I try to hide my movements, not wanting the female beside me or anyone else to judge me more than they already have.

Chapter Thirteen

"Hi, Aria," Theon says as he, Nox, and Chase sit down for lunch. I had purposely picked a seat in the dark back corner to try and avoid them. But it looks like they aren't going to leave me alone that easily.

"How was your morning?" Chase asks.

None of them ask why I ran away from them last night, and I don't offer up the reason why either.

"It was alright." I push my salad around with my fork. I don't feel like eating.

I felt the looks as I walked into the grand hall earlier. Everywhere I walk, I can feel the stares and whispers about me. The first years are talking about me to everyone. I fear the whole school will hate me by the end of the day, not just the first years.

"What's wrong?" Nox's voice is full of concern.

I'm almost certain I'm projecting my feelings to him. But I'm too upset to care.

"Did your classes not go well this morning?" Chase asks when I don't respond to Nox.

I open my mouth to tell them it's nothing, but Jace and Carter join us before I can.

Jace's brows are furrowed as he sits across from me. "I heard someone say that you called on your water magic without being in the water. Is that true?"

The others all turn to me, with mouths gaping open in surprise.

I clear my throat. "Um, yes, it's true. Lucas asked me to try after I could create a dome and freeze it." I squirm in my seat. The guys don't say anything. They just sit there, looking at me funny, like they don't believe I am real. "Can you please stop looking at me like that? It's bad enough that everyone else hates me. I don't want you guys to as well."

Even though I was trying to avoid them, I must admit that as much as it scares me that Jace is a prince and the others are council members' children, I need them. I would be all alone without them.

"We aren't going to hate you," Carter says gently as he wraps his arms around me. "We were just surprised."

Jace growls. "What do you mean everyone hates you?"

Jace glares at the arm Carter has wrapped around me. His jaw is clenched tight, and he looks seconds away from removing Carter's arm.

What is with Jace? He barely talks to me, doesn't try to get to know me, but gets pissed when his friends touch me.

I can't keep up with him and his moods.

Ignoring Jace's reaction, I keep Carter's arm around me. I like the comfort of it.

"They're all mad because magic comes naturally to me. They think I'm showing off or something. I'm not, I swear. I don't even know what I am doing half the time." That's the truth, too. I don't know what I'm doing.

I've only been practicing my magic for two days now. Besides that one night with Felix, I'd never used my magic.

"They'll come around. I'm sure they are just annoyed that the new girl is showing them all up." Nox says, trying to make me feel better. "Besides, you don't need them. You have us."

The others nod in agreement, even Jace.

My chest swells with emotion. "Thanks, that means a lot." I mean it, too.

I don't know what I would do if I didn't have them. They've wormed their way into my heart in the two days I've known them, working past the defenses I've spent years building.

"Things will get better, you'll see," Chase says with a smile. "Besides, we have the welcoming ball on Saturday."

"Welcoming ball? What's that?" This is the first I have heard of any ball.

"It's the ball Nightfall puts on every year at the beginning of the school year," Nox explains.

"Isn't it kind of late, though? The school year started a month ago."

"The academy always waits until October to have it. They say it's so we have time to settle into a routine." Theon explains.

That makes sense.

"The ball is a big deal around here," Carter says. "The guys wear suits or tuxedos, and the girls wear fancy dresses."

My fork hovers in front of my mouth. "Fancy dresses?"

"Oh yeah. Some girls will wear ball gowns, others a little simpler, and some try and show as much skin without getting in trouble." Theon's eyes light up thinking about the girls with so much of their bodies revealed.

"I don't have anything fancy." I've never been to a fancy event before. The most dressed-up I get is for Killian's winter solstice party he has every year. "I don't think I'll go." I don't particularly like the idea of going to an event where so many people will be hostile to me anyway.

"Attendance is mandatory," Jace says in a flat tone.

When I look over at him, he wears his usual mask, all emotions absent from his face. Gone is the anger I saw earlier. At this point, I would rather see anger than no emotion at all.

"If it's mandatory, why is this the first I've heard about it?" Surely, if the headmaster expected me to attend, he would have told me about it when I arrived.

"He probably just forgot since it's usually announced at the assembly when we arrive for the start of term." Theon shrugs. "If you need a dress, you can head into the city and get one. We could take you. We have our cars here."

My stomach drops. The idea of heading into Oxynmire makes me sick. Being at the academy, on the outskirts, is bad enough, but I don't think I can handle going into the capital to shop. Not to mention that Ajax recommended that I don't go into the city.

"Oh, that's okay. I'll think of something." I wave the idea off.

I feel Jace's eyes on me. I turn to find him looking at me with his brows drawn together. "Why don't you want to go into the city?"

"I just don't like to shop." I lie. It's a horrible lie. Anyone who knows me would know I love to shop. I also love fancy dresses; I just never needed to buy one.

Jace lets it go but moves on to a more dangerous topic. "Why did you panic last night when we told you Nova's father was on the council?"

My heart starts pounding. I can't tell them the truth. I can't tell them that I suspect that one of their parents killed mine and kidnapped me. I can't tell them that even though I want to be their friend, I can't ever let their parents find out I am alive.

"I...I.." I can't think of a good lie to tell him. The panic I felt last night bubbles up again.

"Aria?" Jace says my name. His rough voice brings my focus back to him. His magic wraps around me in a protective cocoon and warms my soul.

"I can't tell you," I whisper past the lump in my throat.

Jace cocks his head to the side, studying me. Between not wanting to go into the city and freaking out about the others being council members' children, I know I'm acting strange.

"Aria, you know that Chase, Carter, Theon, and I are council members' kids, right?" Nox asks me gently.

"Yes."

Jace is still staring at me. His face is blank, but his eyes tell the truth. I didn't notice it before. But I can see that one eyebrow is slightly raised, giving away his confusion. It is such a slight lift in the eyebrow that I would have never noticed if I wasn't studying him like I am now.

Jace opens his mouth like he wants to say something, but I beat him to it. "I'll see you guys later. I better head to my next class." I stand before the guys can ask me any more questions.

Chapter Fourteen

I t is the day of the ball, and I never found a dress to wear. I searched online, but either the shops wouldn't deliver to the academy or deliver on such short notice. It didn't help that the dresses were crazy expensive. Killian gave me money for helping around the farmhouse and sharpening blades, but it wasn't a lot, and I can't justify using the emergency credit card on a dress.

I finally decided on a short black dress with a cowl neckline that hugged my figure, which I already owned. It's nowhere near as fancy as I would've liked, but it's better than nothing.

I'm pinning my hair back when there is a knock on my door. I grab my robe from the back of the bathroom door since I'm only in silk shorts and a matching camisole.

A delivery man with a large box is waiting for me when I answer the door.

"Can I help you?"

"Aria Umbra?" He asks me. I nod my head in response. "Delivery for you." He holds out the large white box with a bright red bow on it.

I didn't order anything, and the box looks too big to be anything that Killian would send me. So, the question is, who sent me a package and why?

Curiosity has my hands reaching for the package.

"Thanks."

The box is heavy and awkward to carry, so I kick the door closed with my foot and walk over to the coffee table to set it down. I carefully undo the pretty red bow and pull the lid off.

I gasp as I pull the tissue paper away to reveal the most gorgeous dress I've ever seen. Gently pulling it out, I push the box aside to lay the dress on the table to get a better look.

The dress is made from the softest midnight blue material, with layers of tulle on the skirts. The A-line style dress has a deep V neckline, held up by thin tulle straps that tie into bows, and a slit going up one side of the skirt, stopping midthigh. The back of the dress matches the front, dipping low to expose more skin.

But the best part of the dress is the bottom.

Starting out heavier at the bottom before fading out as it reaches the top, tiny gold gems are sewn into the tulle to look like individual stars, constellations, and moons.

The design is stunning.

I set the dress down and turn back to the box. Nestled between a pair of matching gold heels is a note written in a masculine scrawl.

*So you don't feel
out of place tonight.
—J*

My heart flutters.

I know no one else whose name starts with a J besides Jace. I bite my lip while excitement and confusion war inside me.

Why would Jace send me a dress? He acts like he can barely stand me most days. Why bother doing something so thoughtful?

I shrug. It doesn't matter why, I guess.

Accepting the gift, I finish getting ready for the ball.

I make my way through the packed halls, following the flow of students to a set of large wooden doors thrown wide open. An orchestra playing a soft melody can be heard over the crowd.

As students push past me, I'm even more grateful for the dress Jace sent me. The males are dressed in full three-piece suits or tuxes, and the females are all in extravagant dresses.

My mouth drops open as I take a hesitant step toward the top of the stairs leading down to the ballroom.

The room is remarkable.

The oak stairs, with gold railings, lead into the massive ballroom. The black marble floor, veined with gold, gleams under the glass chandeliers that hang from the vaulted ceiling. The walls are cream, with gold lining the windows and doors leading to the gardens. Tables line the outskirts of the room, leaving the center for dancing.

"If you think this is impressive, you should see the one at the castle." The sound of Nox's voice causes me to jump. I didn't hear him come up beside me.

Since I ran away from them the other day, the guys haven't asked me again why I panic at the mention of the council. To which I will forever be grateful. I know eventually, I'll have to tell them, but I'm not ready yet. For now, I'm happy just to pretend I don't know who their parents are.

"The one at the castle is better than this?" I ask him.

"Oh yes, this is almost shabby compared to the castle's." I can hear the smile in Nox's voice.

I finally tear my eyes away from the ballroom to look at Nox. He's wearing a black tux with a forest green bow tie. His copper hair is gelled back to keep it from falling into his eyes, highlighting his sharp cheekbones.

"You look handsome." I compliment him.

"And you look beautiful." Nox whistles at me. He's yet to remove his eyes from me. His attention makes my cheeks turn pink.

I decided to pull my hair into an updo, displaying the daring back of the dress. I braided the top half of my hair into a crown, pulled the rest into a low bun, and left a few waves to frame my face.

"Thank you."

Nox scrunches his face, "I thought you said you didn't have anything fancy. That dress is definitely fancy."

I smile softly. "I was able to get one short notice." I don't know why, but I don't want to tell him that Jace sent it to me.

"Well, are you ready to descend into the ball, my lady?" Nox holds his arm out for me to take.

Laughing, I accept his outstretched arm.

My nerves have made my legs feel like jelly, and my hands shake.

"I can feel your nerves. It's like you are shouting at me. What's the matter?" Nox asks as he leads me down the stairs.

Ah, I was wondering if he could feel that. The whole way here, I was shaking because I was so nervous about attending. But with Nox by my side, some of that jittery feeling has dissipated.

"Sorry, this is all new to me. I've never been to anything like this, and I don't know how to dance." I tell him honestly.

While most girls my age were taking dance lessons to prepare for the chance to attend court, I was training with a sword. I'd never expected that dancing was a skill I'd need to have. It never bothered me until now.

"Don't worry about that. We can show you how to dance." Nox reassures me as we stop at the bottom of the stairs. Carter, Chase, and Theon are waiting for us. Jace is nowhere in sight.

"He's right," Carter says, hearing the last of mine and Nox's conversation. "It'll be fun!"

I don't doubt the guys will find a way to make it fun.

"You all look very handsome." I compliment them. They all have tuxedos on. Carter and Chase wear slim black ties, and Theon has a burgundy bow tie.

"You look beautiful," Theon says. Chase and Carter chime in their agreement.

"Why don't we go find a table?" Chase offers.

Keeping my arm tucked into Nox's, we follow Chase to a table in the back corner, close to one of the doors leading to the gardens.

"We'll have dinner first, then the dance portion starts," Chase explains as he pulls out a chair for me.

"Where is Jace?" The question pops out of me as I sit. My eyes dart across the ballroom, looking for him.

Nox chuckles. "Are we not good company?"

"What?" I stop searching for Jace and turn to look at the guys. They all share knowing smiles. "No, you're great company. I just haven't seen him yet, is all."

As I say that, the tugging sensation starts in my chest. My eyes are drawn to the grand stairs to find Jace at the top.

He's breathtaking in a fitted tux with a navy bow tie. With his hair styled back and a gold crown with different phases of the moon depicted on each spike and stars made of little diamonds lining the base, he looks the part of a prince.

Jace's eyes land on me and darken. A hungry look overtakes his features as he sees me in the dress he sent me. He strides over to the table, not once taking his eyes off me.

I can't remove my eyes from him, either.

I can hardly breathe by the time he reaches the table and takes the seat on my right. I could have sworn someone had been sitting there before he came over.

Jace opens his mouth to say something when headmaster Nickolas stands from the head table lining the wall opposite the stairs. "Good evening, students and faculty, and welcome to another opening ball. Dinner will be served now."

An army of servants holding trays on their shoulders come rushing in from hidden doors along the wall with the stairs.

A mixed green salad with some type of honey dressing is placed in front of me. I look at the place setting to find three fork options. Why are there choices?

I thought a fork was a fork. My hand hovers over the largest fork.

"It's the smallest one. The one closest to the plate." Jace whispers to me.

"Thank you," I say under my breath.

Choosing the smallest fork, I try the salad. The honey flavor dances along my taste buds, mixing with the nuts in the salad.

"There you are, Jace!" I groan internally at the sound of Nova's high-pitched voice. I watch Nova take the open seat on Jace's other side. "I have been looking all over for you."

I now understand Theon's comment about some of the females' dresses, looking at what Nova is wearing. Her dress is made from a deep burgundy fabric. The top is two panels of silk crossed over her breasts, exposing most of her chest. The skirt flares out from the waist, with a slit on each side that stops at her hip bones.

I don't understand how Nova doesn't flash anyone in that dress; it's so revealing.

"Nova, what are you doing here?" Carter asks, not afraid to be rude to her.

"Silly Carter, we always sit together." She says with a giggle.

No one responds to her.

Nova turns her attention back to Jace. "Jace, you look exceptionally handsome this evening." Nova purrs. She leans into him and places her hand on his arm.

I have to hold back the growl that works its way up. Uncontrollable anger crashes through me, and my eyes shift colors. My fork bends in my grip. I can't take my eyes off Nova's hand. I'm imagining ripping it from where it rests on Jace when I feel his arm brush against me.

I take a deep breath. The haze of anger clears from a single touch from Jace.

I lower my head until I feel calm again, hoping no one saw my eyes change color. I can't explain where that anger came from.

Jace shifts away slightly so Nova is no longer touching him. "Thank you, Nova. You look nice as well." Jace seems to choke on the compliment.

I have to hide my smile behind a napkin.

Of course, Nova doesn't notice Jace's struggle. "Thank you!" She squeals. "I had this dress specially made for me. Isn't it stunning?"

I have to stifle a snort. It looks like the others are also struggling.

Jace is spared from having to answer. The servants come around to clear our empty plates, replacing them with the next course: a butternut squash soup with maple syrup drizzled on top.

"The biggest spoon," Jace whispers.

I pick up the larger of the two spoons.

"Aww, how cute. Aria doesn't know what spoon to use." Nova coos.

My face turns flaming red from embarrassment. Nova was probably taught etiquette from a young age. I must look like I grew up in a cave compared to her.

"Nova," Jace growls in a warning.

"What?" She bats her eyes at him innocently.

Jace shoots Nova a glare. She pouts but doesn't say anything else to me for the rest of the dinner.

Chapter Fifteen

"This is when the real party begins," Nox whispers beside me as the servants clear our dessert plates away.

"What do you mean?"

"See how the teachers are leaving?" He asks. I watch the teachers all stand, moving towards the stairs. "They only join the supper portion, then leave and let us have fun without them watching."

They trust us to leave us alone?

Once the adults leave, the orchestra starts up again, and students flood the dance floor. I keep my head down, trying not to draw attention to myself. I know Nox said he would teach me to dance, but now the idea of dancing in front of all these strangers makes me incredibly nervous.

"Dance with me?" I hear Jace ask. Thinking he's talking to Nova, I don't lift my head. I can't stomach watching them dance together.

"Aria?"

My heart pounds as I look at Jace. He stands beside me with his hand outstretched. "I... I don't know how to dance." I whisper quietly in hopes that Nova won't hear.

Of course, she hears me, and I notice her giggling behind Jace. "Oh, Jace, you should have known she wouldn't know how to dance. She didn't even know what cutlery to use. I'll dance with you."

Jace still stands facing me with his hand outstretched, ignoring Nova. "I'll teach you." He offers. He smiles warmly at me. It's the first time I have seen a smile on his face.

It's his smile that does me in. I tentatively place my hand in Jace's. His hands are rough from years of using a sword.

Keeping my hand in his, he leads me to an open spot on the dance floor.

"You need to place one hand on my shoulder and the other in my hand." Not letting go of my hand, he pulls me close. Jace places his free hand on the small of my back while I set mine on his shoulder. "The moves of a waltz are simple. It's a 1, 2, 3 movement in a box shape. I'll lead us."

I nod my head as he begins to move us. Following his lead, I step back when he steps forward and step forward as he steps back.

After a few times, I find myself getting the hang of it.

"You're a natural." He praises me.

"Thank you. The guys were right; this is fun." I smile up at him.

As his lips part and a look of wonder crosses his face, I realize it's one of the first times I've had a full smile on my face since arriving at the academy.

"You look gorgeous." He says gruffly. His pupils are blown wide, so much so I can only see a strip of gold.

When Nox complimented me, it made me feel good, pretty even. But Jace's compliment has my heart fluttering, and warmth spreading through me. His compliment makes me feel special. Maybe it's because he doesn't seem like the kind of person to give a compliment to many people. Or maybe it's because he took the time to get me a dress, showing me the person he is under the mask. Either way, his compliment means more to me than any other one.

"Thank you." My voice comes out husky. I clear my throat. "And thank you for the dress."

"You're welcome." Jace's lips tilt up in the barest hint of a smile. I memorize it, commit it to memory, so I can look back on it later.

"I have never seen a more gorgeous dress."

Jace twirls me away. When he pulls me back in, we dance much closer together. My skin tingles from the contact. "I'm glad you like it so much. I had it made for you."

My jaw drops. "You had it made for me?"

"You deserve to own a beautiful dress." He says as if that is an explanation.

Butterflies take flight in my stomach. They dance around, making me feel fluttery and lightheaded. At the same time the tug in my chest gives a sharp pull, urging me to be closer to Jace.

Jace didn't just buy me a dress to make me feel like I belonged tonight. No, he went as far as having a custom dress made for me. He made sure that no one else would be wearing what I was. His simple act of kindness has made me feel more special, more cared for than ever before. Don't get me wrong, Killian did everything for me. He gave me a life that I didn't know I could have. He gave me a family. But what Jace has done for me is different. He's made me feel like a princess, even if it's only for the night.

This prince is breaking down all my defenses. He's smashed the walls I've spent years building around my heart, obliterating it in one single act. The thought of staying away from him now seems impossible.

There's a thread pulling us together, winding our fates together before our eyes.

Jace dips me, interrupting my thoughts. I instinctively bring my leg up, exposed with the slit, to rest on his hip. He has one hand on the small of my back, and the other goes to my bare leg.

I can't help but shiver from the contact. Jace must have felt it because a hungry look crossed his face. Still bent over, he pulls me closer to him. My chest brushes against his, our mouths only a couple of inches apart. The tugging sensation in my chest turns wild as everything else in the room fades away into the background.

His eyes dip to my lips, then flick back up to meet my eyes. He lowers his head even further, almost closing the space between us.

Applause starts up for the orchestra, breaking the spell. Jace slowly brings me up, running his hand up my thigh. I'm nearly panting by the time I'm standing upright.

We stand in the middle of the dance floor, staring at each other, not saying anything.

"My turn." Nova coos beside us, interrupting our moment. "You have done your charity work for the night, Jace. Now you can have fun."

Nova has a way of knowing where to hit. Her words cut deep.

I try to step away from Jace, but he won't let go of my waist.

Jace shakes his head slightly, telling me silently that he doesn't think of me that way.

"Don't speak about her like that," Jace replies sharply.

"Fine." Nova huffs. "Will you please just dance with me?"

Jace finally lets go of my waist and offers his hand to Nova.

My heart breaks a little as I watch him glide Nova around the dance floor. I don't understand why I'm so possessive of Jace. I barely know him.

"Trust me, he would much rather be dancing with you," Nox says, walking up beside me.

"They look like they belong together," I say quietly. I rub my chest, trying to relieve the pressure building.

"Dance with me." Nox doesn't give me time to respond. Instead, he grabs my hands and spins me around the room.

I throw my head back, laughing. He makes up the dance moves as we go.

"It's probably best that Jace danced with you first." He says after a few twirls around the room.

"Why is that?"

"Because he would teach you how to dance. I'm just going to show you how to have fun."

I laugh at him as he passes me off to Theon.

I dance for hours with Theon, Chase, Carter, and Nox. Every so often, I get a glimpse of Jace. Each time, he is dancing with a different girl. A courtly smile sits on his face while the girls chat away with him. But he never showed a genuine smile or held them as close as he had held me.

My feet are aching by the time the clock strikes midnight.

"I need some air," I tell the guys.

"Do you want company?" Carter asks.

I wave him off. "No, that's okay. I'll only be a moment."

I leave the dance floor, walk over to our table, and remove my heels, leaving them there. I sigh once they are off my feet.

I exit the door closest to our table, walking into the gardens. I breathe in the night air. People lounge around on the stone benches, but I ignore them.

I wander through the gardens, coming across a maze hidden at the back. The maze butts up against the forest and doesn't seem well maintained. The hedges that make up the maze grow in every direction, with weeds and thorns poking out. Little fae lights line the top.

Even though it doesn't seem to be used much, I want to check it out. I always liked mazes and puzzles.

Trailing my hand along the maze's wall, I choose random turns, not paying attention to where I am going.

All the sudden, everything turns eerily silent, and the maze grows darker. I can't even hear any crickets anymore. I've lost all sense of time and direction in the maze.

I stop moving, letting my hand that was touching the wall fall to my side.

I will my heart to remain calm. I can find my way out. I just have to retrace my steps.

I turn around and take the first left, thinking it's the way I had come. I take a few more turns before I realize I have brought myself further into the maze. It's when I see a stone water fountain, I figure I must be in the middle of the maze.

Now that I have found the maze's center, finding my way out shouldn't be too hard.

The water fountain catches my eye as I make my way closer to it. In the center, made of stone, is a male holding the hand of a female. I tilt my head, looking at the couple. They vaguely resemble the first king and queen. It would make sense since Nox told me this used to be their castle.

The first king and queen were said to be ruthless and evil and treated their subjects like servants. The kingdom suffered greatly under their wrath. Fae starved, children were orphaned, and people were executed for no reason other than for their enjoyment.

Many fae tried to assassinate the king and queen, but none could get past the wall of guards surrounding them at all times. They didn't have the magic or weapons to defeat them.

When that failed, they tried to use poisons, thinking if they could weaken them, then they would be able to attach the magic-suppressing cuffs and throw them in prison. But all that did was kill the innocent fae who were tasked with testing their food.

No one was powerful enough, smart enough to defeat them.

The gods and goddesses heard the kingdom's pleas for help. The goddess Nyx wept when she saw the destruction the king and queen were causing. She always favored the kingdom of Noctem and decided to intervene. Choosing Alexander, Jace's great-grandfather, to bless with extra magic, she gave him the ability to kill the king and queen.

No one knows why Nyx chose Alexander. He was only a simple farmer when she came to him. Nevertheless, she decided correctly, considering he single-handedly slayed the evil king and queen and led the rebel army to defeat their supporters. The kingdom rejoiced and crowned him king the next day.

The wind picks up, blowing stray pieces of my hair into my face. As I push my hair away, I hear whispers. I try to make out what they are saying but can't.

"Hello?" I call out, thinking it's a couple of students who also wandered into the maze.

"Aria." A sing-song voice whispers from further in the maze.

I walk around the fountain in a daze, following the voice. Behind the fountain, there's only one opening. No light comes from inside that section of the hedge. It's as if all the light has been sucked out; it's so dark.

"Aria." The voice calls again. I feel my feet move on their own accord, leading me further into the new section of the maze.

Chapter Sixteen

All light vanishes as soon as I enter the new part of the maze. It's so dark I can't even make out my hands in front of me. I try to turn around to leave, but instead of where the opening was, a hedge blocks my way.

Before I can panic, I hear the voice again. "This way, child of darkness."

I blindly follow the voice. I trail my hand along the hedge so I won't run into anything.

I walk for what feels like just a few minutes, only turning when I have to. The longer I walk, the more I stumble over what feels like sticks or logs. Twice I falter and catch myself before I fall on my face.

"This way. This way." The voice chants, getting increasingly more urgent the closer I get. I pick up my pace.

Finally, after what seems like an hour, I can make out a speck of light in the distance. I break into a run, desperate to find out where this leads me.

"Come here, my child." The voice beckons.

I pause. The closer I get, the more the voice sounds like what I imagine my mother would sound like.

"Mom?" I call out. My heart pounds with anticipation.

"Yes, my child. Come to me."

I break into a sprint. Tears stream down my face. My mother is at the end of the maze. I don't know how, and I don't care either. My mother is alive, and that is all that matters to me.

"Mom!"

"Aria!" A voice behind me roars. "Stop!"

I don't listen to the voice behind me. I can't. I have to get to my mother.

"That's it, my child. Come home to me."

"I'm coming." I cry.

I reach out my hand, almost grazing the light, when strong arms wrap around me from behind, pulling me away.

"No!" I scream. I squirm, kick, and punch the person holding me, doing everything I can to escape their embrace.

The person behind me grunts from the assault. "Aria. Stop, it's me."

I stop moving at the sound of Jace's rough voice. I pant, unable to get a full breath in. It's like a veil has been lifted from over me.

"What happened?" I ask through chattering teeth. I'm freezing.

Jace sets me down and turns me to face him, not removing his hands from my shoulders. A little fae light bobs beside his head, highlighting the concern on his face.

"You've been wandering around the maze for hours," Jace says as I rub my arms, trying to warm up. Jace tracks the movement. "Here, take this." He removes his tuxedo jacket and helps me put my arms through it.

"Thanks." Jace's sandalwood and pine scent wraps around me like a warm hug, bringing warmth back into my body. "I've been out here for hours?"

It didn't feel like that much time had passed.

Jace nods his head. "What were you doing?"

"I was just exploring the maze when I heard a voice. I thought it was my mom, so I followed it." I explain.

I realize how stupid that sounds as I say it aloud.

Of course, the voice I heard wasn't my mother's. There are all sorts of fae creatures that will lure you in with false desires, only to find yourself at their mercy. I feel my heart crumble with the realization.

"I'm sorry, Aria." Jace crushes me against him. I melt into him, sobbing. Jace doesn't say anything. He holds me while rubbing small circles on my back, silently comforting me. I appreciate that he doesn't try to talk, to try to fill the void growing inside of me.

The tears slowly dry up. However, the ache in my heart doesn't seem to want to leave.

Jace stiffens. "Are you hurt?" He pulls me away from him, checking me over.

I feel an ache in my feet now that Jace has said it. "I don't know." I lift my skirt to check.

Jace kneels and lifts one of my feet. I hiss in pain as he does. Now that the adrenaline has worn off, my feet are throbbing with pain.

The fae light bobs closer for Jace to see. "Your feet are a mess. There are cuts all over them, and some look pretty deep." Jace looks up at me with his jaw clenched. I can tell he's mad. However, I don't know if he's angry because of the situation or at me.

Jace gently places my foot back down and stands up. Then, without saying a word, he slides one arm around my back and the other behind my knees, picking me up.

"I can walk." I protest.

Jace glares at me. "No, you can't."

"I'm sorry," I whisper.

Jace sighs, tucking me in closer. I rest my head on his chest, snuggling into his warmth. "It's not your fault. I take it no one ever warned you not to wander into the maze at night?" He asks. I shake my head no. "There are boggarts, pookas, and other creatures in this maze that would rip you apart in seconds if given the opportunity."

I shiver at the thought. "Why doesn't the academy get rid of them, then?"

"Because the maze was their home long before the academy was here," Jace explains. "The first king and queen let the creatures live in the maze. They used the maze to torture fae, who disobeyed them. The creatures have nowhere else to go."

"Oh." I understand now why the academy would let them stay.

As I look ahead, I catch sight of what cut my feet. I suck in a sharp breath. "Are those bones?"

"Yes."

My bones would have joined the others if it hadn't been for Jace. "Thank you. For finding me."

Jace looks down at me with such intensity. His eyes are a dark shade of gold in the fae light. "I will always find you."

My breath whooshes out of me.

Voices ahead stop me from responding.

"You found her," Theon says with relief. Headmaster Nickolas, the twins, and Nox stand with him.

"Wait, why didn't it take as long to get out of the maze?" I ask. Jace said I had been in there for hours.

"The maze moves. It didn't take as long to get out because it knows not to mess with me." He says the last part with a smirk.

I can't help the small smile that works across my face. I still feel hollow and lost from the maze, but Jace's joke thaws some of the icy feeling spreading through me.

"Are you okay, Aria?" Nickolas asks.

"Her feet are badly cut," Jace replies for me, but Nickolas looks at me, expecting an answer.

"I'm okay, sir. My feet are the only thing that is hurt." Well, that and my heart. But Nickolas and the others don't need to know that.

"I need to apologize to you. I didn't think to mention the maze when you arrived. I'm very sorry for my mistake."

"All is forgiven, sir," I reply. As much as my heart hurts right now from my experience in the maze, I won't blame Nickolas for it. I have a feeling that even if he had warned me, I still would have found my way there.

Nickolas still looks guilty but nods his head.

"Bring her to the healing wing. I'll call Isabelle to come and check on her." Nickolas instructs Jace.

Jace nods his head in response and continues to walk back inside.

The ballroom is empty as we walk through it.

"Where is everyone?" I ask.

"It's five in the morning. The ball ended hours ago." Carter explains.

It seems all the guys will be walking me to the healing wing.

"I was in there that long?" I knew it had been a while, but I didn't think it had been five hours.

"Yes." I can feel the rumble of Jace's chest.

I don't say anything else as we make the short walk to the healing wing. Isabelle is already waiting for us when we arrive.

"Place her here, please." Isabelle points to the first bed.

Jace does as she instructs, carefully laying me on the bed. He moves so he will be out of the way for Isabelle to work but still close to me. The others stand off to the side.

Isabelle gets right to work cleaning my feet. I hiss out a breath from the touch of the cloth.

"Sorry, these cuts are deeper than I expected." Isabelle apologizes. "I need to pull some things out of the deeper ones. I'll try to be quick."

Jace sits on the chair beside the bed, picking up my hand and undoing the tight fist I held it in as he does. He gives it a gentle squeeze. I try to focus on the feel of Jace's hand on mine instead of what Isabelle is doing. However, it's hard. I can feel her digging into my foot to remove whatever is stuck.

I shudder, thinking about what it could be.

"Focus on me, Sweetheart." Jace's rough voice brings my eyes to him.

"I really hate that nickname." I scowl at him.

He grins. "You might hate it, but it brought your attention to me, didn't it?"

I'm about to respond when Isabelle pulls a particularly deep piece of debris from my foot. I clench my jaw to prevent myself from crying out in pain. How I didn't feel whatever was in my foot before Jace found me is beyond me.

"Eyes on me, Sweetheart." Jace commands.

I didn't realize I had closed them. I open my eyes to get lost in Jace's golden ones. His magic snakes out and wraps around me. It feels like being wrapped in a warm hug.

Isabelle finally finishes removing the debris from my feet. A warm glow emits from her hands, bringing my attention back to her. Her healing magic seeps into my feet, and I sigh as I feel the pain leave.

"There, that should do it," Isabelle says as she finishes. "You are good to go."

"Thank you, Isabelle. I'm sorry for making you get out of bed." I say as I stand up. My feet feel much better.

"You're welcome, dear. Now, get some sleep, all of you." She shoos us out of the healing wing.

"I'll walk you to your room." Jace offers as we leave.

"Thanks," I say goodnight to the others and lead Jace to my room.

Jace doesn't try to get me to talk, choosing to walk in silence beside me. It's a comfortable silence I'm happy to spend time in. I still feel hollow from the maze, and words won't help that.

"This is me." As I turn to say goodnight to Jace I find him much closer than I expected. My chest brushes up against his.

"Thank you again for finding me and for the dress. I hope I didn't ruin it." My voice comes out breathier than I want.

"You're welcome." His voice has gone husky. "If you give the dress to me later, I can have the royal dressmaker do any repairs on it."

"I'd like that, thank you." I hadn't noticed we had stepped closer togeth-er. We stand like that for minutes, touching but not touching.

Jace clears his throat, "I should let you sleep."

"Right," I nod. "Goodnight, Jace."

"Goodnight, Aria."

Chapter Seventeen

Early the next morning, I lay in bed, replaying everything that had happened the night before.

I can't help the smile that spreads across my face as I think about my dance with Jace. He hadn't danced with the other girls the way he danced with me. He held me close and talked with me. With the other girls, he was the polite courtly prince. I don't want to read anything into it, but I am having a hard time not, especially since he was the one who found me.

My smile vanishes with that thought. I don't want to dwell too much on that part of the night. I feel stupid now for believing my mother would call me into a maze. I don't even know the sound of her voice. If it weren't for Jace, I would have ended up like those other fae whose bones I saw.

I hadn't gotten much sleep after Jace walked me to my room. I had slept for only a couple of hours before the nightmares woke me. I kept dreaming of being in the maze, someone chasing me, and a female's voice calling for me, calling me a child of darkness. Whatever that means.

I push off the covers, shake off the dark thoughts, and pad over to the glass doors. I open the curtains to look out to the mountains. The sun is shining, tinting the mountains orange. My eyes are drawn to the waterfall I saw on my first day.

Needing to be in nature, I decide today is the perfect day to explore the mountains.

I shower and change into a pair of black leggings, a sports bra, a black short-sleeved t-shirt, a lightweight army green sweatshirt, and my favorite sneakers. I grab my bookbag to load with snacks and water from the grand hall.

With everything ready, I set out to get breakfast.

"Good morning, Aria." Theon greets me as I walk over to where he sits with Nox and Carter.

"Good morning." I place my tray down and take a seat beside him. "Where are Chase and Jace?"

"They aren't morning people, so they're still in bed," Carter explains.

"That's too bad. I was going to invite you to come with me today." I bite into my breakfast sandwich, sighing at how good it is. The academy sure knows how to make good food.

"Where are you going?" Nox asks, clearly interested.

"There's a waterfall in the mountains that I can see from my bedroom that I wanted to check out. So, I thought it would be fun if you came with me."

"Sounds good to me. I'll give Chase and Jace a call and wake them up." Carter says, pulling his phone out to make the calls.

The guys and I finish breakfast while waiting for Jace and Chase.

"Whose bloody idea was it to go hiking at ten in the morning on a Sunday?" Jace snarls as he takes a seat at the table fifteen minutes later.

I try to hold back a giggle at his appearance. His hair, damp from the shower, is sticking out, his shirt is on backward, and he looks like he is still half asleep. Chase, unfortunately, isn't much better. He sits down, leans his head on his hand, ignores the breakfast he got, and closes his eyes.

I can't help it. The giggle escapes.

Jace's head snaps to where I am sitting. He pins me in place with his golden eyes. "Something funny?" He asks in a low, gruff voice.

"I don't think I have ever seen you look so un-princely." My smile widens when his scowl deepens.

Jace mockingly snarls at me and takes a bite of his breakfast sandwich. "So, I suppose I have you to thank for getting me up this early?"

"It's not that early. Besides, it's a beautiful morning for a hike."

"Sure, if we hadn't gone to bed past five this morning, I might agree." Jace keeps his golden gaze on me, assessing me. "Did you get any sleep?"

I just shrug. "Enough." I don't want to tell him I only had two hours worth. He doesn't need to know that. "Are you ready to go?"

Carter shoves Chase, causing him to smash his face on the tables. "I'm up." He cries.

I leave an annoyed Chase to gather us water and snacks.

"This should lead to the waterfall you saw," Jace says to me after leading us to a path behind the academy.

The path leads to a steep incline up the mountainside. The trail looks twisty, and some parts are on the mountain's edge.

I remove my sweatshirt and put it in my bag. Even though it's October, the sun is warming me enough that I don't need it.

"Okay. Let's do this."

Hiking up the mountains, the trees thin out the higher we get so we can see the entire capital. The sun beats down on Oxynmire, bathing the city in its gold glow, making the brightly colored house even prettier.

The trail twists after an hour of hiking, bringing us to the backside of the castle.

I stop to get a better look at it.

When I entered the capital a week ago, I thought the castle was foreboding, but standing on top of the mountains, I can see why others would find it beautiful.

The back of the castle is made up mostly of large windows overlooking the mountain range. Ivy climbs up the sides of the stone walls and gold-trims the window frames. Behind the castle are sprawling gardens that put the academy's ones to shame. There is also a glass pool house attached to the castle. The barracks for the soldiers are along the outer wall, with a training arena beside it.

The twins, Nox and Theon, settle on the rocks behind me, taking a break. Jace comes to stand beside me, looking towards his home.

"What was it like growing up in a castle?" I ask him.

"Lonely," Jace says. When I turn to look at him, he is stiff, with his hands shoved into his jean pockets. "At least it was until Theon, Nox, the twins came to live at the castle. But that wasn't until I was twelve. Before that, I only had the guards to keep me company. With my parents busy running a kingdom, I was left to do as I pleased."

"The guys lived at the castle with you?" It explains the brotherly bond they all share. It would also explain why Jace only relaxes when they are around.

"None of the nobility had kids that would have been suitable playmates. And Mother thought it was unbecoming of a prince to play with someone below their station. So I wasn't allowed near the servants or the guards children." Jace spits out the words. I can tell from the grimace on his face that he disagrees with his mother. "So, when my father suggested to the council members that the guys come to stay, they obliged. We've been inseparable ever since."

"That was nice of your father to do that for you." I think about how different our lives were.

If it weren't for what happened to my parents, would I have grown up with him?

"What about you? Where did you grow up?" He asks, turning to look at me.

"Well, as you know, Killian took me in, so I grew up in Lockwood. It was just the two of us and the soldiers he trained. He taught me everything I know." I turn back to looking over the capital, not wanting to look at him.

"What about before that?"

Such an innocent question, and yet it makes me tense. "I went to live with Killian when I was five. He's the only home I've ever had."

"I'm sorry." He whispers. I finally turned to look at him. He is standing close enough to touch now. When had he moved closer?

"Don't be. Killian became my family. I wouldn't have become who I am without him." It is true. I will always be grateful for Killian.

I step closer to Jace. I always feel drawn to him. A pull in the center of my chest, always urging me to be close to him. I've never felt this way towards anyone before him.

Jace doesn't ask more about my parents. Instead, he reaches out like he wants to touch me—his hand hovers beside my face. I want to close the distance between us, but I don't move, afraid it will scare him away if I do.

"Are you guys ready to keep going?" Theon calls over to us.

Jace's face closes off with the sound of Theon's voice. He drops his hand and clenches his fist.

I quickly step away from him, cheeks turning pink from embarrassment. I'd forgotten the others were even there.

We join the others and continue to hike up the mountain.

Another hour passes before I can make out the sound of rushing water.

The waterfall that comes into view a few moments later is massive. It towers twenty feet in the air, with water flowing down the side of the mountain to land into a crystal-clear pool at the bottom. It's even more magnificent up close.

I walk over to the edge and dip my hand in.

"It's warm!" I turn back to the guys to find them taking their shirts off.

My mouth goes dry at the sight of Jace's chest. He is built like a god. With strong shoulders and chest, a six-pack with the v indent at the bottom, and thick biceps. I can't take my eyes off him.

"Aria, I think you might be drooling." Chase teases me.

I quickly avert my eyes, my cheeks turning pink again. "What are you doing?"

"You said the water is warm. Why not go for a swim?" Jace replies.

I keep my eyes on the pool as they remove the rest of their clothes.

"I don't have anything to swim in."

"Just wear what you have underneath," Theon says.

A splash from the left sends droplets landing on me.

I lift my head enough to look over to find Carter already in the pool.

"Come on, it'll be fun," Jace says, his voice coming from beside me.

I sigh. I want to get in with them. "Fine, but turn around." I don't want to get undressed in front of them.

The guys oblige, turning their backs to me. I quickly remove my boots, socks, leggings, and t-shirt. Leaving me only in my sports bra and underwear. I dive into the pool.

When I reach the bottom, I kick off and burst through the top.

My muscles relax, and my nightmare from last night melts away.

Carter and Chase are already starting a water fight between themselves. Theon is floating, and Jace and Nox are talking a little way over.

I raise my hand, forming little seals and sea horses with water magic. I have them jumping in and out of the water, dancing around me. I cast more magic, sending a sea horse over to Jace, making it dance in front of him.

Jace smiles warmly at the sea horse. It is one of the few ungraded smiles I have seen from him. It changes his whole face, making him go from a severe prince to a young male enjoying himself.

He reaches out his hand, touching the water animal gently. I can feel the caress like he touched my skin. I shudder and lose focus, causing the sea horse to burst, soaking Jace and Nox.

I toss my head back and laugh deeply at their scowls.

Jace turns to me, expression turning mock murderous. "You think that was funny?"

Instead of answering, I call my magic forward, making a small wave and sending it over to him. He doesn't have time to block it. I drench him again.

The next thing I know, a wave is knocking me over, sending me underwater.

I sputter when I come up for air. I push my hair out of my face and find Jace howling in laughter at me. My lips part at the sound. It's like music to me. The sound is deep and rough.

Before I get distracted further by the sound, I call forward my magic again to send another wave at him to get back, but he deflects it with air magic, causing Nox to get the brunt of the wave.

Nox turns to me when he comes back up. "Now you've done it."

Gathering water to throw back at me, Nox tries to fling it in my direction. But, at the last second, I use my air magic to push it toward Theon.

Theon sends wave after wave, dragging us all under.

We spend the rest of the day hiking, relaxing, and just having fun. It is the first time since I arrived at the academy that I have felt truly happy.

Chapter Eighteen

I stand at the entrance of the maze again.

"Aria, come to me." A woman's voice calls to me.

"Mama?"

The maze entrance is just as dark as it was the first time. The only thing is, I don't remember walking to the maze.

"Come to me, child of darkness."

Without conscious thought, I step through the maze entrance.

Instead of staying in the maze this time, I'm transported to another place.

The darkness clears the way to the scene of a small cottage in a forest.

Standing at the threshold of the cottage, my hand reaches forward to open the door to go inside.

The cottage opens to a small living room painted in a soft gray, with exposed beams, a brick fireplace, and a small couch in the center of the room. I turn around on the spot. A small kitchen is visible through an archway on the left.

"Hello?" I call out.

How did I get here? A better question is, what is this place?

Walking further into the cottage, I pass a door open to an office, another to a bathroom, and one to a guest room. I stop at the second-to-last room in the house.

It's a baby room. There's a wooden crib in one corner, a rocking chair in another, and soft carpets cover the floor with the walls painted to depict the mountains.

My heart stops as soon as I step inside. I don't understand how, but I know, without a doubt, this room is mine.

I back out of the room, turning to the only other room in the house. I rush down the hall to what has to be my parents' room.

Excitement pumps through me. All these years were just a nightmare. My parents aren't dead; they are alive and well. I'll wake them up and tell them about it. They tell me everything's okay as they make me a cup of hot chocolate.

I shove the door open only to find my parents lying in a pool of blood, their throats slit.

Screaming, I fall to the floor, my body unable to hold me up. I curl into a ball, sobbing uncontrollably.

They're dead.

I feel my whole world crash down around me, hope shattering.

I don't know how long I lay on the floor at the foot of my parents' bed when suddenly, hands roughly grab me by the hair from behind. The person drags me from the room. I kick, scream, and claw at the person. But nothing gets them to release their hold.

"You belong to me, child of darkness." A male voice says.

A cold feeling spreads through me. I recognize that voice, but don't remember where I've heard it before.

"What do you want from me?" I whisper.

The male doesn't answer. Just continues to drag me by the hair. I panic more as he starts to pull me out of the house.

The setting changes once more. This time, I'm hanging from shackles in a dark dungeon. The only light comes from a fae light that bobs outside my cell.

Something warm and sticky slides down my back.

A whistling noise fills the air seconds before it feels like someone douses my back with fire. I scream, my throat tuning raw. Pain like I could never imagine courses through me.

I realize, seconds too late, that the whistling sound is coming from someone pulling their arm back with a whip in hand.

"Why?" I cry out.

I don't understand why this is happening. Why would someone want to whip me?

"This is the only way." The same male voice as before says.

The following crack of the whip causes the room to go dark.

I wake with a scream lodged in my throat.

I run to the bathroom, barely making it in time to throw up.

When I have nothing left in my stomach, I slide down to rest my head against the cold tile floors. My whole body is vibrating. I can still feel the phantom pain of the whip.

Dark thoughts flow through my mind. Was that only a dream, or was it a memory? Am I starting to remember what happened to me when I was kidnapped? Or am I seeing my future?

A shudder rolls through me.

It takes ages, but the cold tile cools my skin, and I can breathe a little. I'm still shaking, but I'm no longer on the verge of hyperventilating.

I slowly peel myself from the floor, checking my watch. It's only three thirty in the morning. I sigh, knowing I won't be getting back to sleep. I decide to change into my workout clothes and go for a run to clear my head.

I'm still shaking and an overall mess by the time I get to the grand hall for breakfast. I skip the food and go straight to the coffee. The idea of food makes my stomach roll.

"Morning, Aria." Nox greets me as I sit down beside him.

I give a little wave, not saying anything.

I'm too busy trying to hold myself together to pretend to be in a good mood. I can't shake the realness of the nightmare.

Jace sits across from me, staring at me intently. "What's wrong?"

"Nothing," I reply, my voice barely over a whisper.

The look in Jace's eyes says he's not buying it.

I imagine I look about as good as I feel. After my run, I took a quick shower, put on the bare minimum makeup, and threw my hair into a messy bun. I'm not even sure if I buttoned my shirt correctly.

"Aria." I lift my head at the tone in Jace's voice. He's now sitting beside me in Nox's spot. "What's the matter?" He asks again, this time in a low, gentle voice.

I sigh. "It was just a nightmare. I'm fine." I don't want to explain any more than that. Jace must understand that since he just dips his head in response.

"You need to eat."

I shake my head. "I'm not hungry." I lie.

Jace doesn't look happy but doesn't push the matter. He leaves me alone for the rest of breakfast but keeps a close eye on me.

I'm dragging my feet by the end of the day.

The nightmare played through my mind all day, distracting me and causing me to perform poorly in all my classes. And I had to listen to the other first-years laugh at me and say it was a fluke that I did so well the first few days.

But I only have combat class left for the day. After this, I can shut the world out and wallow.

"Hi, Aria." Carter waves at me as I sit on the floor to start stretching. "Want to be my partner today?"

"Sure."

Sparring has always had a way of clearing my mind. Maybe this is what I need to get the images of my parents in a pool of blood out of my head.

"Okay, everyone, you know the drill. Partner up and begin sparring." Emmett says as he walks into the room.

I follow Carter to the weapons rack.

I eye the different types of swords. I've been challenging myself to try a different one each time I spar with someone, ensuring I'm still proficient with each one. This time, I chose my favorite, two short swords, while Chase picks out a long sword.

With our weapons in hand, we move to any empty spot on the mats.

Carter brings his sword up to a ready position. I fall into a fighting stance but keep my swords low as I assess Carter. A slight shift of his feet tells me he favors his left side.

I roll my shoulders back, already feeling slightly better.

Carter rushes me, bringing his sword down in an arc. I dance out of the way. Landing on his left side, I use the flat of one of the short swords to smack his side. The side he left open. Carter grunts.

Twisting back around to face me, he tries to bring his sword down on me again. Since it's so long, I don't have time to dart out of the way. I bring my swords up, blocking his hit at the last second. I push him off, using my whole body weight, causing him to stumble. I kick out my leg, catching him in the left leg, making him lose his balance. Using the flat slide of my sword again, I hit the wrist holding his sword. He curses. Losing his grip on the sword, it clatters to the ground. I point one sword at his neck and the other at his heart.

I'm panting by the end of the round. The lack of sleep is starting to catch up to me. Usually, a round like that, I wouldn't have even broken a sweat. Today, everything seems more challenging.

I extend my hand to help Carter up.

"How do you move so fast?" Carter asks as he accepts my hand.

I shrug, "I don't know. I've always been able to move fast."

"You're like a blur when you get going." Carter shakes his head. "Again?"

Carter and I go a few more rounds. I win each one. However, Carter gets a few good hits on me.

By the end, I'm bent over, sweat dripping down my face, trying to breathe normally. I'm exhausted.

"Want to go another round before class is over?" Carter asks me.

I groan. The last hit I had taken to my ribs had done some damage. I'm not sure I can go another round.

"She's done, Carter," Jace says, coming up beside us.

I straighten, the movement causing my already aching ribs to shift. I hold in a whimper.

"Aria?" Carter looks at me to see what I have to say.

"I'm done." I don't want to appreciate Jace stepping in to stop us, but I do. I would've pushed myself to go another round if he hadn't said anything.

"Are you okay?" Jace's eyes search my face for an answer.

"Fine." I hold onto my left side, the side that I'm pretty sure I either cracked or severely bruised a rib. I don't know how to heal anything besides minor cuts, so I'll have to go to Isabelle to fix it.

"Liar." He frowns at me. "Here, let me." He steps in close to me, not giving me a chance to protest. Removing my hand from my ribs, he replaces it with his own. Warmth spreads from his hand, healing my ribs.

My eyes flutter from the sensation of Jace's magic flooding my system. I sigh in relief.

Jace's magic feels different from Isabelle's. His magic feels like an inferno. Like I've been lying out on a hot summer day, baking in the sun. Heat spreads from my ribs to the rest of my body, warming all of me.

"How's that feel?" He asks gruffly when he is done.

I open my eyes to find Jace staring at me intently. His eyes are liquid gold, fastened on my face. "Better. Thank you."

I lick my lips. Jace tightens the hand, still holding my side. His eyes flick down to my lips before moving back to my eyes. My pulse picks up. He pulls me closer so our chests brush with each inhale.

The tugging sensation I always feel around him grows tenfold with his proximity.

"Are you two coming?" Theon calls from the male changing room door.

I take a step back, not realizing that everyone has already left.

I clear my throat, suddenly embarrassed. "Thanks again for healing my ribs."

Without waiting for a response, I rack my swords and rush to the female changing room.

When I open the door, I look over my shoulder, finding Jace standing in the same spot, watching me with that unreadable expression.

Chapter Nineteen

Chase was wrong when he said things would get better for me.

Having finished classes for the day, I'm waiting for Nickolas in his office. My two weeks are up. It's time for me to tell Nickolas my decision.

The door to his office opens behind me, letting me know Nickloas has arrived.

"Good evening, Aria. How are you?" He asks as he joins me in the sitting area.

"I'm okay." I lie.

Truth be told, I'm not. I'm exhausted from classes every day and very lonely. The only bright spot in my days–the only time I didn't feel so alone–is when I see the guys during mealtimes, combat class, and defensive magic class. I don't have anyone to talk to or pair up with during my other classes. Everyone in my year avoids me like the plague. I try to be friendly and make conversations with them, but nothing works.

I also miss Killian desperately. This is the longest we have been apart since I started living with him. Even though he traveled for work, Killian always made sure to be home after a few days. We've spoken a few times since I arrived, but it's not the same. I could use one of his hugs right now.

I've continued to have nightmares every night since the ball. They're always the same thing, the night my parents died. I was too young to remember anything of that night, so I assume my brain is making up what happened.

After seeing my parents with their throats slit, the nightmare will shift to someone torturing me. I wake up every night from them, screaming, covered in sweat. I can never get back to sleep after the nightmare. I lay there for hours, waiting for the sun to come up. Sometimes, I run or go to the gym to try to clear my head, but it never works.

Most days, I am an overall mess.

"I'm sensing that's not the whole truth. You're not looking too good. Are you sure that everything is okay?" Nickolas looks genuinely concerned.

I know I look terrible. I have purple bruises under my eyes from the lack of sleep, and I've lost weight since the nightmares started. It's probably due to the fact that I have lost my appetite entirely.

All laughter and smiles have dried up, too. Every so often, one of the guys will be able to pull a smile out of me, but it's rare. I know they're concerned about me. They've asked me a few times what is going on, but I turn them down each time. Now, they just offer their support, telling me they're here for me when I'm ready to talk.

"I'm still trying to adjust to being here. I had a few bad dreams recently, but nothing to worry about. I'm sure they will go away." I hope that's enough of the truth to appease him. I know Nickolas only wants to help, but I don't want to talk to anyone about the nightmares. Actually, it's not that I don't want to. It's that I don't think I can.

"Well, please come to me if the dreams continue. I can have a sleeping potion made up. You need your sleep." Nickolas still looks at me with concern but must know I don't want to talk about it. "Anyway, have you decided what you want to do concerning joining the second-year courses?"

I have thought long and hard about it, mainly when I can't sleep. "I think taking second-year classes would be a good idea. You were right. It's worth the risk." I can't let my fear of the council finding out I'm alive stop me. I need my magic if I'm going to stay alive.

The thought of running away now seems ridiculous to me. As hard as the last two weeks have been, I know I need to stay at the academy.

"Wonderful." Nickolas beams. "I'll have your new class schedule sent to your rooms, along with your books. You'll be in all second-year classes now. The only two that will remain the same are your combat and defensive magic classes. I think you're making the right decision."

I hope Nickolas is right.

My stomach is in knots, thinking about telling the guys tomorrow.

I sit in the grand hall the next morning, reviewing my new class schedule. I didn't bother getting any food. My stomach is too twisted to even try eating.

"What do you have there?" Nox asks, taking a seat beside me.

Jace sits on my other side. He hasn't said much to me since the day he healed my ribs in combat, but he always sits close to me, watching me.

The tugging sensation I felt when I first saw Jace has grown stronger. I find myself absentmindedly rubbing my chest at times to relieve the tension. I've caught Jace doing the same. I want to understand what it means but haven't had the time or the energy to investigate it.

"Good morning to you, too." I joke with him. "It's my new class schedule. Nickolas has decided it would be better if I joined the second-year classes." I expect the guys to be surprised or even annoyed, but instead, they look relieved.

"Pay up, suckers! You guys owe me fifty dollars," Theon says, looking smug.

The guys groan and fish out their wallets to pay Theon.

My mouth pops open in shock. "You guys bet how long it would take me to join the second-years?"

"Of course we did. We bet as soon as we heard you could use your water magic out of the lake," Carter explains.

I laugh a little at that. I guess it shouldn't have surprised me as much as it did.

"So, who bet what?" I'm curious as to how long they thought I'd last in the first-year classes.

"Well, Nox said three weeks, Carter said a month, Chase said two months, and as you know, I said two weeks," Theon says.

"And Jace, did you bet on me too?" I turn in my seat to find him looking at me with so much heat in his eyes that I forget to breathe for a minute. The tugging sensation is frantic.

Jace doesn't respond at first but then says in a low, gruff voice, "I bet you would join the second-years after the first day."

The little air that I had left in my lungs vanishes. I didn't know Jace had that much faith in me.

One of the guys clears their throat. I didn't realize how much time had passed while Jace and I were staring at each other. I look away, my face turning scarlet, as I pick up my mug and take a sip.

Jace slides a plate of food in front of me as I place my mug down.

"You need to eat if you are going to join the second-years." He gives me a pointed look. Ah, so he has noticed the lack of food lately.

"Yeah, we won't go easy on you in class." Chase winks at me. "Sadly, you won't get to see Jace in action, though. Just the rest of us."

"Oh, why not?" I take a bite of the eggs from the plate.

"I also skipped my first year, so I take third-year classes," Jace says.

I choke on my eggs, not expecting that. But it makes sense. From the little magic I have seen him use in defensive magic class is clearly at a high level.

Nox taps my back and hands me water. "Thanks." When I turn to look at Jace, he has a grin on his face. He is clearly enjoying that he managed to surprise me. "You skipped your first year?"

"I did." He nods for me to keep eating. "I'm sure you have heard the rumors that my father is only sitting on the throne until I am done at Nightfall. They are true." That was something Ajax had said when we first met. "I'm only here to fill the requirement to sit on the throne. My father does not wish to rule anymore."

"Really? But he's such a good king."

Since King Baston took the throne, the kingdom prospered even more than before. Even with the demon attacks, the kingdom is well-fed, has money, and is generally happy. No one questions that he isn't doing everything to try and stop the demons.

In the last ten years, the demon attacks have almost come to an end, with only a few here and there. He has made the kingdom a safe place, one filled with laughter and a sense of ease that wasn't present before his family line took over.

Jace raises his eyebrow at me. With a start, I register how that sounded. "Not that you won't be a good king. You'll make a great king. The best." I bite my lip to stop rambling.

Jace's grin shows off a dimple I have never seen before. *A dimple.* I can't look away from him. His grin stretches into a full smile. It changes his face, making it more boyish. Gone is the princely mask I'm accustomed to seeing.

"Thank you for the vote of confidence. But my father wishes to enjoy his remaining years and teach me how to run the kingdom from the side. He says he has done it long enough that it's time to pass it on to me. He will become my advisor when I'm king. I hope that with his help, I can become half the king he is."

I feel down to my bones that Jace will make an excellent king. The fact that he knows he needs help and can't do it on his own speaks volumes.

"Does that mean you will graduate early? Wait, does that mean I get to graduate early?" I hadn't even considered that by skipping a year, I would be able to leave the capital sooner.

The thought brings a sinking sensation to my stomach. I thought I would be happy about leaving the capital sooner. But the idea of leaving the guys, especially Jace, makes me incredibly sad. I would miss them. When I first arrived, I wanted nothing more than to leave. But now, only two weeks later, I find I don't want to.

Jace chuckles at me, oblivious to my inner turmoil. "Yes, you will get to finish the academy early."

"Do you have any plans for when you are done?" Chase asks me.

I shrug. "Not really. I never thought about it before coming here."

What I'm not saying is I didn't think I had a choice before coming here. I always assumed I would need to stay in hiding and not draw attention to myself.

I ponder that for the rest of breakfast. Thinking that maybe now I could have a normal life. Nothing bad has happened since I started at the academy two weeks ago. Maybe the person who had my parents killed has forgotten about me. Maybe I can make something of myself.

Chapter Twenty

I join the guys, minus Jace, in the potion's classroom for the first class of the day.

Potion class is held in the academy's basement, so there are no windows, making it dark and damp. Shelves line every wall, containing ingredients and other equipment we might need. Wooden tables fill the center of the room, with a desk in the front of the classroom for the teacher.

Nox and I stand at a table with two cauldrons suspended over a little pit for a fire.

Timothy, the older male who teaches the class, stands at the front. He's hunched over from age and requires a cane when he walks. He must be ancient to show signs of age. It takes thousands of years for fae to look old.

"Today, you are going to be making healing potions." Timothy begins the class. "Now, I know we all have the ability to heal, but it's important to have healing potions on hand for the times when your magic is depleted. It could mean life or death."

It takes a while for powerful fae's magic stores to diminish, although not as long for those with less magic. But it can happen. Especially when in a battle and using magic that requires more power.

"The recipe is on page two hundred and four. You may collaborate with the person at your table since it is a more complex potion, but I want you to each have a potion by the end of class."

I open my text to the page and glance at the list of ingredients.

"Do you want to get the first half, and I'll get the second half?" Nox offers.

"Sure."

I follow Nox over to the shelves. I grab mint, ginger, and morning dew while Nox gets distilled water, elderberry, and ginseng.

Bringing our ingredients over to the table, we divide them between us.

I go back to my text to read that the healing draught requires ingredients to be added at specific times. If done incorrectly, the potion can have the opposite effect.

I flick my hand, bringing magic to the surface to light the pit under the cauldron. Using the mortar and pestle, I start crushing the ginger, elderberry, and mint while I wait for the water and morning dew to boil. I then chop the ginseng as finely as I can.

"Make sure everything is crushed into a fine dust. It will make the potion smoother." Nox tells me.

"Thanks."

I do as Nox suggested.

Once the base is at a boil, I add everything else and stir in a clockwise motion. I recheck the recipe and let it simmer for fifteen minutes before removing my fire magic from the pit.

Once it's cool enough, I ladle some into a glass vial. The rest I leave in the cauldron for Timothy to check.

I look over at Nox to see him finishing up his potion, too.

I scrunch my brows. My healing draught is a pale green, whereas Nox's looks sky blue.

"Why is yours a different color? Did I do something wrong?" I whisper to him.

"No, I'm pretty sure I did something wrong." Nox scratches his head, trying to figure out where he messed up. "Well, looks like we're about to find out." Timothy hobbles over to our table with dry, dead-looking leaves in his hand.

"I'm going to drop a leaf in each of your cauldrons. If the leaf turns green and healthy again, you have a working healing potion."

He drops a leaf in Nox's potion first. The leaf turns slightly green with still a few brown spots. "Almost Nox. I suggest a little less time over the heat next time. But it is very good for your first attempt. Not many even get it to turn green the first time."

Nox beams. I smile along with him, happy he has a half-working potion. Although I can't help but worry that if Nox's only half worked, what would mine do?

"Now for yours, dear." I'm nervous as Timothy drops the leaf into my cauldron. I watch the leaf float on the top, slowly turning bright green. "Well done! That is how a healing potion should work. Good potency, not too much, but enough to heal someone properly."

The class gives me a round of applause for being the first to have a fully working healing potion.

"Good job." Nox praises. "Maybe next time, I will get you to give me tips instead of the other way around."

"Yours worked, too! You just need to take it off the heat sooner next time. You did great."

Timothy goes around the room checking everyone's potions. The twins came close like Nox, along with a few other students I don't know yet. But Theon is the only other one who gets their potion perfect.

Our next class of the morning is fire elemental magic.

Fire class is held in a fireproof room with no windows, large enough that we have enough room to work and not worry about hitting someone with our magic.

I change into the clothes I wear for combat and defensive magic class: black combat pants and a black t-shirt. We have the option to stay in our regular uniform or change. But I prefer not to wear a skirt when practicing fire magic. I quite like to keep my legs the way they are.

"What is she doing here?" Nova comes up to where I stand with Chase and Carter. Nova cocks her hip out and places a hand on it. "She's not a second-year. She's only a first-year."

I find it rather annoying that Nova is talking about me like I'm not standing here. I'm also surprised that she didn't notice me in potions class. Or if she had, that she refrained from saying anything till now.

"Aria is a second-year now," Carter explains.

"WHAT!?" Nova screeches.

Hearing Nova's outburst, Theon and Nox jog over to join us.

"Headmaster Nickolas thought it would be better for me if I joined the second-years." I don't feel like explaining myself to Nova, but if I don't, she'll make a bigger deal out of it.

"You cannot be that powerful." She says with a sneer.

"She is that powerful. She could beat us if we went against her with our magic." Theon comes to my defense.

"Alright, class, let's begin today's lesson." Clark, the teacher, interrupts.

In my first class with Clark, I thought he was terrifying, but then I learned that even though he looks scary with his pounds of muscles, a permanent scowl, and dark blue eyes, he's nothing but a softy. He just likes to intimidate us at first.

Nova huffs and turns away to join her friends. I'm glad to see her go, but I know she'll be back.

"Today, I want you to work on creating whips of fire," Clark explains. I have to suppress a shudder at the mention of whips. I still wake up from my nightmares and feel the phantom pain of the one I dream about.

"I know you might think this will be easy, but it's not." Clark continues. "The idea is to cut the target in half, not catch the whole thing on fire. Go ahead."

I find a target and call forward my fire magic. My arm gets warm as my magic races down to my fingers before shooting out in front of me in a whip form. I take a second to marvel at how quickly I can call forward my magic now.

Focusing on the task, I bring my arm back and shoot the fire whip toward the target.

My fire hits the target with a crack but doesn't break it. It only leaves a burn mark. I try a few more times to no avail.

"Looks like you don't belong here after all." Nova snickers from beside me. I glare in her direction, seeing she hasn't broken her target yet, either.

"The key is to ensure your fire is hot enough," Clark says, trying to offer help as he walks around the room.

I call forward my magic again, this time increasing the heat. Instead of its typical orange hue, my fire shines rose gold.

Interesting. I didn't know it could change colors with the different levels of heat.

This time, when I bring my whip down on the target, it breaks with a resounding crack through the room.

"That was so cool." Theon cheers from my other side.

I smile as I watch him break his target, too.

Nova huffs, "So what? You can break a target. It's not that impressive."

"If it's not impressive, you try it." I can't help snapping back at her.

Nova gets under my skin. Any chance she gets, she'll be found bad-mouthing me to others or saying nasty, hurtful things to my face. In fact, thanks to her, most of the female population hates me, choosing to believe the lies she tells them. They all sneer when they see me now.

I can think of only one reason why Nova is so nasty toward me, and that would be because she's jealous that Jace pays attention to me, not her.

"Fine." Nova creates a whip of fire so hot it's green. She raises her arm toward the target and whips her magic at it. The whole thing lights up into flames instantly.

Nova yelps. "Sir!"

Theon and I descend into a fit of laughter. Sure, it isn't very nice of us to laugh at her, but seeing her taken down a peg is nice.

Clark rushes over and uses his water magic to put out the flames. "You have water magic. Use it next time." He says to Nova sternly.

Nova turns scarlet. "It's not my fault. Aria distracted me!" She points in my direction.

I stand up straight. Is she really trying to blame me for this?

"That is no excuse for why you used that much magic. You will stay and clean up the mess you made." Clark turns to the rest of us. "Alright, everyone, if you have broken your target, I would like you to follow me. The rest stay where you are till you do."

Leaving the targets and a fuming Nova behind, I stand where Clark pointed.

"I would like you to all partner up," Clark explains when we join him. Theon looks to me to be his partner. "We are going to be doing something a little different today. I want one of you to throw fire at the other person. The second person is going to try and absorb it. I'll demonstrate." Clark looks around the room before stopping when he comes to Carter. "Carter, if you will throw fire at me, please."

We all take a few steps back, giving Clark and Carter room to work.

Carter summons his fire magic, creating a ball, and throws it at Clark. As Clark extends one of his hands in front of him, the fireball disappears into his skin.

My eyebrows shoot up.

Holy shit, that was cool! I didn't know we could do that.

"When trying to absorb the fire, you must think about pulling the fire into yourself. Fear will make you lose concentration. So try your best to stay calm and believe you can pull the fire into yourself. It's an exceedingly difficult technique that I don't expect everyone to get today. Give it a go."

"You try to absorb it first," Theon says when we're away from everyone.

Gathering his fire magic, Theon creates a large fireball before tossing it at me.

As the fireball sails through the air, I raise one of my hands and concentrate on absorbing the fire. I keep the fear that wants to rise at seeing a fireball fly at my face, shoved down deep, and take a few breaths to keep my heart rate steady.

But when the fire hits my hand, it scatters around me instead of absorbing into my skin like it did with Clark.

"Are you okay?" Theon jogs over to check on me.

"Fine, it didn't hurt my hand." I flip my hand over to show Theon that I'm okay. However, I find it strange that I didn't get burnt by his fire magic.

"You blocked the fire instead of absorbing it," Clark says as he comes around to check on us. "Try again."

Theon moves back to where he was standing and summons his magic again. This time, when he throws it, I'm ready. His magic hits my outstretched hands, molding with my magic and absorbing into me.

"Nicely done." Clark praises.

Theon and I switch places. I throw a fireball at him once he is ready.

Extending his hands in front of him, Theon pulls my magic into him, absorbing the fire on his first try.

We go back and forth a few times before Nova joins us.

"I'm partnering with Aria." She declares with her hands on her hips.

Theon shakes his head at me, telling me silently that it's a bad idea. I agree, but Nova will just annoy me into agreeing. It's better to just get this over with.

"Sure." I finally say.

Theon steps a few paces away, so he's out of the way but still close in case I need him.

"I'm going first," Nova says once we are in position.

I create a smaller ball of fire than the ones I was with Theon before tossing it in Nova's direction.

Nova shrieks and ducks down. "I wasn't ready!" She snaps. I barely manage not to roll my eyes. Nova had plenty of time to be ready. "Do it again."

I make another fireball, holding it in my hand for a second, waiting for Nova to nod her head that she's ready. When I throw the fire this time, she absorbs the magic.

"Your turn." She throws a fireball at me the second the words are out of her mouth. I don't have time to try to absorb the fire. I don't even have time to duck. The fire hits me square in the chest, shattering around me.

Thank the gods, I was able to block the magic without thinking about it.

"Sorry, were you not ready?" Nova sneers at me. "How about this time?"

She gathers more magic, this time creating two fireballs. She throws them at me simultaneously.

Knowing I can't absorb the magic again, I bring my hands forward, throwing the magic away from me and everyone else.

Nova scowls, clearly not impressed that I could move so quickly. She gathers her magic again, throwing fireball after fireball in my direction. Each one I deflect, throwing them in different directions each time, hoping I'm not hitting anyone with it.

My nostrils flare as my anger spikes.

My hands itch to call on my own fire magic and throw it back at her. But my well of magic has dipped dangerously low from defending myself, and I'm exhausted from trying to catch her magic before it hits someone else.

"Nova!" Clark roars. "That is enough!" He stomps over to us.

One last fireball flies my way before Clark can stop her.

My arms shake, and sweat slips down my spine from the effort as I try to absorb Nova's magic one last time. But I'm too tired to pull her magic into me. So when the fire hits my hands, it scatters, raining ashes around me.

Theon rushes over to me. "Are you okay?"

"Fine." I'm bent at the waist, trying to catch my breath.

"You could have seriously injured her. This is a training exercise, not the real thing." Clark scolds her.

"She is fine." Nova protests.

"Barely. This was not the intention of today's lesson." Clark says. "Go clean up the mess you made earlier."

Nova huffs before walking over to the targets to clean up.

"That's all for class. You are dismissed." Clark says.

I turn to leave but see Nova glaring at me. The look in her eyes is nothing but hatred.

I don't know what her problem is. She didn't even get in trouble for attacking me like that.

I glare back at her, showing her she doesn't scare me.

Chapter Twenty-One

C ombat class is still my favorite since it reminds me so much of Killian and home. But also because it's been nice to spar with people my own age and level and not against soldiers who've been training since I was born.

So, as I stretch my muscles out on the mat, I look around the room and try to find someone new to spar with. But the only person left is Jace. He's made a point of avoiding me during this class. Even though Jace sits close to me during every meal, he still barely speaks to me or even looks in my direction. Since the ball, he's pulled away from me, putting even more distance between us.

And for the life of me, I can't figure out why.

"Today, pick someone you've never sparred with. It's important to learn from each other, not just me." Emmett instructs.

I roll to a standing position, pulling my hands over my head to finish stretching before grabbing two practice swords and going over to where Jace is standing with Jace in the corner.

Jace's jaw clenches, and his eyes narrow when he sees me walking toward him.

He says something low to Chase without taking his eyes off me. I just raise my eyebrow at him. He is going to have to get over not wanting to spar with me.

I thrust one of the swords out to Jace when I reach him. "Are you ready to spar?"

"Fine," he grumbles, taking the sword from me and sauntering over to one of the mats.

Chase smiles at me. "Good luck. He's in a mood." He pats me on the back and goes to find his partner.

I join Jace on the mats, bringing my sword up to a ready position. I know from watching Jace spar with other people he is lightning-fast.

Jace doesn't waste any time, striking first. His sword comes down hard against mine, forcing me to step back. I push off with my sword and dart out of the way. Not fast enough, though. Jace quickly brings his sword up, not giving me time to recover. He hits me with brute strength, making my grip loosen. Jace uses the flat side of his sword to knock mine out of my hands before bringing it to rest against my neck.

The match is over in under two minutes.

I growl at him and stomp over to where my sword fell.

"Again," I say once I'm back to face him. Jace just shrugs and brings his sword up again.

I take up an offensive position this time. Bringing my sword down in a wide arc, I try to hit his open right side. Jace moves out of the way at the last second, bringing his sword down to meet mine. The swords hit with an ear-piercing ring. I clench my jaw and dart behind him. Using the flat side of my blade, I smack the back of his knees. Jace only stumbles. So, I help him by kicking his legs out from under him. He rolls, landing on his back. I stand over him, pointing my sword at his heart. I go to kick his sword out of his hands but don't get the chance. His sword is already meeting mine.

Jace swings his feet at the same time, kicking mine out from under me. He straddles me as soon as I land. I buck my hips fast, causing Jace to fall forward and twist so I'm on top. As Jace tries to bring his sword, I grab the blade and yank it out of his hands with a snarl, throwing it across the room. I rest my sword against his throat. The match is over.

Jace looks up at me wide-eyed and in shock.

The whole room has gone silent. I glance around to find everyone watching us with varied expressions. Some expressions are shocked that I can take down the prince, while others seem almost disgusted.

"Oh, poor baby! Are you okay?" Nova comes rushing into the room. She crouches on the floor where I'm still straddling Jace. "What do you think you are doing, attacking a prince like that!" Nova spits at me. With barely controlled rage, she shoves me off Jace. I slide off, landing in a pile beside him.

Stunned, I stand and walk a few steps away.

"Get off me." Jace stands, pushing Nova out of the way.

"But she hurt you," Nova says, putting her hands on Jace's chest.

I fist my shaking hands as my eyes shift to their deep violet color. Uncontrollable anger rushes through me at the sight of Nova's hands on Jace.

I want to rip her hands off him and then detach them from her body so she can't ever touch him again.

The possessiveness I feel toward him is confusing, to say the least. But in this moment, I'm willing to let the beast my possessiveness out if it means Nova will remove herself from Jace.

A flash of surprise crosses Jace's face as he cocks his head to the side, studying me.

I don't know how, but I have a feeling he picked up on where my thoughts had gone.

Jace finally pushes Nova's hands off him and walks over to stand before me.

"Are you okay?" He asks me.

I just stare at him, not responding. I'm still worried that if I open my mouth, I will start throwing insults at Nova and try to attack her.

"Aria?" He asks again. I just tilt my head.

Jace gently picks up the hand I used to take his sword from him. He undoes the fist I have it in to show me a long, deep gash in the center of my palm.

Blood drips from my hand onto the floor, adding to the small pools that are already there.

"Oh." I breathe out, forgetting about my anger with Nova. Now that Jace has brought my attention to it, my hand is hurting a fair amount.

"What are you doing in my class, Nova?" Emmett comes over to where we are standing.

"I was thinking of joining next semester." She twirls her hair. "Could Jace maybe show me a few moves? See if I like it?"

Without taking his eyes off me, he says, "No."

Out of the corner of my eye, I watch Nova's jaw go slack.

This is the first time since I've been around that Jace has ever been this direct with her.

"Come on, I'll clean this up and heal it." Jace lets go of my injured hand, moving so he places his hand on my lower back, guiding me out of the room and into the male changing room.

I want to argue that I can do it myself, but he doesn't give me a chance.

A buzzing sensation starts where his hand is placed on my back before spreading outwards. The sensation pushes the rest of my anger away.

He stops in front of a wooden bench in the middle of the room. "Take a seat. I'll be right back."

I sit down, placing my injured hand in my lap. It's starting to throb in pain now.

The practice swords are dull, so we can't do significant damage. However, as I just learned, the blade will still cut you if you grab it hard enough and yank on it.

After a couple of minutes, Jace returns with a steaming bowl of soapy water and a few towels. He kneels in front of me and places the bowl beside me on the bench. He dips one of the clothes in the water and begins cleaning the wound.

I hiss when the cloth touches the cut. "Sorry, it'll only sting for a minute. I just need to make sure it's clean." Jace apologizes. His hair falls forward into his eyes while he works. I itch to move it out of the way for him. But I fist my free hand to stop myself.

Once he is done cleaning the cut, he replaces the cloth with his hand. His big hands envelop mine, and a soft golden glow forms. Just like the last time he healed me, I feel his magic flood my system. It feels like laying out in the sun on the hottest day. Warmth spreads throughout my whole body from it.

"There, all better." He says once he's finished.

My breathing hitches as Jace looks up at me. His hair is still forward, falling to his eyes that look like two pools of liquid gold. He keeps my hand in his larger ones, now rubbing small circles across it. The tugging in my chest turns insistent, commanding me to not ignore it anymore.

"Thank you," I say low and husky.

"That was impressive. I haven't had anyone beat me in a very long time." He doesn't say it as if he is boasting, merely stating a fact.

I keep very still. Worried that if I move, he'll notice he still has my hand and drop it. I don't want to lose the comfort that he's bringing me just yet.

"Really? No one?"

I don't know why I'm surprised. The rough calluses on his hands speak of years' worth of training.

"No one," He agrees. "Growing up, I loved to spar. I'd sneak out of the castle to the barracks and practice with the soldiers. Usually, when I was supposed to be in some princely lessons." I can picture a little prince, Jace, running around with a tiny sword. "My mother hated it. But my father encouraged it. He gave me a sword at five and had the weapons master at the castle teach me."

"Killian did the same for me. He was the one who taught me." I smile softly at him.

"Killian was a good teacher. I've heard that he is one of the best the kingdom has ever had." He doesn't smile back at me; his brows are furrowed in thought. "Why did your eyes change color? To a deep violet."

145

I'd been hoping that no one saw that.

"They do that when I get angry." I'm startled to realize that I trust Jace enough to tell him. The words are out of my mouth without me thinking about it.

I never knew why my eyes changed color. I only know it was unusual.

"Interesting." Jace looks into my eyes again. I know they are my regular lavender. I'm feeling multiple different emotions at that moment. However, anger is definitely not one of them.

Carter walks in, pulling his shirt off as he does, breaking the moment. He stops abruptly when he spots the two of us. Jace is still holding my hand and kneeling in front of me.

Carter smirks at us. "Unless you want to see a ton of half-naked guys, I suggest you leave Aria."

"Right." I jump up from the bench at the same time Jace stands. We are so close our chests brush. "Thank you again for healing my hand."

"You're welcome," Jace says with that dimpled smile again. He steps out of the way so I can leave.

As I pass Carter, he gives me a knowing smile. I blush as I run out of the male's changing room.

Chapter Twenty-Two

A month has passed since I arrived at Nightfall Academy.

I'm acing all my classes and becoming stronger daily with my magic. My days are filled with learning about my magic, classes, and spending time with the guys.

I've also become closer with Theon, the twins, and Nox. They've been helping me catch up in my non-magic classes by studying with me in their free time. But the best part about them is that they've chased some of the loneliness away, making me feel less isolated. They pulled the rare smile out of me and have quickly become people I'd consider family.

With them by my side, I can handle the hostile looks I get from the other females at Nightfall and Nova when she tries to ruin my day.

But everything good happening is overshadowed by the nightmares that have plagued me relentlessly since the night of the ball.

It's the same thing every night: fall asleep, only to wake up a couple of hours later, screaming and rushing to the bathroom to throw up.

The nightmares have made me a mess. I try my best not to let the others see, but I'm not doing a very good job. Purple bags have become a permanent fixture under my eyes, and my clothes hang off me now. Most days, my hair is scraped up in a bun, and I don't bother with makeup because I'm too tired to do it.

The guys watch me like hawks during meals, making sure I eat something. But it's hard to eat when I feel so nauseous from the nightmares.

Jace is the worst out of the bunch.

Speaking of Jace, I've barely seen him since the day he healed my hand. He isn't avoiding me, per se, but he also seems to make himself scarce when I'm around. The only time I see him now is during the two classes we have together and mealtimes. And even then, I'm pretty sure he only joins us to eat so he can track the little food I consume.

He turns down all our invitations to hang out in the evenings and turns mute when I join them for anything. He's also refused all my attempts at sparring together. He won't talk to me, won't sit near me, and he definitely won't touch me.

I don't know what happened to make him pull away even further. I thought we were making progress, but I guess I was wrong.

And even though Jace has distanced himself, the tugging sensation has only grown stronger. The tug doesn't hurt; it feels oddly warm and pleasant, but I still find myself massaging my chest to relieve the pressure from it more and more.

Sitting in the library, with my school work spread out around me and a book open in my lap, I can't help but wonder if it would have the answers to as why I feel this way towards Jace.

Not that it's had any of the other answers I've searched for.

I found the library after a week at the academy. I originally came here to find information about my parents. But like Ajax and Isabelle said, there is no mention of them anywhere. All the history books from seventeen years ago have been altered to remove their names from everything. Not even a single picture of the council exists from that time. Even though I found this insanely frustrating, the library still became my favorite place.

The library is three stories, with oak bookshelves lining every wall. Tables and chairs, made from the same oak, are spread throughout the ground level, with a spiral staircase in the middle leading to the other levels.

I'm sitting on the third level in a small seating area tucked in the back corner in front of a large window overlooking the lake. It is cozy up here, with the low lighting and rain pattering on the window. I find that not many come to the library. It's the one place I can slip away from the prying eyes and the insults.

My phone rings, pulling me from my thoughts. I fish it out to see Killian's name on the screen.

"Hey kid, how are you doing?" Killian asks when I answer the phone.

I laugh at him. "You realize I'm not a kid anymore, right?"

"You'll always be a kid to me. But really, how are you doing? I haven't heard from you in a few days."

"Sorry, I've been pretty busy. I have a big potions test coming up and a history report due tomorrow." I feel bad for not calling him sooner. "I'm good, though. I still get tired easily from using my magic so much, but it's getting better."

"And are you sleeping?" Killian asks. I can hear the concern in his voice.

After the first few nightmares, I told Killian about them. I didn't want to initially, but I needed to talk to someone about them.

"Enough." I don't want to lie to Killian, but I also don't want him to worry about me. Even though I told him about the nightmares, I didn't tell him the amount of sleep they cause me to lose or the weight loss. I love Killian, but he turns into a mother hen when it comes to me.

"Okay, but tell me if the nightmares get worse again. You should consider getting that sleeping potion from the headmaster."

"I'll let you know if they do. And I'll think about asking Nickolas for it."

The only reason I haven't asked Nickolas for one yet is because I don't like the idea of being in that deep of a sleep. The sleeping potion doesn't just help you fall asleep; it keeps you asleep. I'm worried that if I take it and have a nightmare, I won't be able to wake up. The idea of being trapped in the nightmare almost scares me more than just having the nightmare.

"How are you?" I ask him, changing the subject from myself.

"I'm good. I plan to be in the capital in two weeks." Killian replies.

I squeal, "Really!? Why didn't you start with that? Does that mean I'll get to see you?" This is the longest I have ever been apart from Killian.

"Yes." Killian laughs at my excitement. "I'll call when I'm done with my job there and can come to visit."

"I can't wait. I've missed you."

"I've missed you too. I must go, but I'll see you soon. Love you." Killian says goodbye.

"Love you too." I hang up the phone.

I'm so happy I'll see Killian soon that a massive smile sits on my face. This is one of the few times I feel like smiling.

"What has you smiling like that?" Jace stands in front of me.

I yelp, placing one hand on my now-racing heart. "Jeez, you scared me." I'd been too distracted talking to Killian to feel the tugging start in my chest to let me know Jace was around.

"Sorry, I thought you heard me walking up the stairs." Jace grins at me. "Who were you talking to?"

"Killian. He's coming for a visit soon." I beam.

I can't contain my happiness.

Jace's lips part slightly. His pupils are blown so wide that only a thin strip of gold is visible.

"Beautiful." He breathes in a low whisper.

I feel my heart flutter at the compliment.

"What?" My voice comes out no more than a breath.

"You're beautiful." He still looks at me with this almost awed expression.

I don't know how to respond. "Th-thank you." I finally stammer out. I feel my cheeks go red.

"You're welcome." Jace takes the chair opposite me. The low table that I have my feet propped against separated us.

I raise an eyebrow.

Why is he sitting down? He makes sure he's never alone with me. Why is he willing to be now?

Jace clears his throat. "How are you?"

Both my brows are up now. He wants to know how I am? What is going on?

"I'm good," I reply hesitantly, curious about where this is going.

Jace nods his head. "Are you sure? I'm only asking because I overheard Killian ask if you were sleeping."

Stupid fae hearing.

"Were you listening to my conversation?" I feel my anger rising. I know the library is a public place, but I still thought Jace would give me privacy and not listen to my conversation with Killian.

"No!" He runs his hand through his midnight-black hair. "I'm sorry. I should have explained myself better. I was walking up the stairs when he asked you that. When I recognized your voice, I walked back down until you were done. I didn't mean to hear that. I'm sorry. Really, I am."

My anger dissipates as soon as Jace explains himself. "Okay."

"I know it's none of my business, and you don't have to answer, but are you okay? I've noticed that you hardly eat anything anymore. And now I hear you aren't sleeping either. Why not? What is going on?" Concern fills Jace's eyes. He looks genuinely worried about me.

I take a deep breath, letting it out before I answer. "I've been having nightmares every night since the ball." Something in me tells me I can tell Jace the truth. That my secret will be safe with him. "I think being in Oxynmire is causing them. I never used to have them."

"Why is being in Oxynmire causing you to have nightmares?" Jace pulls his eyebrows together in confusion.

I tuck my feet under me, looking out the window to the darkening sky. "This is where my parents lived." I take a shuddering breath. "Because it is where my parents died. Well, not here, but close. It happened in their summer home in the Bellvista mountains."

The Bellvista mountains are located further in the mountain range but are still the closest town to Oxynmire. I hear Jace's sharp intake, but I don't turn to look at him, not wanting him to see the tears in my eyes.

"You said you went to live with Killian when you were five. Was that when they died?" Jace asks softly.

I shrug. "No, I think I was closer to six months old. I don't know what happened to me between the ages of six months and five."

"I'm sorry." Jace comes over, kneeling in front of me. He reaches up and wipes a stray tear away.

My breathing is shallow as I turn my head to get lost in his golden eyes.

"It's not your fault," I whisper. I'm afraid if I move too suddenly, he'll leave again.

He takes my hands in his, gently pulling them open. I hadn't noticed I held them in fists so tight my fingernails left half-moon circle indents on my palms.

"I know I've asked before. But who were your parents?"

"I wasn't lying that day. I don't know who they were. No one will tell me their names." I would have told him if I knew.

"No one will tell you their names?" Jace seems shocked. I just shake my head. "Well, what do you know about them? Maybe I can find out who they were for you."

My mouth parts, "you would do that for me?"

"Of course I would," Jace says with absolute certainty.

I want to fling my arms around his neck and hold him close. But I stop myself at the last second.

"Why, though?" I ask him. "I thought you didn't like me." I clamp my mouth shut. I hadn't meant to say that last part.

Jace's eyebrows draw together again. "Don't like you?" He says it like he doesn't understand the concept.

"I just mean, you hardly talk to me, you tend to avoid being alone with me, and you never touch me unless it's a mistake." Except for right now.

I remove my hands from his and stand to move away.

I need space from him. He's confusing me, acting like a different person tonight. Acting like the same person when he danced with me at the ball, when we went hiking, and when he healed my hand. Not the cold, distant person he's become.

"Wait." Jace shoots up and grabs my arm, turning me around. The movement causes us to stand so close that every inhale makes our chests brush. "I'm sorry I have been distant."

Now, it's my turn to draw my eyebrows in. "You've been more than distant. You've been cold towards me."

"Please sit. I'll explain." He pleads with me. His please does me in. I don't think I've ever heard that word from him.

I retake my seat. I want to hear his explanation. Jace sits on the edge of the table in front of me, our knees touching. "I acted that way because I felt something for the first time in my life." He begins. "I was taught to tuck away my feelings. That princes were not to show emotion. So, I did what I was taught. I learned to wear a mask when out in public. Shutting myself off from any real emotions. Not letting people see the real me. I only ever showed them the strong prince that I was told to be. I could only let the mask slip when I was alone with the guys. Even then, the longer I acted that way, the harder it became to remember who I was."

My heart aches for the way Jace was raised. It's not right that he wasn't allowed to be himself.

"But then I saw you, sitting in the grand hall that first day, and you were the most beautiful female I had ever seen, and I felt this pull towards you. It scared me. No one before had made me want to let go of the mask and just be myself. I wanted you to know the real me. I wanted to be awarded with one of your rare smiles. But I was reminded of the consequences every time I let myself be real with you in the last month."

My heart pounds in my chest. "Consequences?"

"I started to notice the looks the other females were giving you. They saw how I was around you and were becoming jealous. I heard some whispers about wanting to do something to you to get you out of the picture. I didn't want to risk you getting hurt, so I pulled away. I couldn't live with myself if something happened to you."

So the glares I've been getting are because of Jace, not from Nova talking about me.

"I don't care about the risks," I tell him fiercely. As much as I appreciate that he was trying to protect me, I also hate it. It meant that he was pushing me away.

Jace groans, running his hand through his hair. "You should. If I openly courted you, it would put a target on your back at the academy and throughout the kingdom. There are some who would use you to hurt me. I can't let that happen."

"Don't you get it?" I half yell at him. "You are worth every risk."

Jace looks like he stopped breathing. "What?" His voice comes out no more than a whisper.

"You are worth every risk," I say again. "You said that I make you feel. Did you ever consider that you make me feel too? I may not have had to hide away my feelings, but I still guarded my heart. Before coming here, I didn't let anyone in besides Killian. Then I met you. You were the first person who made me want to live. Really live. Not just hide away from the world. You make me laugh when it's not something that I do easily."

Jace opens his mouth to say something, but I'm not done.

"I've seen behind your mask, and I like that person." Jace scrunches up his face, not believing me. "It's true. Who else would heal me multiple times now? Who else would get up early to go hiking with me because you knew I wanted to go, even though you had hardly any sleep? Your voice was what stopped a panic attack one time. And only you would send me a dress so I wouldn't feel out of place. No one else would do that because no one else is as kind, caring, and compassionate as you are. Yes, you can be a pain to spar with, and you watch me like a hawk when I eat. But I still like that about you. So, I will say it again: you are worth every risk."

I'm out of breath by the time I'm finished. I want him to see that he is not a prince to me but just Jace.

Jace swallows once, twice, before saying anything. "I don't deserve you." His voice comes out hoarse.

"Yes, you do."

He lifts his hand, letting it hover over my cheek. "You mentioned earlier how I never touch you. That's because I was afraid if I let myself, I would never stop."

"Who says I would want you to?" I whisper.

His eyes widen before he lets his hand rest on my cheek. Warmth spreads from the contact. He brings his other hand up, twirling it through my hair. I reach out my hand, letting it rest on his chest.

Noses pressed together, Jace's eyes flick down to my lips before moving back to my eyes. Desire swirls through his eyes. He leans forward, our lips almost touching.

"There you are!" Nox yells behind Jace. I jump away from Jace, scooting back against the chair. "I've been looking everywhere for you."

I push a hand against my chest, trying to will my heart to stop racing.

Nox stands beside us now. Jace's nostrils flare. He narrows his eyes at Nox. "What do you want?" It comes out more of a growl than anything.

I stifle a smile behind my hand. Jace turns his icy glare on me, only making me smile more. For some reason, I immensely enjoy seeing Jace riled up.

Nox looks between us. My face is flushed. Jace's posture is rigid.

"Oh, never mind. It wasn't important. Come find me later." Nox shoots me a wink and quickly runs back down the stairs.

My face is hot from how red it is.

Jace sighs. "Sorry."

The moment's ruined. It's probably for the best anyway. I'm not sure if having our first kiss in the library for everyone to see is a good idea.

"It's okay." I smile at him. "It's getting late anyway. I should probably head back to my rooms."

"I'll walk you back," Jace says.

"What's your favorite food?" Jace asks me as we walk.

For some reason, the question makes me want to laugh. I never thought the prince of Noctem would be asking me what my favorite food is.

"Chocolate chip cookies." I answer him. "Yours?"

Jace doesn't answer right away. His brows are slanted down in thought. "Pizza."

"Really?" I ask with laughter present in my voice. "I never pegged you as a pizza lover."

Jace smiles at me, showing off that dimple of his. "Hey, pizza's the best."

"I'm not saying it isn't. I just didn't expect a prince to love pizza."

"Favorite flavor of ice cream?" He asks.

"Cookie dough."

"Hmm, I'm sensing a theme." Jace comments. "Mines chocolate."

We come to the top of the stairs, turning towards my room.

"What's your favorite book?" I ask. My steps slow the closer we get. Jace matches my pace, slowing along with me.

"I've never had the pleasure of being able to pick up a book simply to enjoy it. All the books I've read are about politics or history. So, I don't have a favorite."

My smile slips away. "That's sad." I couldn't imagine a life where I didn't read for enjoyment.

Jace shrugs. "Maybe one day, when I don't have to meet certain expectations, I'll have time to read."

"Well, when that day comes, I'll have recommendations for you."

"Thanks."

Before I can say more, we reach my door. I find my stomach sinking in disappointment that we've already made it. I've enjoyed getting to know this side of Jace. I've enjoyed getting to talk to Jace without him wearing that mask I've come so accustomed to seeing.

I turn in place to face him.

"Goodnight, Jace." I love how he's so much taller than me that I have to tilt my head back to look at him.

Jace walks in close to me, putting his hands on the door behind me and boxing me in.

"Goodnight, Aria." His breath ghosts over my face.

His eyes are firmly locked on my lips.

The intensity of his stare and his proximity make it impossible to breathe. I want nothing more than to grab his shirt and close the distance between our lips.

A door closed nearby, breaking the spell. Jace closes his eyes and sighs.

He steps away from me and says, "I'll see you in the morning."

"See you in the morning."

Jace stands in front of me like he doesn't want to go. I want to ask him to stay, to come inside. But I don't get the chance. He shakes his head after a moment before shoving his hands in his pockets and turning to leave.

Chapter Twenty-Three

I'm finishing getting ready the next morning when I feel a tugging sensation in my chest. I smile, opening my door to find Jace leaning against the opposite wall. He has his hands in his pockets, with one foot kicked against the wall.

His eyes run down my body, darkening as they do.

Today, I'm wearing a button-up black cardigan, a short black plaid skirt, and knee-high black boots. Fortunately, the school uniforms are kind of cute.

"Good morning. You look beautiful." He says as I close my door. Jace pushes off the wall and crosses the hall to me.

"Good morning. And thank you." I smile softly at him.

Jace places one hand on my waist and pulls me close. It isn't quite a hug; he is just holding me close. I rest my hand on his chest.

"What happened to you wanting to keep me safe?" I ask with a raised brow.

Our conversation never really went anywhere last night. When we parted last night, I figured he was still in the mindset of wanting to protect me.

Jace pulls me flush against him. I wrap my arms around his neck in the new position.

"I'm still going to keep you safe, but I thought of a plan last night."

"What's the plan?"

"We can just keep it a secret." He suggests. "Since we hang out already, it won't seem unusual for me to be spending time with you. I won't be able to show affection in public, but I can when we are alone. I know it's not ideal, but it is the best I can come up with right now."

I think it through. I don't care if the other students know about us. I only want to be with him. However, I don't like that we won't be a normal couple. Although, I have a feeling no matter what, we would never have a normal relationship.

"Okay."

Jace sighs in relief, and some of the tension melts from his shoulders.

Was he really that nervous I would disagree?

"So. My question is, will you be my girlfriend?" He asks with his dimpled smile.

"Yes," I whisper without hesitation.

He leans down towards me for a second before abruptly pulling away. I hear the voices coming down the hall a second after he does.

I already miss the contact.

"We'll have to tell the guys. They would figure it out too fast anyway." Jace says as we make our way to the grand hall.

I laugh. "Yes, they would. Then they would find some way to tease us about it."

Jace laughs along with me. I love that sound. It is deep and masculine and sounds like it comes from his soul.

"Why don't you take a seat with the guys? I can get your breakfast." He says as we enter the grand hall.

"Thanks." I walk over to join the twins, Theon and Nox.

"So, Aria, have anything new to tell us?" Chase asks as the others snicker.

Nox is such a gossiper. I should have known he'd tell the others about seeing Jace and me last night.

"I don't know what you are talking about," I reply coyly. I know Jace wants to tell them, but I want to have fun with them first.

"So, are you telling us that Nox didn't catch you and Jace in a compromising position last night?" Theon asks.

"Compromising position? Seriously?" I laugh at them.

"Were you, or were you not kissing Jace in the library last night?" Carter asks.

They all stare at me, waiting for an answer.

After leaving them in suspense for a minute, I give them a devilish grin. "Not."

It's the truth, not that they seemed to think that.

Jace joins us before they can pepper me with any more questions. He places a cup of coffee and a large plate of eggs, sausages, and toast in front of me.

I smile at him in thanks.

"Hey, why don't you get my food for me?" Theon teases.

"Because you're not pretty enough," Jace replies seriously.

Theon pretends to be hurt while we all laugh at him.

Jace hooks his hand through the leg of my chair and drags it as close as he can to his own. Warmth spreads from the contact through my leg to the rest of my body.

"So, Jace, do you have anything you want to tell us?" Theon raises his brow at him.

Jace looks down at me, a silent question in his eyes. If I changed my mind and didn't want them to know, he would respect that and not tell them. I appreciate that he wants to make sure. But the guys are his family and are becoming mine, too. I trust them more than I thought possible.

I dip my head slightly.

"We are dating," Jace tells them quietly.

"Can't say we didn't see that one coming," Nox says with a smile.

"It's about time!" Chase says at the same time.

"We would rather no one besides you know about it right now," Jace explains.

They all nod their heads in understanding.

"I forgot to ask you last night, is it okay if they know about me looking into your parents? They might be able to help." Jace whispers into my ear.

I chew on my bottom lip. I want them to help, but I don't want word to get to their parents about me. "Okay. But only if they promise not to tell their parents." Jace's brow furrows in confusion. "It'll make sense when I tell you what they did for a job." I had forgotten to mention it last night.

"Jace?" Nova's voice comes from the end of the table.

Jace closes his eyes and lets out a breath before turning his head in her direction. I look over at her as well.

Today, Nova has her shirt unbuttoned even more than usual, showing a black lacy bra off. She twists her golden hair with one finger, attention fixed on how close Jace and I are sitting together.

"Yes?" He replies. Annoyance makes his voice come out rough.

"I was wondering if you are going to the winter solstice ball at the castle again this year?" Nova asks, batting her eyes at him.

"Of course. Seeing as I'm the prince, I'm required to be there. Why are you asking? It's a month and a half away."

"Well, I was wondering if you had a date yet. I wanted to see if you would go with me again. We had so much fun last time." She purrs. Nova bends over, leaning closer to Jace. "Remember the fun we had on the balcony?"

It feels like Nova punched me in the heart. What fun on the balcony? What was she talking about? I bring my hand up to massage the ache in my chest.

"Nova, enough. I'm not going with you." Jace narrows his eyes at her.

"Why not?" She leans in even closer, bringing her lips so they are close to Jace's ear. "Do I need to remind you of our fun?"

I tense.

Whereas only a moment ago, I felt hurt by Nova's words, I now feel rage.

My eyes shift to their deep violet color, and I fist my hands in my lap to prevent myself from doing something stupid, like attacking Nova. But I can feel the leash on my magic slipping—fire dances around my knuckles.

I try to take a deep breath, but it feels like it gets stuck in my lungs. I want to growl at her that Jace is mine. But that would be ridiculous. First, I only just started dating Jace today, and second, it would mean exposing our relationship.

But logic doesn't seem to matter to me because I open my mouth to say the words to her anyway.

Before they come out, though, Jace places his hand on my leg under the table, squeezing it. The contact snaps me out of it. The haze of possessiveness lifts from me, and I feel like I can breathe again. The fire around my knuckles dims.

"Nova," Jace growls in a warning. "Please leave before you ruin my entire breakfast."

Nova huffs and turns away, but not before glaring at me.

I push the rest of my breakfast away. I don't feel like eating anymore.

"Aria, what she said is not what it seems." Jace grips my chin, turning me to look at him. "I was drunk for the first time last winter solstice, and Nova took advantage of that. She kissed me, and I pushed her off me after a second. Nothing else happened, I swear. You can ask the guys; they were there too."

"It's true," Nox says. The others all chimed in their agreement.

I don't need the others to confirm Jace's story. I know he wouldn't have done anything with Nova without reason.

"I believe you." My eyes shift back to their normal lavender. I need to be more careful that others don't see my eyes changing color. I thought I had a handle on my anger, but Nova seems to bring it out again.

Jace lets go of my face, pulling my food back to me. "Eat."

"So bossy." I tease him.

"Well, I am a prince." He flashes me a grin, showing off his dimple.

The guys all make fake gagging noises around us.

"About what we were talking about earlier," I say, changing the subject. "I would like to not talk about it in a public place. Can we do it later?"

"How about my room after classes? No one else lives on the top floor beside us. It'll be safe to speak up there." Jace offers.

"That would be perfect. Thank you."

"Can you meet us in my room after classes today? Aria would like to talk to us about something." Jace asks the guys.

"Sure." Carter and Chase say at the same time. Nox and Theon nod their heads, too.

Hopefully, Jace and the others will be able to help me find some answers as to who my parents were.

Chapter Twenty-Four

After classes, I run back to my room to change out of my uniform before meeting with the guys. I pull on my favorite jeans and a cozy cream sweater and head back out.

Just as I'm finishing locking up, I'm shoved into the door. My face takes the brunt of the hit.

I cry out in pain and shock.

The hit causes stars to dance along my vision and warmth to run down my face. Asshole must have broken my nose.

The person grips my hair and shoves me to my knees before twisting me around. When I look up, I don't recognize the male who's holding me. But I know the other person with him.

Nova.

"You must think you are so special," Nova says. "Getting the prince's attention like that. It doesn't matter, though. He'll get over this little infatuation soon enough."

"What are you talking about?" I try grabbing the male's hands to shove him off me.

"Ah, ah." Nova tsks.

One look from Nova, and the male pulls my hair harder. I can't help the whimper of pain that escapes. It feels like he is ripping my hair from my scalp. He takes both my hands into his free, beefy hand. I try to tug on them, but he only tightens his grip, grinding the bones in my wrists together.

I've never felt so hopeless before. I'm typically good at self-defense, but the male surprised me. He is also much bigger and stronger than me. I usually could use his weight to my advantage, but he had attacked me from behind. Taking the coward's way out and not allowing me time to defend myself.

"I saw you two this morning. The prince is mine. Stay away from him." Nova continues.

I'm fully struggling now, trying to move anyway to get the male to relax his grip.

"The prince makes his own decisions." I know as soon as the words are out of my mouth, they are the wrong thing to say.

Nova rolls her eyes and gestures to the male holding me. He roughly pulls my head up before smashing it against the floor. Black spots dance across my vision. The male drops me into a pile of limbs on the floor. I groan.

Nova crouches down in front of me. "I'm only going to say this one more time. Stay away from the prince. I'd hate to see you get hurt." Nova smirks at me as she stands. "I don't even know what he sees in you. You're not even pretty, with your weird hair and eyes."

"I may have unusual eyes and hair, but at least I have a personality." I try to smile at her, but it hurts too much. I know I shouldn't be goading her, but I'm so fed up with Nova that I can't seem to care.

Nova screeches, "you little bitch!"

Without waiting for direction from Nova, the male kicks me in the ribs with his heavy boots repeatedly.

After his third kick, I feel something snap. I try to hold in my cries of pain, not wanting to get them satisfaction. I curl myself into a ball to protect my ribs from further damage. But that only makes the male move onto a different body part. He stomps on my left leg, putting his entire weight on it. I scream in agony as he continues to stomp on my leg, shattering the bones.

"You deserve this," Nova says.

The male kicks me in the jaw for good measure.

I feel blinding pain for a second before everything goes black.

"Aria!" I hear a voice from far away.

I try to move but can't get my limbs to respond. I can't even open my eyes.

"Don't move. I've got you." The voice says again. Strong arms lift me. I whimper from the movement. "I'm sorry."

Pain courses through me. I try to remember what happened but can't. Everything is too hazy.

"You're okay now. I've got you." The voice tries to reassure me.

I try to hold onto consciousness, but it slips through my fingers.

Everything goes dark again.

Blinking my eyes, I find myself lying in my bed.

How'd I get in here?

I let out a soft groan as I try to shift into a sitting position. Damn, everything aches.

"You're awake!" Jace's voice comes from beside me. There's relief in his eyes when I turn my head to see him sitting on a chair beside the bed, holding my hand. "How are you feeling?"

"My leg still hurts, and I'm a little achy. But besides that, okay." I croak. My throat feels raw.

"Here's some water." He helps me sit up enough to take a few sips of water. "Isabelle said she would be back to check on you soon."

"Thanks," I say as Jace helps me lay back down. "How long have I been out?"

"About two hours since we found you." Jace moves so he can sit on the edge of the bed. He starts gently rubbing circles on the back of my hand that he is still holding.

"Who did this to you?" Jace demands. His voice is hard and growly.

I have to think for a moment to remember. Everything still feels hazy. But it slowly comes back to me. "Nova and some male came behind me when I locked my door and attacked me. I didn't get a chance to defend myself. The male was too strong."

I've never known what it was like not being able to fight back. But today, I learned. And I don't like the helpless feeling of it. I don't like that I feel like a failure.

"Nova had this done to you?" Jace asks through clenched teeth. "Did she say anything?"

I sigh. This was the part I didn't want to tell him. "She said she saw us this morning and to stay away from you. That you're hers."

Jace stands abruptly, running his hands through his hair before pacing beside my bed. He does this for a while, wearing a path on the floor, not speaking. I stay quiet while he does, giving him time to process.

"She must have seen us outside your room." Jace finally breaks the silence.

"I guess so." I agree. "I didn't think anyone was in the hall besides us."

"Neither did I," Jace says.

"This is why I didn't want people to know about us. I should have never shown affection to you in the hall. It was too public of a place. I'm so sorry, Aria." Jace collapses back onto the bed. He faces away from me with his head in his hands.

I scoot up further in the bed, wincing from the movement, and place my hand on Jace's back. "It's not your fault, Jace. Nova is using you as an excuse. She's hated me from the first day."

Jace still won't look at me. "I don't know."

My heart stops and my breath won't come.

I massage my chest, trying to relieve the ache that has bloomed from his words. But it doesn't help.

What doesn't he know? Does he not want this? Does he think it's not worth it? Does he think *I'm* not worth it?

Tears stream down my face. I don't want to lose him already. We haven't even begun to explore the connection we share. I whimper, unable to contain the noise.

Jace finally turns around, eyes wide, when he sees my face. "No, please don't cry. That came out wrong." He pulls me into him, careful not to jostle my injuries. He rubs soothing circles on my back. "I didn't mean it like that. I'm sorry. I'm upset you got hurt."

"What did you mean?" I hiccup.

Jace pulls away far enough to see my face. He tucks a stray piece of hair behind my ear. "I just mean that we need to be extra careful."

"Okay." I don't mind being more careful if it means I won't lose him. Jace opens his mouth to say more when someone knocks on my door.

"Come in," I call out.

Jace lets go of me to move back into the chair as Isabelle walks in.

"How are you feeling?" She asks, lacking her customary smile.

"I'm okay. Everything aches, but the only thing that still hurts is my leg." The longer I'm awake, the worse I feel.

Isabelle nods. "That's to be expected with the amount of healing I did." She explains. "I had to heal three ribs, your nose, jaw, and leg. I thought I healed everything in your leg, but I must have missed something. I would like you to shower first and wash off the rest of the blood so I can get a better look. Once you are done, I'll come back and finish healing you. Then, headmaster Nickolas would like to speak with you. He'll meet you in your sitting room once I'm done."

"Thank you, Isabelle," I say. Isabelle nods her head and leaves.

Before I can get out of bed, Jace is there, scooping me in his arms and carrying me to the bathroom. I appreciate it. I'm not sure I could have walked the short distance to the bathroom. Not with the amount my leg is hurting.

"Thank you," I say once he sits me down on the edge of the tub.

"You're welcome. Do you need anything else?"

"No, but could you stay for when Nickolas comes, please?" I'm not ready for him to leave yet.

"Of course." Jace softly kisses me on the head and leaves, giving me some time alone.

Chapter Twenty-Five

I take a bath and wash off the excess blood from my skin and hair. Apparently, blood is a pain to remove when your hair is white-blonde. I'm pretty sure a few strands are still stained pink.

Once clean, I dress in leggings and an oversized deep green sweater and lie on the bed for Isabelle.

She gets to work by running her glowing hands over me from top to bottom. She takes her time on my leg, ensuring it is completely healed.

"It looks like I got it all this time. You'll be sore and tired for a day and probably limp a little since the bones in your leg were shattered. It's why I had to heal you a second time. It's much more complex when the break is not clean." Isabelle says once she is done. "I'll go let Nickolas know you are ready."

"Thank you, Isabelle."

Isabelle nods her head and shows herself out.

I slowly make my way out to the sitting room. Sure enough, as Isabelle said, I walk with a limp.

When I make it to the doorway separating the living area and bedroom, I see Jace, Theon, Nox, and the twins spread out on the couch and chairs. I expected Jace to be here, but not the others. The fact that they are here, with concern etched on their faces, makes my heart swell. I've only ever had Killian who cared about me. I never thought there would be more people who would come into my life that would feel the same way.

As soon as Jace notices me, he jumps up and helps me walk the rest of the way.

"I'm glad to see you are okay," Nox says as soon as I take a seat. He sits beside me and hugs me gently, trying not to squeeze my ribs too hard.

"Thanks." I yawn. I'm ready to get this meeting over with Nickolas.

"While we wait, do you want to fill us in on what we were going to meet about?" Theon offers.

Right. I'd completely forgotten the reason I was even leaving my room this evening.

I quickly fill them in to catch up to what Jace already knows.

"What was it that you couldn't say in public earlier?" Jace asks. He sits with his arm around me, drawing small circles on my shoulder.

"I'm sorry I didn't tell you this sooner. I trust you, but I was scared." I start. "The only thing I know about my parents, and I only just learned this, is that they were second in command to the king." I look at Jace to see his reaction. He seems confused, with his brows furrowed. He has no idea who I'm talking about like I hoped he would.

"My father hasn't had anyone second in command for at least seventeen years. The last couple must have been your parents. I don't know anything about them, though. I would have only been one year old when they left." Jace says. "I'll look into it. See what my father's records say."

"Thank you," I blow out a breath before saying the next part. "There is one other thing. I also learned someone on the council betrayed them.

Whoever it was came to our home in the Bellvista Mountains, killed my parents, and kidnapped me."

"Why would they do that?" Carter's voice is just a whisper.

I shake my head. "Because of some prophecy about me," I tell them. "That's why my parents gave up their positions on the council and took me to live in the Bellvista Mountains. They were trying to protect me, and it cost them their lives."

Just explaining that little bit to them hurts more than I expected.

Jace pulls me closer to him. "It's not your fault." He whispers into my hair.

I wish more than anything that I could believe that. But I don't. It's my fault they are dead. Sure, it was someone on the council who killed them, but it was because of me that they did.

"How do you know someone on the council who killed them?" Nox asks. He and the others look concerned about the mention of their parents.

"From Isabelle and Ajax. The king told them that he and the council were the only ones who knew my parents had a home in the Bellvista Mountains and were the only ones who knew about the prophecy back then. He never told Killian any of this. The king just showed up on his doorstep with me and asked him to hide me."

"What does the prophecy say?" Carter asks.

I shake my head against Jace's chest. "I don't know. Only the king and the council know what it says. Until a month ago, I never even knew a prophecy existed."

"Well, it was important enough that someone on the council felt they needed to kill your parents over it." Jace muses. "I'll see if maybe my father can give me any information about it. Don't worry, I'll be discreet."

"There is no way it was any of our parents who did it. That doesn't sound like something they would be capable of doing." Chase says. "That only leaves Nova's father and Charles."

"Who's Charles?" I ask.

"He's the oldest council member. Never married or had children. Once he retires or dies, his spot will open for someone else." Theon explains.

"We'll have to keep an eye on Nova. Make sure she doesn't tell her father about you." Jace tells me.

Before I can panic about that, Nickolas walks in without knocking.

"How are you feeling?" He asks as he makes his way over to me.

"I'm okay, sir," I say. I just want to get this over with.

Nickolas nods. "I'll make this quick then. I just need you to explain what happened, please."

I quickly go through everything for him.

"My dear, I'm so sorry this happened to you," Nickolas says after I'm finished. He looks distressed.

"What are you going to do, sir?" Jace asks him with his arm still wrapped around me. I expected him to let go when Nickolas came in. But I'm glad he didn't. I'd be a mess if he weren't holding me right now.

"I'm going to talk to Nova now. She'll be given detention, but I am afraid that's all I can do. There's nothing I can do about the male since you don't know who he is."

"That's not good enough," Jace says through clenched teeth. "She had Aria attacked for no reason."

"I understand that. But neither Nova nor the male used magic, so I can't expel them. And I can't make more of a fuss without alerting her father about what happened." Nickolas says sympathetically.

Jace glares at Nickolas. He opens his mouth to say more.

"It's okay, I understand," I say before Jace can speak.

I can't let Nova's father know what happened. It's too risky. So, I'd rather let Nova go unpunished.

Jace runs his hand down his face but doesn't argue.

"I would like to move you, though. There's an empty room on the top floor. This way, Nova won't know where your room is anymore." Nickolas offers. "You'll be placed across from Prince Jace."

"Thank you, sir. But could I move tomorrow night? I'm pretty tired." I say. I don't think I can walk more than to my bed without collapsing from exhaustion.

"Yes, of course. I'll have the room cleaned and prepared for you. Just stop by my office tomorrow for your new key." Nickolas moves to leave. "Oh, one other thing. You should call Killian. We had to call him when you were attacked. I'm sure he would appreciate hearing from you that you are okay."

"I'll do that now."

Nickolas nods and shows himself out.

I limp to my bedroom, waving off Jace's offer of help. I want a minute alone to talk with Killian. Closing the door softly behind me, I dial his number.

"Are you okay?" Killian asks as a greeting. I can hear the worry in his voice.

"I'm okay," I tell him.

"Tell me what happened, please," Killian asks me.

"Before you say anything, I'm sorry I didn't defend myself," I say after telling Killian what happened.

"You have nothing to be sorry about," Killian says sternly. "It sounds like you didn't have an opportunity to defend yourself. Short of using your magic, which I understand you are not allowed to use outside the classroom, I don't believe you could have done anything differently."

A weight is lifted off my shoulders, knowing that Killian isn't disappointed in me. Some of that failure I felt earlier leaves as well.

"You go rest now," Killian says. "I will see you in a few weeks. Love you."

"Love you too."

Chapter Twenty-Six

I'm exhausted by the time I get off the phone with Killian.

I make my way out of the bedroom to let the guys know I'm going to bed. But when I open my door, I find only Jace—no sign of the others.

Jace lies on my couch, reading one of my books. He looks so relaxed for once.

"I told the others to leave. I figured you were probably exhausted by now." Jace sets the book down. When he reaches me, he tucks a stray piece of hair behind my ear.

"I am, thank you." I move closer to him, placing my hands on his chest. He settles his hands on my hips and pulls me flush to him.

Jace's eyes darken as they flick to my lips again. All thoughts of sleep vanish. My pulse picks up. He doesn't hesitate this time. He crashes his lips against mine. The kiss is far from gentle. It's the most earth-breaking, soul-shattering kiss I have ever experienced.

I gasp against his mouth. Jace uses it as an opportunity to deepen the kiss. I run my hands up his chest to push them through his hair. It's as soft as I always thought it would be.

Jace lifts me with ease, and I lock my legs around his hips, holding him close. Without breaking the kiss, Jace walks us over to the couch.

Laying me down beneath him, Jace pulls his lips from mine to run kisses down my throat. I tug on his shirt. I want his lips on mine, not my neck. I feel something click into place as we kiss. Something I didn't know I had been missing my whole life until this moment.

Jace pulls back abruptly, lips swollen, eyes wide. "You're my mate." He breathes. His statement resounds within me.

Everything makes sense now. The tugging sensation in my chest, the tingling feeling when we touch, and the constant need to be close to him.

Jace is my mate.

"Mate," I whisper.

Jace growls low in approval before crashing his lips to mine again. This time, he takes his time with the kiss. There is less urgency in it.

When we break for air this time, Jace sits up, pulling me with him to straddle his lap.

"I should have realized sooner. It all makes sense now." His dimple shows as he smiles. There is a brightness in his eyes that I've never seen before.

A black band on Jace's left-hand ring finger catches my eye. I lift his hand to hold closer to get a better look.

Up close, I notice that the band is not solid black like I thought, but a row of tiny stars that spans around his finger.

"It's our mate mark. See." He lifts my hand for me to see the same on my left ring finger. "As our relationship grows, so will the mark."

The mark is beautiful but noticeable. "We won't be able to keep our relationship a secret now," I comment.

Jace furrows his brows. "I can glamour it for now."

Jace's magic seeps in, warming me as he runs a hand across the mark.

When he pulls his hand away, the mark is gone. In its place is my normal pale skin. He runs his hand over his mark, concealing it too.

I frown at my hand. I don't like my mate mark not being there. It feels wrong not to have it on display.

"What's the matter? I can feel conflicting emotions coming from you."

I lift my wide eyes to meet Jace's. "You can feel my emotions?"

"Of course I can." He laughs softly at me. "What do you know about mates?"

I shrug. "Not much. I only knew mates have a visible mate mark, unique to the couple. I've never been around a pair of mates. There were none in my village."

Jace nods, "that's not surprising. They're rare now. It used to be that fae would find their mates at a young age. Now, most don't find their mate, and if they do, it's not until later in life." Jace explains. "Along with feeling each other's emotions, mates can feel the other's pain. We can also find each other through our link. However, we wouldn't be able to do that yet. That requires our connection to mature. But we can communicate telepathically."

Just like this.

Jace's voice weaves through my mind.

My mouth pops open. "That is so cool!" I scrunch my face in concertation, trying to talk to him through my mind.

Laughing deeply at me, Jace smooths out the lines on my face. "It's not like that. Close your eyes." I do as he says. "Look for the link that connects you to me and follow it. Once you get to the end, you can talk to me."

I find the link he is talking about. It looks like a string, with one end lavender and the other gold. The colors meet in the middle, twisted together to represent us. I follow it to the end, finding Jace.

This is incredible.

I open my eyes to see Jace grinning at me. "Did it work?" I'm honestly not sure.

"It worked." He looks at me with awe, like he can't believe this is real. "You never answered my question. Why were you upset a minute ago?"

"Oh." I had gotten distracted by learning we can talk telepathically. "I don't like not seeing our mate mark. It's perfect, and I don't want to cover it up."

Jace sighs, running his hand through his hair. "I don't want to either, but I am only doing it for your protection. Just for a little bit, please."

I consider his request. "Do you really think I am in danger?"

Jace's eyes turn hard. "You were attacked tonight. Of course, you are in danger!" He grinds his jaw and runs his hand through his hair again. I've noticed that he only does that when he is frustrated.

I cringe. "Right, sorry."

"No, I'm sorry. I didn't mean to be harsh with you. It's not your fault." He pulls me so I can lay my head in the crook of his shoulder. "How about this? When we are alone, we will have them un-glamoured."

I lift my head enough to look up at him, my eyes lighting up. "I'm good with that."

"Gods, you're beautiful." He whispers, placing a soft kiss on my lips. I smile against his mouth.

His happiness bleeds through the bond, mixing with my own. The feeling creates a high within me, making me feel lighter than I ever have before.

Jace pulls away. "You know this means you'll have to live in the capital, right? Because I can't leave, and there is no way you are going anywhere without me. You're mine." The last part comes out more of a growl than actual words. I can feel his happiness switch to possessiveness and worry.

I place my hand on his face. "I'm not going anywhere," I say, trying to calm him down. "I never wanted to live in the capital, but that's only because I was scared. Scared of finding out who killed my parents and kidnapped me, scared of them trying to kidnap me again, and scared of finding out what the prophecy says."

Jace's hold tightens on me, "I'd like to see them try." His eyes are murderous at the thought of someone taking me.

"But." I start bringing his attention back to me. "I'm not scared if you'll be by my side. I know you will keep me safe."

Something deep within me tells me that I'll be safe if I have Jace by my side and won't be harmed. It's not the mate bond that makes me think that, either. The feeling goes even deeper than that.

Jace's eyes soften. "I will always protect you."

"I know." I can't stop the yawn that slips out. The lack of sleep and healing magic is starting to catch up to me.

"You need to sleep." Jace stands with me, placing me gently on my feet. "I'll go."

"Wait!" I chew on my bottom lip.

Jace pulls my lip out of my mouth. "What is it?"

"Can you stay, please?" I look down, slightly embarrassed I am asking him to stay.

Jace places his hand under my chin, tipping it up so I have to look at him. "Of course I will."

I sigh a breath of relief. "Thank you. I know no one can get into my room, and I'm safe. But I haven't been sleeping anyway, and tonight scared me. And your presence has always made me calm and relaxed. So, I thought maybe if you are close, I might sleep better." I ramble.

"Aria," Jace says softly. "You don't have to explain. I'd love to stay."

I nod my head. "Okay. I'm just going to get ready then. I'll be just a minute."

I limp to my bathroom to wash my face and change into pajamas. I pick out my favorite black silk shorts and the matching silk tank.

Returning to my bedroom, I find Jace in bed, shirtless, and if the pants folded on the nightstand are any indication, only in his boxers.

I don't get in the bed when I reach in. I stand there, staring at Jace with shaky hands. I've never shared a bed with anyone before. I didn't think about that when I asked him to stay.

"Aria, I can feel your nerves." Jace sits up in bed. "We are only going to sleep."

"Sleep," I repeat.

"Yes, sleep. Come here." The softness in his voice is what gets my feet moving. I climb into bed beside him. Jace tucks me in close so I can rest my head on his chest.

"Thank you," I whisper sleepily. My eyes are already feeling heavy.

"Anything for you." Jace vows. He rubs lazy circles on my shoulder, soothing me.

"We should tell the guys we are mates," I mumble.

"We can tell them when we have a moment alone with them tomorrow." He replies. "Now, go to sleep. I've got you."

"Goodnight, Jace." I say just before sleep claims me.

"Goodnight, Sweetheart," Jace whispers into my hair.

Chapter
Twenty-Seven

I wake up feeling refreshed for the first time since arriving at Nightfall Academy.

There were no nightmares last night. I didn't wake up screaming or run to the bathroom to expel the contents of my stomach.

And it's all because of Jace.

Still asleep beside me, Jace holds me tight against his body. One hand is wrapped around my waist, and the other is tangled in my hair. I'm lying half on top of him, with my legs twisted in his. I've never been more comfortable.

I wiggle out of his grip to slide my arm out to check my watch.

Five-thirty in the morning.

I need to get up and get ready for classes. Slowly, to not wake him, I begin to untangle myself from Jace. I only make it a couple of inches before he pulls me back tight to him.

"Where do you think you are going?" Jace growls sleepily.

I laugh softly at him, remembering Carter explaining that Jace isn't much of a morning person. "I need to get ready for classes."

"Not yet." He pulls me so I am fully lying on top of him.

"We need to get up now. I need to get ready, and you need to leave before anyone else wakes up and sees you leaving my room."

Jace grumbles. "Fine." He opens his eyes to look at me.

I smile down at him, pushing his hair away from his eyes. "Good morning."

"Good morning." He kisses me.

I lean into him, deepening it.

Jace abruptly rolls us, pinning me beneath him. I wind my arms around his neck, keeping him in place.

I gasp for air when Jace pulls away after a few minutes.

I touch my still-tingling lips. "We should always say good morning that way."

Jace gives me a devilish grin. "I agree." He kisses my head and rolls off me.

"How did you sleep?" He asks as he gets out of bed.

"Good, no nightmares. Thank you again for staying." I also slip out of bed, going to the closet to get my uniform. As I walk, I notice that my limp from last night is absent, along with all my aches.

Jace follows me and leans against the doorway to my closet. "You never have to thank me for that, Sweetheart."

The nickname he used last night makes me smile. And to think, the first time he called me that, it annoyed me.

Words can't begin to express the gratitude I feel. So, instead of stumbling over my words, I just walk over and wrap my arms around his waist. His large arms envelop my tiny body, holding me close. I let our mate bond speak for me and send all my emotions down the bond.

"I better go," Jace says after a few moments. "I'll wait for you at the entrance to the grand hall." He kisses me on the head again and leaves.

Jace is exactly where he said he'd be thirty minutes later as I walk to the grand hall for breakfast.

Gods, you are gorgeous. Jace speaks into my mind as I draw closer to him.

I blush at the compliment.

I'm wearing a simple black skirt, a white button-up with the academy logo on the pocket, a long black cardigan, and my combat boots. I feel good in the outfit.

Thank you.

I can tell it's taking everything in him not to pull me close to him. He flexes his hand at his side like it will prevent him from touching me.

"Ready?" I ask aloud.

"Yes." Jace exhales sharply and rolls his shoulders. "Go sit. I'll get your breakfast."

"Thanks." I make my way to where Nox, Theon, and the twins are sitting.

"Morning." I greet them with a bright smile.

"Good morning, Aria. How are you feeling?" Carter asks me as I sit down. There's concern in his sea-blue eyes and his mouth is tilted down slightly.

His worry for me warms a small part of my heart, reminding me that I've found a special type of friendship with these guys. The kind of relationship that is rare, and extends past just being friends. The kind where I'd call them family.

"Much better." It's amazing what a good night's rest will do for a person. I feel lighter than I have in ages.

"Sleep well?" Nox gives me a knowing smile.

"I did." He must be able to feel how happy I am right now.

Jace walks over and places a large plate of food in front of me. Today, he chose pancakes, eggs, bacon, and coffee.

"Thank you." I smile at him. Jace smiles back at me—one of his rare, genuine smiles. Jace never smiles like that in public. My stomach goes all fluttery seeing it.

I can see the guy's exchange looks out of the corner of my eye.

Theon clears his throat. "If you guys don't want people to know about you, then I suggest stopping looking at each other like that."

That makes Jace's smile vanish. His eyes go cold. "Right." He turns to his breakfast, attacking it with his fork.

When do you want to tell them? I ask Jace through our connection.

Tonight, when we move your things to your new room.

"Would you guys mind helping me move my things tonight after classes? I don't have much." I ask them.

"Of course," Chase says. The others chime in their agreement.

"Aria." my blood turns cold at the sound of Nova's voice. I look up to find her standing at the end of the table. She's lacking her usual confidence today. Her eyes are downcast, and she twists her hands in front of her. "Can I speak with you, please?"

"Whatever it is that you wish to say to her, you can say here," Jace responds before I can say anything. His tone brokers no arguments.

Nova nods her head in understanding. "I just wanted to say that I don't know what came over me last night. What I did is inexcusable and will never happen again. I hope you can find it in yourself to forgive me."

I look at Nova closely. I can tell from the hardness of her eyes that she doesn't mean a word she is saying. She's most likely putting this show on for Jace's benefit. Or maybe Nickolas is making her. Either way, it's fake.

"All is forgotten." I can't lie and say that I forgive her, but I can say I've forgotten about it. If given the opportunity, Nova will do it again.

Nova must pick up what I meant because she stops fidgeting and narrows her eyes at me. She opens her mouth to say something, but Jace beats her to it.

"If that is all, we would like to get back to our breakfast."

"Yes, of course. Enjoy your breakfast, your highness." Nova purrs.

I have the sudden urge to throw my food at her.

"Thank you, Nova." Jace dismisses her.

Nova looks at me one more time before she leaves, giving me a hateful smirk.

Nox sighs in relief once she is gone. "I can't stand her. And to think, we'll have to work with her when we run the council."

Nox's words make my anger disappear and be replaced with panic.

I haven't even considered that because Jace is a prince, it will make me a princess when we announce our mate status. It's one thing to stay in the capital to be with him. It's another to become a princess. Someday, a queen. Having to work with Nova when she takes her spot on the council.

I try to shove the panic down, but it doesn't want to go. It bubbles over and makes my chest tight. My breaths come in short little pants; warning me that I'm on the verge of hyperventilating.

"Aria, are you okay?" Jace asks, concern bleeding through his voice.

"You're a prince." It's the only thing I can say.

He raises his eyebrow. "Yes, you knew that."

"That... that... would make me a..." I trail off, not wanting to finish the statement.

But Jace understands what I'm trying to say. His eyes soften. "Yes, it does. But I'll teach you everything you need to know. It'll be okay."

"You promise?" I plead.

"Promise." He vows.

Sweetheart, you have nothing to worry about. You'll be an amazing princess.

His gold eyes hold so much warmth, letting me know he means every word.

Being a princess is not something I ever thought I'd be or wanted. But if it means being with Jace, I'm willing to try.

Thank you.

"Would either of you like to share with the group?" Chase asks. His easy teasing dispels the rest of my panic.

"We'll tell you tonight when we help Aria move everything," Jace explains, ending the conversation.

Chapter Twenty-Eight

"**G**ood morning, class." Natalie, the basic magic teacher, greets us as she enters the classroom. She has long black hair, a slim figure, and deep green eyes. Natalie is one of my favorite teachers because she's always bubbly and upbeat. "Today, I want to teach you how to do glamours."

I straighten in my seat.

It'll be useful to be able to create glamours. That way, if something ever happens, like the glamour fails and Jace isn't around, I'll be able to do it myself.

"Now, glamours are tricky and don't last forever. To do it, you must concentrate the magic on one specific area or thing you want to be glamoured. You must focus on keeping the lines sharp around the glamour, making it harder for anyone to see through it." Natalie explains. "I want you all to practice the hand motion with me first. Taking your right hand, simply swish it to the left."

Natalie demonstrates the motions. I follow her lead. Using my right hand, I swish it to the left.

After a few times, Natalie brings our attention back to her. "Excellent, everyone. Now, you will see a gold coin on the desk in front of you. I want you to try and glamour that. Making the hand motion I just taught you, infuse your raw magic into the movement. Once you have the hang of it, I will show you how to reverse it."

I slide the coin closer to me.

Swishing my hand to the left, I infuse my magic into the motion. But nothing happens. I try again, concentrating more on the magic, but still nothing.

I furrow my brows, trying to figure out what I am doing wrong.

Nova snickers from the table beside mine. "Having trouble?"

"No." I grit my teeth. I try again, ensuring I have enough magic at my fingers. As I swish my hand to the left, the coin disappears. I glance at Nova to see her glaring at me. "I'm good, thanks for your concern," I say with mock sweetness.

Nova narrows her eyes at me. She looks back at her own coin and tries again. Nova huffs in frustration, unable to get it.

"Now that most of you have gotten it, I will explain how to reverse it," Natalie says. "Instead of moving your hand to the left, you move it to the right. Still infusing your raw magic, I want you to concentrate on reversing the glamour." Natalie shows us the motion.

I look down to where my coin sat. I swish my hand across it, going to the right like Natalie said. My gold coin returns instantly.

I beam.

I can't wait to tell Jace that I can do glamours.

I stand outside with the guys for our last class of the day, air magic. The class, usually held in one of the glass buildings attached to the main castle, was changed to be held outside today.

"Good afternoon, class." Emmett, our combat and air magic teacher, addresses us. "We are going to be doing something a little different today. I'm going to teach you to create lightning."

My eyes widen. "We can create lightning?" I whisper to Theon beside me.

Theon chuckles. "Not all fae can since it takes quite a bit of magic to do it."

"Theon is right." Emmett chimes in, overhearing our conversation. "Not all of you will be able to create lightning. It is a skill only the more powerful fae have been able to master. But it's important to try and push yourselves to see if you can."

"Now, I want you all to spread out. I don't want any stray lightning bolts to hit another student." I move so I am far enough away from everyone. "To create lightning, you need to bring your hands together in front of you. Next, you need to slowly pull them apart, infusing your air magic into the palms of your hands."

Emmett demonstrates.

He reaches his hands out in front of him and pulls them apart. As he does, little bolts of lightning begin to form, which turn into larger bolts of lightning the further apart his hands are.

"Give it a go." He says once he is done.

I lift my hands in front of myself and call upon my air magic. I then slowly pull my hands apart. At first, I think nothing is happening, but then I see a little spark. I slow my movements down and call more magic to my hands to get better bolts. As I continue pulling my hands apart, I start to see bigger lightning bolts. By the time my hands are shoulder-width apart, I have multiple bolts. The lightning is contained in a ball shape, moving around and throwing off bolts in every direction.

"Holy shit, this is cool." I hear Chase say over the crackling of the lightning. Looking over at him, I see his hands spread apart with lightning between them.

"Nicely done, Aria." Emmett praises me when I have my arms as wide as I can get them. The bolts of lightning between my hands span roughly four feet across. "Don't let it get any bigger for today. I want you to bring your hands back together now. Think about removing the magic from the lightning and bringing it back into yourself."

I do as Emmett instructed.

Pushing my hands back together, I slowly make the ball of lightning disappear.

"That was insane!" Nox says as soon as I finish dispelling the magic. He tosses a small ball of lightning between his hands, keeping it controlled.

"It was very impressive," Emmett agrees.

"Thank you, sir," I reply.

"That is enough for you today. You just used an amount of magic you've never had to use before. You're going to be tired after this. I suggest sitting and watching for the rest of the class."

"Okay." I gratefully take a seat on the grass a distance away. I can feel the drain from using so much magic.

I observe for the rest of the class. The only other people who can create lightning are Nox, the twins, Theon, and another girl I don't know.

Nova struts over to where I'm sitting when she fails to create anything more than sparks. "You don't listen very well, do you?"

I knew her apology this morning didn't mean shit. I'm not surprised that she's bothering me again since Jace isn't around. She really does hate me.

"What are you talking about?" I ask her.

"I told you to stay away from the prince last night." Nova sneers.

"Yes, and I told you he makes his own decisions," I tell her.

Nova clenches her fists, clearly annoyed I'm not cowering in fear in her presence. "He'll lose interest in you soon enough and move on to someone with more status. He and I are meant to be together, and we will be."

I clench my jaw. The idea of Nova with Jace makes me want to rip the realm apart. I have to breathe deeply to prevent my eyes from shifting color. The last thing I need is for Nova to see that.

Nova smirks. She knows how much her words are affecting me.

I force myself to shrug. "Maybe he will lose interest in me, as you say. But the thing is, Nova, you may think you are better than me, but you're not. And Jace can see that. So, I can guarantee that if he picks someone else, it won't be you." I lie. I don't want to give her a reason to suspect we are mates.

Nova's smile slips from her face, and her eyes turn murderous.

"Everything okay?" Theon takes a seat beside me on the grass.

Nova's expression turns from cold to sweet in seconds. "Fine, I was just complimenting Aria on her display of magic." Nova smiles sweetly at Theon.

"All right, class, excellent work today. You are dismissed." Emmett says.

I stand with Theon and join Carter, Chase, and Nox.

"Has Nova always been possessive of Jace?" I ask once we are a distance away.

"Oh yeah." Nox snorts. "Although, it got worse after she kissed him at the Winter Solstice ball last year. Ever since then, she has been obsessed."

I chew on my lip. "Have they ever been a thing?"

"No way." Chase wrinkles his nose as if the idea disgusts him. "You are the first female he has ever shown any interest in. There were a couple of females he flirted with, but nothing serious."

"Okay, thanks."

"Trust us. You have nothing to worry about." Carter says.

Chapter Twenty-Nine

After class, I picked up the key for my new room from Nickolas before heading to pack up the few things I brought with me.

"How's it going?" Jace asks me as he, Nox, and Chase join me in the bedroom.

Since it's only the guys around, Jace doesn't hesitate to show affection. He walks up behind me, wraps his arms around me, and kisses me on the head.

I lean into his warmth, letting his sandalwood and pine scent wrap around me. "Good, I only have a little left in my closet to pack."

"What do you want us to do?" Nox asks, making himself comfortable on the bed.

"Can you bring those bags up, please?" I point to the three bags sitting at the foot of the bed. "Here's the key." Reaching into my pocket, I pull out my new key.

Nox hops off the bed and takes the key from my outstretched hand. "Sure thing."

Nox and Chase grab the bags and leave.

"Is this all you have?" Jace asks me.

He moves from behind me to stretch out on the bed. His shirt rides up with the movement, giving me a glimpse of his abs. I remember seeing them when we went swimming, but I had been too shy to look for long. Now that we are mates, I don't care if he catches me looking.

"Aria?"

"Mhhh?" I can't form proper words. Too busy thinking about running my hands down his chest and over his abs.

Jace chuckles at me as he sits up to pull me to stand between his legs. He's so tall that I barely meet his eye level with him sitting.

I give into my desires, fuse my mouth to his, and run my hands along his chest. Jace moans from the contact and kisses me back just as hungrily. I sink into him, letting myself get lost in the heat of the kiss.

"Seriously, you two? We leave you for five minutes, and this is how we find you?" Nox scolds us.

I jump back from Jace at the sound of Nox's voice.

Jace scrubs his hand down his face. "You have the worst timing." He glares at them.

I turn, expecting to see Nox and Chase, but Theon and Carter are also here.

Great. The guys will never stop teasing me about this. I just know it.

My cheeks are pink as I turn away and finish gathering everything.

It only takes a few more minutes before I have everything packed. "That's all of it."

Jace picks up my last bag for me. "Do you mind coming up with us? We wanted to talk to you about something."

"Okay," Theon says skeptically as Chase and Carter share confused looks.

The guys follow behind as we walk up the three flights of stairs from my old room.

Unlocking the door, I step inside to my new room.

The room is a carbon copy of my old one, from the wall color to the layout and furniture. I even have the same view of the mountains and waterfall from my bedroom balcony.

"Have a seat," I tell them.

Jace sets my bag down with the rest just inside my bedroom. Theon and Carter take the two chairs while Nox and Chase share the couch.

Jace and I move to stand in front of the fireplace so we can face them.

"What's going on?" Carter asks.

"Yeah, you guys are acting weird," Chase adds.

Jace looks down at me, confirming I'm still okay with telling them. I smile and nod my head. I want them to know. They have become like brothers to me in the last month.

Jace takes my hand and removes the glamour concealing our mate mark.

I look at our mate mark to see it has grown since last night. The band of stars has spread up my finger, stopping halfway across the back of my hand. The pattern depicts constellations.

"We're mates." Jace's voice conveys his joy. He wraps his arm around me, pulling me into his side. His smile lights up his whole face, showing off his dimple.

"Pay up, suckers." Nox cheers.

I laugh, looking over to Chase and Carter, paying Nox and Theon. "You bet that we are mates?" I don't know why I'm so shocked. They bet on how long it would take for me to join the second-year classes.

"I have never felt happiness like I feel from the two of you when you are around each other. I figured you had to be mates." Nox says.

Jace shakes his head at him, laughing softly. "There is no hiding anything from you, is there?"

"Nope." Nox grins.

"Congratulations," Chase says. He and the others get up to give us hugs.

Jace growls low in his throat as they move closer to me. He gently shoves me behind him. The guys stop moving instantly, stepping back slowly from us. None of them look worried about the way Jace is acting.

I, however, am. I peer up at him to find his attention fixed on the guys. His lips are curled back, showing off his teeth, and his eyes are narrowed. I gently place my hand on his arm to bring his attention back to me.

His body lets out the tension it was holding with my touch. "Sorry." He looks at me sheepishly. "I don't want males to be close to you now."

"It's a newly mated thing. I'm sure you would respond the same if a female came close to him." Theon explains.

My lip curls at the thought of another female getting close to Jace. My eyes shift to their deep violet, and a low growl escapes me.

"Yours," Jace whispers into my ear.

I shiver at the possessive note in his voice. "I'm yours," I whisper back to him.

Jace inhales sharply, lips parting. He grips my waist harder.

As Jace leans down to kiss me, the other guys gag, interrupting the moment.

"Are we going to have to deal with this now?" Chase complains.

I pull away from Jace, blushing. "Sorry, we'll try to behave."

Jace clears his throat and takes the open spot on the couch, pulling me to sit on his lap.

"Speak for yourself." He grins mischievously.

I lightly smack him on the shoulder, silently loving this playful side of him.

"Are you going to tell people now?" Carter asks, bringing my attention back to the conversation.

I shake my head. "No, Jace and I agree that it would be best if we keep it between us for now."

"What about your parents, Jace? Or Killian?" Theon asks.

"We haven't discussed it yet. But am I right to assume you would like to tell Killian?" Jace asks me.

"I would. But I understand if you don't want anyone else to know."

"If I could, I would announce it to the whole damn kingdom." Jace's words warm my heart. "But for now, we can just tell my parents and Killian."

"Thank you. We can tell Killian when he visits in a couple of weeks."

"Sure." Jace makes small circles with his fingers on my hip.

"Aria, did your eyes change color a few minutes ago?" Chase asks me.

"Oh, yeah, they do that when I get angry. I usually try to hide it when I am around other people."

"Strange," Theon muses. "I wonder why."

Jace's phone rings, interrupting our conversation. He fishes his phone from his pocket. "Dad?" He answers the phone. "What's wrong?" I can't hear his father's words but I feel Jace's worry. "Is everyone okay?" More words I can't make out. "Okay, I'll be there." Jace hangs up and runs his hands through his hair.

I place a hand on his arm, squeezing it. "What's wrong?"

"There was a demon attack in the city. They lit several businesses on fire and killed innocent people."

I cover my mouth. "That's horrible."

"They are getting bold." Nox comments.

"I thought the demon attacks had stopped." I haven't heard of any attacks since I came to live with Killian. I don't know how often they happened before that, though.

"They had. But lately, several attacks have occurred around the city and neighboring towns. Father and the council can't figure out why they have started again or how to prevent them." Jace says.

No one knows how to stop demons from entering our realm.

Our realm borders against the demon realm and the human realm. We call the demon realm the underworld and the human realm Earth. Demons can enter our realm at free will, and we can enter theirs, but we never choose to since their realm is almost inhabitable for us. Their air will slowly kill us if we stay for a prolonged period there.

Demons and fae can create what we call rifts every time we enter a different realm. These rifts are how we travel to different realms. Even though we can both open and close these rifts, only the demon or fae who opened it can close once one is open.

It's also impossible to know when and where demons will enter. Whenever a rift is open, anywhere between one demon and thousands of demons can come through.

The fact that they are attacking again is worrying.

"I didn't know that," I say.

"You wouldn't," Chase explains. "The king and the council have kept it quiet. They don't want people to panic."

"What about the fae who've been harmed? Or those who've lost businesses?" I ask.

"We've been compensating where we can. But that money won't bring back people's loved ones." Jace says, running his hand through his hair again. "I need to go. My father wants me there to help calm the people, show them we care."

"Of course, go," I say. I can't help but worry for those who were hurt tonight.

Jace slides me off my lap and gives me a quick kiss. "I'll stop by if it's not too late when I get back."

"Do you want us to stay?" Theon asks as Jace leaves.

"No, that's okay. I need to unpack my things. Thank you, though." I stand and walk them to the door.

"We are happy for you two." Chase squeezes my arm as he passes.

I close my door behind them and get to work unpacking.

Chapter Thirty

I'm standing in front of my parents' bedroom door.

"No, no, no," I whisper. I don't want to see my parents that way again. But I don't have control over my body. My hand moves of its own accord, opening the door to reveal my parents' room.

This time, my parents aren't dead yet. A large male stands over them with his dagger drawn. Shadows wrap around the male, concealing his features from me. I only know he is male because of his size and build.

"Stop, please," I beg him. I try to move to stop him but can't. My feet are firmly planted on the floor.

"Mom, Dad, wake up!" I yell at them. "You have to wake up!" But they don't hear my pleas.

The male turns his head in my direction but doesn't stop. Still looking at me, he slices through my father's throat, then my mother's. I can hear the soft gurgling of them choking on their blood.

A gut-wrenching scream comes out of me. I drop to the floor, my body no longer able to hold me up, sobbing.

"Why?" I cry at the male.

He doesn't respond.

On near-silent feet, the male makes his way over to me. He grabs me by the hair and drags me from the room.

The scene changes, and I'm back in the dungeon, dangling from the ceiling by chains.

"Please." I whimper. I can feel the breath of someone behind me on my neck.

The person doesn't listen to my pleas.

I can feel the shift in the air seconds before the whip cracks along my back. I cry out in pain, unable to contain the noise. The person brings the whip back down two more times.

"Why?" I pant out. My sweat mixes with the blood running down my back.

I don't understand why anyone would want to harm me. The person behind me responds by cracking the whip against my back again.

My screams echo through the dungeon.

I wake up screaming. Rough hands hold my wrists, and there is weight on my hips. I try to push whoever is on me off by thrashing my body wildly to get away from them.

I can still smell the dank air of the dungeon. I can feel the weight of the chains on my wrists and the pain of the whip across my skin. I feel like I'm still in there.

"Aria, Sweetheart, it's me." Jace's voice pierces the panic. "Shh, you're okay."

I open my eyes to find Jace lying on top of me. His golden eyes stare down at me, full of concern.

I whimper. I push on his chest to get him off me. I jump from the bed to run to the bathroom once he is out of the way. Only just making it in time to retch in the toilet.

Jace pulls my hair out of the way and rubs small circles on my back. He's silent while I empty the contents of my stomach.

I can't shake the realness of the nightmare.

Once I have nothing left in my stomach, I reach up and flush the toilet.

"Sorry," I whisper to Jace.

"Don't apologize. Stay here." Jace orders. He gets up and rummages around my bathroom.

I close my eyes and slide to the floor to curl up in a fetal position.

Just like every night after a nightmare, I can't shake the feeling of it. I use the cold tile floors to try and ground myself. It isn't working, though.

The panic attack sets in, and my lungs stop pulling air in. My vision darkens around the edges from the lack of oxygen.

"Breathe, Sweetheart." Jace's voice pulls at my mind. "I need you to take a deep breath with me." He takes my hand and places it on his chest. "Follow my lead."

I feel Jace take a deep breath. Focusing on him, I try to do the same. I only get half the breath he does, but it is more than I was getting.

"That's it. Keep going." Jace encourages me.

I don't know how long we stay like that, me lying on the cold floor, with Jace holding my hand to his chest. But my breathing stops coming in short pants, and my vision clears.

"I've got some water for you. Do you think you could sit up and take a few sips for me?" Jace says to me.

I open my eyes again to see Jace crouched in front of me with the glass of water he mentioned. I sit up and accept the class with shaky hands. Jace wipes my brow with a cold cloth while I sip the water.

"How did you get in?" I finally ask him.

"I broke your lock."

"What?" My eyes widen.

"I heard you screaming and didn't know if you were being attacked again. So yes, I broke the lock on your door to get in." Jace takes the now-empty glass from my hands. "Do you want to talk about it?"

I take a deep breath. "It's always the same thing, the night my parents were killed. I was too young to remember anything, so I think my brain has started making up what happened. This time, I saw a male slit their throats. I couldn't move, couldn't get them to wake up, couldn't stop him. I just stood there helplessly while he killed them. Then it changed to me being tortured in a dungeon."

Tears stream down my face.

I tell Jace the one thing I have not told Killian. "I'm scared that I'm starting to remember what happened to me when I was missing. I'm scared that the part where I am being tortured has already happened to me."

"It's okay. They can't get you now. I've got you, Sweetheart." Jace moves, so he sits beside me on the floor. He wraps his arms around me, holding me close. I melt into him, sobbing into his chest. Jace doesn't try to fill the void inside me with words. Instead, he does something better. He runs a comforting hand through my hair and holds me close, letting me cry my heartache out in silence.

Only when the tears dry up does Jace let me go to stand. Scooping me up in his arms, he walks out of my bathroom and towards the front door. "Where are you taking me?"

"To my room. Your lock is broken, so we can't stay here tonight." Jace says.

He walks through my open door and sets me down so I can lean against the wall. Jace closes my door and unlocks his before picking me up again and walking into his room.

I want to protest that I can walk, but I don't trust that I can. I'm still shaking.

Jace's room is similar to mine. The only difference is the colors. Instead of blue walls, his are a dark forest green. And his bedroom wall has a painting of a forest behind a king-size four-poster bed.

He places me gently in the bed and crawls in beside me. Jace wraps his arms around me and pulls me in close.

I sigh. I don't usually sleep after a nightmare. But in the comfort of Jace's arms, I know I will.

"Thank you," I whisper to him.

"You don't need to thank me. I'm here for you, always." He vows.

A dreamless sleep claims me quickly.

Chapter Thirty-One

I'm bouncing at dinner two weeks later. My eyes keep drifting to the entrance every two minutes.

"What has gotten into you?" Theon asks me with laughter in his tone.

"Killian should be here by now," I say, without taking my eyes off the entrance.

Jace chuckles, "he said around six. It's only five after. He'll be here." He places his hand on my thigh underneath the table, squeezing it. He pushes my food in front of me, "Eat."

"Yes, Your Highness." I purr as I finally remove my eyes from the entrance. I take a bite of the chicken parm. I have to hold back the moan that wants to escape. I will never get over how good the food is here. No offense to Killian, but he can't cook like this.

Jace growls low in his throat in approval. My blood heats from the desire I can feel through our bond.

Jace and I have taken to sharing a bed at night. I tried to stay in my room the first night after he had woken me from the nightmare, to wake up screaming again. Jace didn't have to break the lock that time. I had given my key to him in case it happened. He carried me to his room and announced that I would be sleeping with him from now on. I didn't argue with him, knowing that if I wanted to sleep, I needed to stay with him.

And I have been. I've gone almost two weeks without a single nightmare. My appetite is back, and I almost feel like myself again. Of course, I still need to regain the weight I've lost. But that will take time.

The guys gag around us.

"Would you two please stop it?" Nox begs.

I blush. I had forgotten other people were around us.

"How long is Killian here for?" Carter asks.

I clear my throat, turning my attention to him. "He said he could only stay for the evening. After that, he needs to head home and train the soldiers there." I'm disappointed I only get the evening with him, but I understand. I'm just happy I get to see him.

"Are you telling him today?" Chase asks.

Jace nods his head. "We decided to tell him alone since he's only here for the evening. We'll tell my parents tomorrow night at dinner. I called my father last week and said there was someone I wanted them to meet and asked if we would come for dinner tomorrow night."

"It might also be better if Killian isn't there. I don't know how the king and queen will react." I add. I'm nervous about telling them. Especially since it was the king who hid me with Killian. He knows what the prophecy says.

"You have nothing to worry about, Sweetheart." Jace reassures me again.

Before I can say anymore, movement by the entrance catches my eye. I turn fully to see Killian's large frame standing there.

Jumping out of my seat, I shove students out of the way to run into his open arms. Killian crushes me into him, lifting me off the ground in one of his signature bear hugs.

"I've missed you." I choke out. My eyes fill with tears.

"I've missed you too, kid." He doesn't let go of me for several minutes.

"I want you to meet some people," I say once he puts me back down. Eyes follow us as I lead him back to our table. Everyone knows who Killian is. So it's no surprise people are curious as to why he's here.

"Killian, this is Theon, Nox, Chase, Carter, and Prince Jace." I point each one out.

"It's nice to meet you, sir." Jace stands and offers his hand to Killian.

Killian bows at the waist before shaking his hand. "It's nice to meet you as well. I've heard a lot about you."

My face heats. "Killian." I scold.

"Let's sit." I sit beside Jace again as Killian takes the open seat beside me.

"Are you well?" He assesses me. Killian never misses anything.

I knew he would pick up on the weight loss right away. I'm just glad the dark circles under my eyes have disappeared, or he'd be really concerned.

"I am."

"Good. Have you been sleeping? Getting enough to eat?"

I roll my eyes at him. "Yes, Killian. Things are better, I promise."

"Just making sure." He pats my head affectionately.

"Killian, can you tell us what it is like to be a weapons master?" Theon bounces in his seat. I'd forgotten that Killian was an idol to them.

The guys spend the rest of dinner peppering Killian with questions, eager to get to know him. Even Jace seems excited to hear his stories.

"You seem good." Killian comments as we walk to my room after dinner. There is no way I'm telling him that I'm actually staying with Jace. He'd freak.

"I am," I say as I unlock my door and show him inside. "Things are going well here. I'm acing all my classes and have made some really good friends. I am happy here."

"I'm glad." He smiles warmly at me. "I was worried you wouldn't give it a real shot."

I snort, "I didn't have a chance not to. Those guys attached themselves to me pretty quick."

"That's good. You need people like that," Killian says. "Now, how about a tour?"

I walk him through my room, showing him everything.

"This is the best part." I lead him to the glass doors in my bedroom. Opening them, I walk out onto the balcony.

"It's nice up here." He comments, looking at the scenery. It's late, so the stars are starting to peek out, and there's a bite to the air that indicates snow will begin falling soon.

"Thank you for convincing me to come here," I whisper to him. "I know I didn't have a choice, but I still appreciate you making it sound like everything would be okay."

He wraps his arm around me. "I'll always encourage you to do what's best for you."

We stay like that for a while, catching up on all we missed over the last month and a half.

A soft knock on my main door interrupts our conversation.

"One second," I say to Killian, running to the door to open it.

Jace stands on the other side, looking nervous. He has his hands in his pockets, and his hair looks like he's run his hands through it multiple times.

I smile warmly at him and try to push through our bond, my happiness and excitement at telling Killian.

"Killian's not scary, I promise," I tell him, extending my hand to him.

"Maybe not to you." Jace runs his hands through his hair once more before taking my hand and following me back to Killian.

"Killian?" I say once we are standing behind him. He turns around. His eyes go immediately to our joined hands and narrow. Jace starts to sweat a little. I give his hand a squeeze to try and calm him down. "We would like to tell you something."

"What?" He asks in his scary commander's voice. The voice that used to send me running but now has no effect on me. Jace, on the other hand, stands up even straighter, and his eyes widen. He looks like he's going to pass out.

I giggle at his appearance, unable to help myself. Jace, the most powerful fae to walk our realm, is scared of Killian.

Jace turns his wide eyes to me, pleading with them to put him out of his misery.

I smile at him, and without taking my eyes off him, I say to Killian, "We are mates."

Jace removes the glamour from our mate mark so Killian can see it.

I finally remove my eyes from Jace to see Killian's slack jaw expression. I don't think I have ever seen Killian speechless.

"Killian?" I'm a little worried he hasn't said anything yet.

"I just need a minute." He takes a seat on one of the chairs and stares at our hands.

We stand there silently while Killian collects his thoughts.

"How long have you known?" He finally asks us.

"Two weeks, sir." Jace answers. He isn't sweating anymore, but he still looks half terrified.

"We wanted to tell you in person," I add.

"Have you told your parents?" He asks Jace.

"No, sir. We are going to have dinner with them tomorrow."

I want to roll my eyes at Jace's use of sirs. But I know he's nervous, so I'll let it go.

"Did you tell them who you are bringing with you?"

"No," Jace shakes his head.

"I don't know how they will respond to you two being mates. I don't even know if the queen knows Aria is alive. King Baston was adamant that no one find out I had her."

"I don't care what they think. She is my mate, and they will have to learn to accept her." Jace says. His body is rigid at the idea of his parents not accepting me.

"Well, I wish you good luck. I truly hope they accept you two are mates." Killian stands. "I'm happy for you two. It just took me by surprise, is all."

Killian's smile stretches across his face. He pulls me from Jace and gives me another bear hug. I laugh in his arms.

The joy I feel at Killian accepting us is overwhelming.

"Welcome to the family," Killian says to Jace once he puts me down. He pulls Jace into a hug, slapping him on the back.

"Thank you." Jace gives him one of his genuine smiles. "And I promise, I'll be good to her. Aria will always be cherished and cared for." Jace pulls me back into his side. His words fill me with warmth.

"I know you will," Killian says. "I don't even have to threaten you either. Because if you aren't good to her, she'll put you in your place."

Jace lets out a nervous laugh, knowing it's true.

Killian looks down at his watch, "I need to get going."

"Are you sure?" I pout.

"It's almost midnight. You have classes in the morning, and I need to portal home. I have to be up early to meet the next batch of soldiers I am training."

"Fine." Jace and I follow Killian back inside. Warmth greets me instantly. I hadn't noticed how cold I had gotten.

"Congratulations. Again, I'm happy for you two," Killian says.

"Thanks." I pull him in for one final hug. "Goodnight, Killian."

"Night, kid, Jace."

I watch him disappear down the hall. Sadness flows through me while watching him go.

"You'll see him again soon," Jace says from beside me.

"I know." I sigh.

"Come on, let's get some sleep." Jace closes my door and leads me across the hall.

Chapter Thirty-Two

I have nothing to wear. I stand in my black silk robe in my closet, staring at my empty closet.

When I agreed to dinner at the castle with Jace and his parents, I had forgotten I don't own any fancy dresses. Well, except for the one Jace gave me. But I figure that's too fancy.

I sigh. The little black dress I had planned to wear for the welcoming ball will have to do. It's not as dressy as I want, but at least it's a dress. I'm sure the queen will have a fit if I show up in jeans.

"Why does it look like a bomb went off in here?" Jace laughs as he walks into my closet.

Even though I spend every night in Jace's room, I've yet to have a chance to move my things into his closet.

I grimace, looking down at the mess I've made. While hunting for something to wear tonight, I threw all the clothes I didn't like on the floor. It really does look like a bomb has gone off. "I was trying to find something to wear."

"Speaking of that. I have something for you." Jace takes me by the hand and leads me back into my bedroom. On my bed sits a large black box with a red bow. "Open it."

I smile at the excitement in his voice. I tug on the bow and push the top to the side. Inside is another gorgeous dress. It is a deep emerald green, slip-style silk dress. The neckline is straight across, with the back open and a slit up the right side. Tiny straps hold it up.

"It's beautiful." I breathe.

"You like it?" Jace asks. I can feel how nervous he is.

"I love it. Thank you so much." I place the dress back on the bed and throw my arms around him.

"You're welcome. I remembered you don't have many dresses and figured you would be stressed about finding something to wear."

My heart warms. No one has ever done something so thoughtful for me. I kiss him deeply, trying to convey the gratitude I'm feeling.

Jace pulls back after a minute. "If we start that now, we will never get there on time." He looks me over. "Or ever." He smiles at me wolfishly.

I blush. "Right. I just need to get dressed, and then I'm ready."

Jace leaves my room to go change as well.

I shimmy into the dress, zipping it up on the side. I walk back into my closet to look in the floor-length mirror. It fits me like a glove. It accentuates my curves, making me feel feminine.

I left my hair down for the night. Only curled it a little to define my natural waves and pinned the front pieces back. I also did my makeup the same as always- winged liner and nude lipstick. I want the king and queen to see me as I am.

I slip on my black strappy heels, completing the look.

I walk back into my room and find Jace looking out the window, waiting for me.

My mouth turns dry when he turns around. He wears a black shirt with the top two buttons undone, sleeves rolled up, black slacks, and black boots. Jace's muscles push against the confines of his shirt. His hair is pushed back from his face, except for that one piece that always falls forward.

He always looks good. But this makes him look like the powerful prince he is.

"You look handsome." I compliment him once I find my voice again.

Jace doesn't say anything for a moment. He's too busy looking me over. "Gorgeous." He finally breathes out.

"Thank you." I blush. Even though Jace tells me I'm beautiful at every opportunity, I will never get used to it.

Jace grabs my coat and helps me into it.

The temperature dropped overnight, bringing snow with it.

Even though I know I can heat my skin with my fire magic since I've accidentally done it before, I would rather not try tonight and risk burning my dress.

"Ready?" He asks.

I nod my head even though I'm not remotely close to being ready. I'm a nervous wreck.

Jace must be able to feel my nervousness because he tucks me in close. "I promise everything will be okay."

I relax into him, trusting his words.

"How are we getting there?" I forgot to ask him earlier.

"My father sent a car along with my personal guards." Jace rolls his eyes. "I usually drive myself, but since I am bringing you and the demon attacks have worsened, he felt it would be better to send someone to get us."

"Why not use a portal? Wait, can you portal? I guess I have never asked."

"Yes, I can portal." Jace laughs softly at me. "To answer your question as to why we aren't using a portal, there are barriers around the castle to prevent anyone from portaling into it. The barrier extends past the castle wall so far that driving is safer."

Before I respond, I hear Nova's voice. "Jace, wait!"

I grumble under my breath.

Sorry. I'll get rid of her. Jace speaks in my mind.

"Nova, what do you need?" He asks when she catches up to us.

She's wearing a short blue mini-dress that leaves nothing to the imagination. I don't understand how she gets away with dressing like that. Isn't there some kind of dress code here?

"Where are you headed?" Nova bats her eyes at him.

I want to gag and punch her all at the same time.

"I have a dinner to attend at the castle," Jace says flatly.

"Would you like some company?" She reaches forward like she is going to place her hand on his chest.

Jace shifts out of the way before she can. "Aria will be joining me."

Nova blinks at me like it is the first time she has noticed me standing here. "Why?"

"Because I want her too," Jace explains no further. "We really must be going. Our car is here." He doesn't give Nova time to respond. Jace places a hand on my back, leading me out the door.

The blast of cold air cools my temper. "She never stops, does she?"

"No, she doesn't."

Jace leads me to the black SUV in front of the steps. Two males are standing at attention beside it. They both wear all-black army uniforms, with a sword strapped to their backs and several daggers attached in various spots.

"Good to see you again, sir." One of the males says. He is a mountain of a male with chestnut hair and deep blue eyes. He towers over even Jace with pounds of muscle. I would find him terrifying if it weren't for his kind eyes and easy smile.

"Enough with the formalities, Conrad." Jace pulls him into a hug, slapping him on the back. "How have you been?"

"Good. My wife and I are expecting our first child." He beams.

I can practically feel his excitement and pride.

"Congratulations!" Jace hugs him again, smiling along with Conrad.

"Stan, how about you?" Jace turns to the other male. He is slightly smaller than Conrad but still huge. He is bald, with eyes so dark they look black, and a nasty scar that runs through his left brow, narrowly missing his eye and stopping just above his lip. The wound must have come from an iron blade if it left a scar behind.

"I'm good, sir." He replies gruffly. His demeanor is not as warm as Conrad's.

"Conrad, Stan, this is Aria." Jace pulls me forward to introduce me to them. "Aria, this is Conrad and Stan, my personal guards."

"It's nice to meet you." I dip my head in respect to them.

"Nice to meet you as well, miss." Conrad flashes me a warm smile.

Stan dips his head in greeting and turns to Jace. "Are you ready?"

Stan clearly is the one who is all about business in his and Conrad's relationship.

Jace nods his head and helps me into the SUV.

Jace chats with his guards while we drive from Nightfall Academy to the castle. I notice that once Stan is in the car and behind the wheel, he is more relaxed and less on guard. He talks to Jace the same as Conrad. Even though there has to be a significant age gap between Jace and his guards, he treats them like friends.

I look out the window, only half listening to their conversation. I only saw a glimpse of the city when we first drove to the academy. Even though it is almost night, the streets are still bustling with fae.

Shops line the road, with brick walkways in front of them. Some places have little seating areas in front of them, with fire bowls to keep the fae warm sitting at the tables. Others have their doors thrown wide open despite the chill in the air and the late hour. Each shop is painted a different color, with some having designs depicting what they sell inside. Lamp posts stand in front of each shop.

Stan turns into the city's center.

"A skating rink?" I squeal. It sits in the middle of the city. The skating rink is massive, with little twinkly lights strung above it and booths around the perimeter selling food and hot beverages. Fae skate around the rink while others sit to the side, enjoying the evening while drinking their hot drinks. Next to the skating rink is a park where kids and their parents still play.

"Do you like ice skating?" Jace asks, amusement apparent in his voice.

"I've only been once when I was younger. We didn't have one in my village, but the village next to ours had one. I loved it." I smile at the memory. It was the only time Killian felt comfortable taking me someplace. We only did it once, but it's one of my favorite memories.

"We will go soon, then."

My smile is so big, my face hurts. "Thank you!"

I press my face back against the window, taking everything in. I can't remember now why I'd been so scared to go into the city.

"Have you never been to Oyxnmire, miss?" Conrad asks me from the front passenger seat.

"No, this is my first time. I haven't left the academy grounds since I arrived."

"You'll have to get Jace to show you around."

"Any time you want." Jace smiles at me affectionately. "I'd love to show you around."

We pull up to the castle's outer wall, halting our conversation. Flags with the kingdom's sigil, a golden sword with eight stars surrounding it, hang on each side of the gate. There is also a tower on each side of the gate, with soldiers standing guard inside them.

The gates open wide with our approach.

Stan drives up the short driveway, coming to a stop in front of the enormous front steps. It looks like there are fifty to walk up.

I look up at the castle, taking it all in. Up close, I agree with my assessment from the day we went hiking. It's beautiful. The castle is bright and open, with large windows lining every wall. Balconies jut out every so often, breaking up the flat stone exterior.

A young guard comes up to the driver's side as Stan starts to get out. Now that I'm not focused on the castle, I can see guards lining the castle walls, standing on the open balconies- and I'm sure- hiding in the shadows.

Conrad gets out of the SUV next and opens Jace's door for him.

Jace turns to me before getting out. "Ready?"

I blow out a breath. I can't seem to shake my nerves. But Jace being close is helping. "Ready."

Jace gets out of the SUV and extends his hand to help me out.

Once we are both out, Conrad takes position beside me, and Stan takes place beside Jace, boxing us in between them.

Are they worried something is going to happen? I ask Jace as we walk.

They are on high alert for demon attacks. They are just being overly cautious.

That makes sense.

A butler opens the large oak doors for us as we finally reach the top.

I gawk as we step inside. The place screams wealth. The floors are polished white marble, with the walls a white stone wash. Stone pillars sit every few feet. Open archways lead to various rooms, and a stone staircase sits in the middle. I strain my neck to look up at the high ceilings. Gold chandeliers cascade down from the ceiling. The gold continues in the banisters and frames the archways. Even the veins in the marble floors are gold.

What gets me is there are no personal touches. No pictures of the king and queen with Jace. No decorations. Nothing. Although the room screams wealth, it also feels cold.

Jace chuckles at my expression. "Not what you were expecting?"

"Not at all." I finally tear my eyes from the room to turn to Jace. "I knew it would be grand, but I didn't expect it to feel like this."

"Like what?" He tilts his head to the side.

"Cold," I whisper to him. I don't want to insult his home, but I want to be honest with him.

Jace nods his head. "Yes, cold is an accurate description. Some parts of the castle don't feel that way. But not many."

"Good evening, Your Highness." The butler bows deeply to Jace, interrupting our conversation. "May I take your coats?"

"Yes, please." Jace removes his and helps me out of mine, handing them off to the butler.

"The king and queen are waiting for you in the private dining room, sir." The butler says.

"Thank you." Jace places his hand on my back, guiding me down the hall to the right. Conrad and Stan follow behind us.

We walk a bit before Jace turns left through an open archway.

Inside is a walnut table that takes up a large portion of the room, with several cushioned chairs lining it. The wall opposite the entry is floor-to-ceiling glass doors that lead to the gardens. At one end, a granite fireplace takes up most of the wall. This room feels cozier compared to what I've seen of the rest of the castle. However, there are still no personal touches in the room.

Conrad and Stan join the other guards and servants lining the walls.

"Hello, son." King Baston greets Jace warmly.

He's not what I'd been expecting. He is a massive male, with ebony hair, and piercing sea-blue eyes. He wears no crown to indicate that he is king.

But he would never need one. His presence alone exudes power. Not to the extent that Jace does, but it is still strong.

"Father." Jace strides over to where he is standing by the fire.

I stay standing just inside the room, giving them a moment.

Baston hugs him tightly. I can tell from the expression on King Baston's face that he loves his son dearly.

My eyes wander over to the female standing beside King Baston, Queen Camila. She is beautiful, with long caramel blonde hair and chocolate brown eyes. She is wearing a long, flowy burgundy dress with a high neckline and a straight skirt. Although she is beautiful, her expression is severe. Unlike King Baston, she does not smile when Jace hugs her. She does not hold him as close, either.

Jace looks almost exactly like his father, all except the eyes. Looking at them, I can't help but wonder where Jace gets his unusual gold eyes from. He is the only other fae I have met who does not have earth-tone eyes.

"Mother, Father, I want you to meet someone." Jace walks back over to where I'm standing. He pulls gently on my hand and walks me over to his parents. "This is Aria Umbra."

I dip into a clumsy curtsy. "A pleasure-"

"Leave." Queen Camila interrupts me.

My head whips up, thinking she is talking to me. But it is the guards and servants that file out of the room.

"Mother?" Jace questions her.

She gives him a sharp look that has him shutting his mouth.

Once everyone else is out of the room and a servant closes the door, Camila speaks again.

"How is she alive?" Camila turns her angry eyes to King Baston.

But King Baston is not looking at her. He is too busy staring at me. "You have grown into a beautiful young female." He says to me.

"Thank you, Your Majesty." I dip my head.

"Baston!" Camila practically snarls his name. "What is she doing here?"

I step back, bumping into Jace, at her tone. She is not happy I'm here, or alive, for that matter. I thought she knew I was alive since King Baston did.

"Mother, what is going on?" Jace demands. He wraps a protective arm around me.

Her gaze narrows at the contact.

I knew this wouldn't go the best, but I didn't picture it going this bad.

"Jace, step away from her." Camila takes a threatening step toward me.

"No." Jace growls at his mother. He pushes me fully behind him, protecting me from her.

"You will listen to your queen." She demands.

"Camila, enough." King Baston finally intervenes.

"Father, will you please explain what is going on?" Jace pleads with him.

I peek out around Jace's side.

King Baston runs his hand through his hair, similar to the way Jace does. "Camila, dear, I'm sorry I did not tell you. But when my soldiers found Aria, I hid her with Killian Umbra to raise."

"You told me she was killed with her parents. Are you telling me this whole time she has been alive and well, living with one of your oldest friends?" Camila's voice has reached that dangerous calm.

"No, not that long." King Baston meets my eye. "She was five when my most trusted soldiers found her."

"What is she doing here now, though?" Camila asks again.

"I had a spot kept for her at Nightfall Academy. Aria needs to learn her magic, and Nightfall is the best place for her." Baston replies calmly.

"Her magic should be bound." Camila spits.

I flinch. Even though that's what I initially wanted, her comment still hurts. What is so wrong with me that she thinks I shouldn't have my magic?

Jace snarls at his mother. "You will not bind her magic." He pushes me further behind him again.

"What has gotten into you?" Camila asks Jace. "You barely know her. Why are you protecting her?"

"I know her better than anyone else." He says.

Jace pulls me gently out from behind him. He wraps his arm around my waist, holding me close. He removes the glamour on our mate mark before I can object.

Our mark has grown again. It now covers the entire back of our left hands and stops just above our wrist. In the center of our hands is a crescent moon with constellations surrounding it. The mark looks like the night sky came to life on our hands.

"She is my mate."

Chapter Thirty-Three

His mother gasps. "What have you done?"

Both mine and Jace's eyes fly to Camila. The hatred that was present in her stare has only grown hotter, changing her delicate features into something hideous. I bury my face into Jace's chest to escape her venomous look, but I can still feel her eyes on me.

What is it about me that she hates? Why does she stare at me like she wants to reach into my chest and rip my heart out?

I peek up at Jace from under my lashes to see his eyes are dark gold. His jaw is clenched tight and his free hand not wrapped around me is held tight in a fist. He opens his mouth to snap at his mother again, but Baston beats him to it.

"Camila, enough." Baston scolds. He pulls Jace and me into a bone-crushing hug. "Congratulations. I am happy for you two."

"Thank you, Father." Jace's voice comes out tight still.

Baston speaks so low to Jace that I barely hear him. "Don't pay attention to your mother. It's not worth the fight tonight, Son. Let us enjoy our dinner together and get to know your mate."

Jace's shoulders drop a fraction and he dips his head in a shallow nod in agreement.

A soft sigh slips out of me. I'm glad at least one of his parents seems to accept me. But I would like to know what Camila's problem with me is.

"Baston, we need to talk about this." Camila urges as Baston lets us go.

"No, we don't." His jaw is locked tight and there's anger brewing in his eyes. Camila is testing Baston's limits now.

"Are you completely forgetting the prophecy?" She asks him with a raised brow.

My ears perk up at the mention of the prophecy. Maybe now is the time to get the answers I seek.

"No, I'm not." He begins slowly. "But it doesn't matter now. Either the prophecy is wrong, or we misunderstood it."

Camila shakes her head, not agreeing with him. She opens her mouth, most likely to launch into all the reasons why he's wrong, but I beat her to it.

"Could I ask what the prophecy says?" I ask King Baston.

He gives me a sad smile. "I'm sorry, dear, I cannot tell you. If I do, it could alter your fate significantly. It's best to forget all about it."

"I understand." I don't, not really. But I am not about to argue with a king.

"Maybe we should tell her. Might give us a better chance of it not coming to pass." Camila comments.

"Please excuse us for a moment," Baston says to us. Grabbing Camila by the arm, he leads her from the room.

Once they shut the doors again, my shoulders drop. "This is horrible."

"I'll admit, it's not the best." Jace agrees. "But my father seems to accept us."

"Yes, it is good to have him on our side."

"Things will get better." Jace kisses me on the head.

"Did you understand anything she was talking about?" I turn in his arms to look up at him.

Jace shakes his head. His brows are lowered in thought. "No, I was hoping you would be able to explain some of it."

I sigh. "Nope."

"It's okay. We will figure out everything together." He reassures me.

Baston and Camila come back in only after a few minutes. Followed by the guards and servants.

Jace quickly puts the glamour back on our mark upon seeing the guards and servants.

Camila shoots a glare at me before huffing and taking her seat, not waiting for the rest of us. She takes her napkin off the table and delicately places it on her lap. Sitting straight, she folds her hands in her lap, and stares out the glass doors, ignoring us all.

Jace's jaw is tight again and his eyes are narrowed at his mother. But he doesn't comment on her rude behavior. Maybe he doesn't want to deal with her right now. Or maybe he doesn't want to ruin our night anymore than it already has been. Either way, I appreciate that he doesn't say anything. It would only lead to more poisonous words from Camila.

"How about we sit down for dinner?" Baston says, completely ignoring the lingering tension in the air.

Jace leads me to my seat, pulling it out for me, before taking his seat beside me. He sits on the king's right hand with me beside him and Camila on the other side of the table.

I can feel Camila's glare, but I don't look at her.

King Baston motions with his hand, and the serving staff brings out the first course.

They place a plate with roast beef, roasted potatoes, vegetables, and gravy in front of me.

What fork? I ask Jace. I can't remember which one it is.

The furthest out. It's the biggest one.

Jace taps the one he is talking about before picking it. I follow his lead.

I take a bite of roast beef. Flavors explode across my tongue. I don't know how it is possible, but the food is even better than the academy serves.

"We will have to get etiquette lessons set up for you immediately," Camila comments.

My face heats. I was hoping no one would notice Jace's help.

"Mother," Jace warns.

"Jace, she needs them. Along with the history of our bloodline, politics, and dance lessons." Camila says.

"She doesn't need anything. Aria is perfect the way she is." Jace growls.

"She is not from court, so she never had to learn these things. It is important to maintain a certain image." Camila chided.

I feel lacking. I put my fork down gently, no longer hungry. I want to speak up and say what I think. But I am afraid it will make Camila angrier if I do. So, I stay silent.

"She may not have grown up in court, but Aria is not incompetent," Jace snaps. His arms are crossed over his chest, and his anger pushes through our bond.

"That is not what I mean." Camila sighs.

"What did you mean then?" Baston speaks for the first time during the conversation.

"I meant that she is expected to talk, walk, act, and dress a certain way at all times. I am only trying to help you, Jace. You need someone by your side that is seen as poised and regal."

Jace shakes his head, jaw clenched tight. "No, I like the way she is. Aria is a breath of fresh air in this place. I don't want to change that." Jace turns his golden gaze to me. "But I will not stop her if she chooses to take any lessons."

I clear my throat, trying to gather the courage to speak. "I don't want to change who I am. Thank you for your offer, though." I hope that is polite enough not to upset Camila further.

Camila shakes her head and doesn't say anymore. But I can feel her displeasure radiating off her. I see Baston smiling at me out of the corner of my eye like he is pleased with me for sticking up for myself.

Jace lets out some of the tension his body is holding. He places his hand on my leg, giving it a squeeze.

I'm sorry. Jace speaks into my mind. I know he feels terrible about how tonight's going.

It's okay. It's not your fault. I tell him. I cover his hand with mine.

I don't feel particularly good right now. But knowing that Jace disagrees with his mother about me needing lessons does make me feel slightly better.

We eat in silence for a while.

I had initially planned on asking Baston for information about my parents tonight. But I no longer think that is a good idea. He didn't want to tell me about the prophecy, and I doubt he will want to tell me about my parents, especially with Camila here.

Camila is the first to break the silence. "I suppose this means the engagement is off."

My heart stops. My fork slips from my hand, clattering to the plate. "What engagement?" My voice is deathly cold.

"Mother!" Jace snaps. "The contract was never agreed upon."

"Jace, it was a done deal. We had it in writing and everything. We were just waiting for you to sign it." His mother replies.

"What engagement?" I repeat.

"Well, the one with Councilman Victor's daughter, Nova."

I can barely make out the king saying something.

Anger becomes a living thing inside me. Jace was engaged to Nova and never told me. My eyes shift to deep violet, and flames burst from my hands. I can't concentrate on containing my magic. The table lights on fire instantly.

The queen screams and pushes back from the table.

Rough hands pull me away from the table while someone uses their water magic to put out the fire.

My fire still coats my fist. I can't dispel my anger. I know, somewhere deep within me, that if what the queen said was true, Jace would have told me.

"Aria!" Jace roars, stepping into my line of vision. He flinches when my eyes meet his. "Please listen to me."

My mind is hazy with anger, but I manage to nod for him to explain.

"I never signed the contract. It wasn't a done deal. It was something my mother wanted. But neither my father nor I agreed to it. There is no engagement. I would have told you if there was. I promise."

I feel my magic slip away from my hands at his words.

"I believe you," I whisper to him.

Jace sighs in relief and crushes me against his chest. "I'm sorry." He says into my hair.

I wrap my arms around him and hold him close. The contact makes the last of my anger vanish. "I'm sorry for getting so mad." I haven't lost my temper like this since I was little.

"Don't be."

I pull away to take in the damage I'd done to the table. There are black handprints where I had lit it on fire. I cringe looking at it.

"I apologize for losing my temper and ruining your table. I will pay for a new one." I say to Baston. I can't look at Camila yet. I don't know how I am going to pay for it, but I will find a way.

Baston grins. "It's okay. We can just make that your spot."

Despite how I'm feeling, a laugh bubbles out of me.

"It is not okay!" Camila scolds. "That table is a priceless heirloom!"

"Camila, enough. You have done enough damage for the evening." The king says with a voice of authority. Jace opens his mouth like he wants to say something to her, but Baston lifts his hand before he can. "We were enjoying a lovely meal before this, and I would like to finish it."

Baston sits back down at the table, and we follow suit.

★★★

The rest of the meal is tense.

Baston engages Jace and me in small talk, but Camila doesn't say anything. She sits there staring at me, not touching her food.

After a while, I stop pretending to eat and politely refuse dessert. Camila staring at me is making me too nervous and uncomfortable. My thoughts are a mess, too. I keep replaying everything she said.

Jace looks at me with concern. "I think it is time for us to head back to the academy. It's getting late." He tells his father.

"Yes, of course." His father stands.

"You go ahead with my father. I'll be along in a minute." Jace says to me.

"Oh, okay." I raise my brow in a silent question.

I just need to speak with my mother, and I don't want you to see me yell at her. Conrad will go with you.

Okay.

I follow Baston out of the dining room. Conrad follows behind me and closes the door, giving Jace and Camila privacy.

"What the hell is wrong with you?" Jace snaps.

I quicken my steps, not wanting to hear Camila's reply.

Baston sighs, running his hand through his hair. "I am deeply sorry about her. I had no idea she would react this way."

"Why did she?" I ask him hesitantly.

"She is scared."

"Of me?" I squeak out. I can't fathom why anyone would be scared of me; I would never hurt anyone.

"Yes." Baston chuckles. "Although, I don't know why either. I knew we misunderstood everything when I met you when you were five."

We come to the front entrance, where the butler is waiting with my coat.

"Thank you," I say as I accept it from him. "How did you find me anyway?" It was something I always wondered about.

"You actually found us."

"I did? How?"

Baston sighs. "That's the thing, I don't know. Do you remember anything from that time?"

"No," I shake my head. "I can't remember anything past you giving me to Killian. I remember standing on his front step with you and you begging him to take me. Nothing before that."

I've tried a million times to remember the time before. But every time I do, I hit a mental wall. I can't even get a murky picture. It's as if my life started on those steps. As if I didn't exist before that.

The only time I feel like I remember something is during my nightmares while being tortured in a dungeon. The fact that I wake up and still feel like I am in that dungeon makes me believe it even more.

"I figured as much."

I wait for Baston to say more, giving him time to collect his thoughts.

Baston gets this faraway look like he is lost in a memory. "I lied earlier to Camila when I said it was my soldiers who found you. I was with them. I was traveling back to the capital from visiting a friend with my guards when one shouted and slammed on the brakes. He jumped out and yelled for me. As I stepped out of the vehicle, there you were, lying in the middle of the road, half dead. You looked like you had been beaten within an inch of your life and were covered in filth. Most of your bones were broken, and you had cut marks covering your body. I don't know where you came from or how long you walked, but your body gave out on you in the middle of that road."

Silent tears stream down my face. All my life, I wanted to know what happened to me before Killian. And now that I am finally getting answers, I find myself not wanting to know anymore.

"You were so tiny," Baston continues, voice cracking slightly. "You were just skin and bones. All I could think when I saw you lying on that road was what monster would do this to a child. Then, after I healed most of your major wounds and patched you up enough to move you, you opened your eyes. And I knew who you were as soon as I saw your eyes and why someone would do this to you. It broke me in a way I will never recover from because I failed you. You were this helpless, scared little girl I failed to protect from the monster who did atrocious things to you.

"I knew I couldn't change the past but could change your future. So, I had my guards re-route to Killian's. I told no one else where I was going. I knew if anyone was going to protect you, it would be Killian. As I am sure you know, Killian had just lost his wife and unborn child, so he refused at first. But I got one of the soldiers to bring you from the SUV. When Killian looked at you, his face softened. I think he saw the same brokenness in you as he saw in himself. I only told him the bare minimum information, enough that he would know how important it was to protect you, but not too much that he would ever be put in danger because of it.

"I have not seen you since. Killian and I agreed it would be best if I stayed away. But he kept me updated over the years. Told me the first time you talked to him, the first time you held a sword, the first time you went to school, all of it. I am proud of the young female you have become. I know you don't remember what happened to you, but something like that changes a person."

By the time Baston is done, I feel like I can't breathe. Tears are still streaming down my face, and my heart hurts. So many emotions are warring inside me. Anger, hurt, confusion, sadness, but most importantly, gratitude.

"Thank you." I choke out.

"It is the least I could do." He says with a sad smile. "I want you to know I never stopped looking for you. After we found your parent's bodies, I sent out search party after search party for you. I never gave up hope that you were alive."

"Why?" I ask. "Why search for me? Why care if I was alive if the prophecy is so bad?"

Baston's eyes soften. "Because, my dear, I will never kill an innocent because of an unknown."

I can't find words to express how thankful I am. How much it means to me that he saved me all those years ago. How grateful I am that he gave me to Killian.

He must be able to read this all on my face because he says, "You know fate has a funny way of working sometimes."

"Why's that?"

"Because we were never meant to take that road. It was a back road that wasn't used often. But a tree had fallen over the one we were supposed to take, so we turned and took the road we found you on."

My lips part in surprise.

"Everything okay?" Jace asks as he walks down the hall towards us.

I quickly wipe under my eyes to remove the last of my tears.

"Everything's good." I smile at him. My smile must be watery, though, because Jace doesn't look convinced. He places a hand on my waist, squeezing it gently.

Aria, Sweetheart, what's wrong?

Nothing, your father just told me about the day he found me. I will tell you when we get back to the academy.

Jace nods his head in understanding.

"Thank you for coming tonight." Baston turns our attention back to him. "Again, I am sorry for Camila's behavior."

Jace sighs, running his hand through his hair. "It's not your fault."

"She'll come around." Baston smiles warmly.

"Thank you for having us." I dip into another wobbly curtsy.

I think I need to work on those.

"You don't need to do that, dear. You are family now."

My eyes water, family. Never did I think I would have anyone besides Killian to call family. Now I can add Baston to the growing list.

We say our goodbyes and head back to the academy.

I'm quiet on the drive. Too many thoughts and emotions are going through me. I don't know how to process everything that Baston told me.

Not to mention what Camila expects of me and that she wanted, or more like, wants Jace to marry Nova.

I can't dwell on that one for too long without wanting to light something on fire.

Jace doesn't try to get me to talk. He just wraps his arm around me and pulls me close so I can rest my head on his shoulder.

Jace is unlocking his door when he finally speaks. "Are you okay?"

I don't know how to respond at first.

I walk into the living area and sit on the couch.

I gather my thoughts and tell Jace everything his father told me. Jace doesn't sit as I tell him. He paces in front of me, getting angrier with every word that comes out of my mouth.

When I'm finally done, my head and heart hurt again. I want to remember what Baston is talking about, but I still can't. I thought maybe if he told me how he found me, it might unlock the other memories. But that wall is still there.

"You almost died." Jace's voice is nothing but a rasp. He finally stops pacing to kneel in front of me. "I want to hunt down whoever did that to you and slowly kill them."

My heart warms at his protectiveness. "I wish I could help you."

"One day, I vow we will find the bastard and kill them."

"Thank you." I kiss him hard.

The fact that he wants to help fight beside me and not hide me away makes me fall a little more for him.

"That's not bothering you the most, is it?" He says once we pull apart.

I knew Jace would be able to tell that's not all that is bothering me.

"I'm not good enough," I admit. I look down, not wanting to see Jace's face.

Jace grabs my chin and pulls my face up to look at him. He is furious. "Not good enough?" He grinds out. "You are the best thing that has ever happened to me."

I pull my face free and stand, moving to look out the window. "I'm not, though. I don't know how to act, talk, walk, dance, what cutlery to use, or even how to curtsy properly. I don't know politics or even the first thing about being a princess. I will be horrible at all of it."

"Aria." Jace turns me to face him. I look at his chest, unwilling to look at him when he says I'm right. "I meant what I said. I will be with you every step of the way. I will teach you everything. We are in this together. I only want you."

My eyes fly up to meet with soft golden eyes. "Why?" It's all I can think of to ask.

Jace's smile is as soft as his eyes. "Because you are perfect the way you are."

The last of the icy chill that had entered my body at dinner evaporates.

"But won't I embarrass you?"

"Sweetheart, you are not going to embarrass me." He wraps his arms around my waist. "If you want to take lessons, that is fine. But you don't have to. We will figure everything out together."

"I wouldn't mind knowing what cutlery to use or how to curtsy and dance."

"I can teach you those."

I shake my head. "I don't want to waste your time."

"You never waste my time," Jace says. "We can start tomorrow. I will show you the most common dances. We will practice every day until you feel comfortable. I will also have a table setting made up so I can explain when to use what cutlery."

"Thank you." I place my head on his chest.

"Anything for you."

Chapter Thirty-Four

"I want to take you on a date," Jace says a week later.

I smile at him from the mirror in our closet, where I'm getting ready for classes. I finally moved my things into his room, making it officially ours. "You do?"

"Yes, we have yet to go on one. Also, you need a break."

Since our dinner with his parents, Jace has been teaching me how to dance, curtsy, and what cutlery to use every night. I am slowly getting the hang of everything. I know what cutlery to use most of the time and how to curtsy properly. I still have to count the steps in my head when we are dancing. But Jace is patient with me. He never gets annoyed when I get the cutlery wrong for the fifth time in a row or step on his feet when we are dancing.

"What do you have in mind?"

He walks deeper into the closet. "It's a surprise." He kisses me on the head.

I toss my head back and groan. "Have I ever told you that I don't like surprises?"

"You'll love this, I promise."

"What should I wear?"

"Something warm." He grins at me as he walks out of the closet, giving me no more information.

I dress warmly, as Jace said. I wear a pair of blue jeans, a gray wool sweater, thick socks, my favorite combat boots, and a long, puffy jacket. It finally started snowing overnight.

"You are going to need these." Jace hands me a pair of mittens and a hat.

"Will you please tell me where we are going now?" I ask for the millionth time. I asked him every time I saw him today, but he wouldn't budge.

"Nope." he grins at me. "Come on." He tugs my hand. I laugh and follow him out.

He drops my hand as soon as we leave the comfort of our room.

"So, I was hoping that we could get away with no guards, but with the demons picking up their attacks, my father requested that I bring Conrad and Stan," Jace explains as we walk to the front entrance. "That also means I can't portal us to where we are going. I can't travel with that many people yet."

"That's okay, I understand."

In the last week, the demon attacks have gotten worse. There are multiple attacks every day. They are killing fae, burning homes and businesses, and even kidnapping some fae. The king requested that none of the citizens go anywhere alone. He also has the army patrolling the city. It won't stop the attacks from happening, but the hope was fewer lives would be lost.

With all the attacks happening, Jace hasn't had a chance to investigate who my parents were. The only time I see him is late in the evenings. He spends most of his free time in the city, helping wherever possible. I don't want to add to his stress by asking about it.

"You won't even notice them where we are going," Jace says as he holds open the main door to the academy for me.

A blast of cold air hits me as I walk out. I pull my hat lower, grateful Jace gave it to me.

A light dusting of snow covers the ground, with more falling. We walk towards Conrad and Stan, who stand at attention in front of the same SUV as last time.

"Good evening, Jace." Conrad dips into a bow. "Aria, good to see you again."

"You too, Conrad."

"Ready to go?" Stan asks.

Jace nods and helps me into the SUV, sliding in beside me.

"Could you two tell me where we are going?" I ask after a few minutes into our drive.

Jace chuckles. "No, they won't tell you where we are going."

I pout. "Fine." I turn to look back out the window. The city looks magical, with the snow covering everything.

I gasp as I get a look at where Stan is pulling in. "Are we going ice skating?"

"I promised we would," Jace whispers into my ear.

"You are the best!" I squeal.

I jump out of the SUV before Stan fully stops.

"Hold on, Aria." Jace laughs from behind me. He catches me by the hand before I can go much further. "We need to get skates first." He points to a little hut on the side of the rink.

Jace leads me to the hut. Conard and Stan follow close behind.

"Your Highness." A thin male behind the counter bows as we approach. "How can I help you?"

"We need to rent some skates, please," Jace tells the male our sizes and hands him cash to pay.

"It's on the house, your highness." The male tries to push the money back toward Jace.

Jace waves him off. "I insist."

He leaves the cash on the counter and walks to an open bench.

"Here, I'll tie them for you." Jace sets aside his skates and kneels in front of me.

I hear people gasp around us. I lift my head to find everyone looking at us. Some are whispering behind their hands, and others are openly gaping at us. At first, I don't understand what has them in shock, but as I look back down at Jace, I see it. The crown prince is kneeling in front of a female.

Jace, everyone is staring at us. Maybe I should tie my skates.

Jace turns to look at the people. I can't see his face from this angle, but his expression must be scary enough because people's faces pale, and they turn back to their business.

Problem solved. Jace grins at me, showing off his dimple.

"Ready?" He asks once he finishes tying his skates.

I nod.

Jace helps me up and heads over to the entrance of the rink. The rink has a half wall surrounding it, so people can hold on to it if they need help.

Jace steps confidently onto the rink. "Here, take my hands. I will pull you for the first little bit until you get used to it."

I follow Jace, much wobblier, onto the rink. I hold onto his hands with a death grip. He skates backward, going slowly, pulling me with him.

After two laps around the perimeter, I get the hang of it.

"Want to try it on your own?" Jace asks me after the third lap around.

"Okay, but don't go far, please."

"Never." He whispers, letting go of my hands.

I take a few steps on my own and instantly lose my balance. Jace catches me around the waist before I fall.

"Thanks." I am pressed flush against him.

"Try again." He steadies me and lets go again.

I skate halfway around before I lose my balance again. This time, Jace doesn't reach me in time. I fall flat on my butt.

I tip my head back and laugh. Even though my butt is now cold and wet, I don't care. I am having the best time.

"Are you okay?" Jace pulls me back up.

"I'm great! This is the best." I let go of Jace and start skating again.

I gain my confidence after going around the rink a few more times.

We skate around the rink for about two hours before we get tired.

"Let's go get something warm to drink," Jace suggests.

I follow him off the rink and pull my skates off. My ankles are sore from skating for so long.

Jace orders hot chocolates and joins me at one of the little tables overlooking the rink.

"Thank you for this," I say, blowing on my hot chocolate. "I don't think I have ever had this much fun."

"You're welcome." Jace's smile is so big it lights up his whole face. I love seeing him this happy.

"Your Highness. What are you doing here?" A male walks up beside us, bowing at Jace. He is shorter than Jace, with golden blonde hair, a dusting of facial hair, and deep blue eyes.

Something about him nags at me. I can't pinpoint what it is, though.

"Councilman Victor, it's good to see you again." My blood turns cold at Jace's words. This is Nova's father. "I wanted to show Aria the skating rink. She's not from the city."

Victor's eyes widen slightly when he turns to look at me. "Aria, nice to meet you." He reaches out his hand to shake mine. I accept it and immediately want to draw my hand back. That nagging feeling grows, and my skin crawls from the contact.

"Nice to meet you too, sir," I reply. I'm surprised my voice comes out even.

Victor lets go of my hand. "Who are your parents? I feel as if we have met before."

"Killian Umbra is my father." I don't say he is my guardian. I don't want him to know anything more about me than he needs to know.

"Interesting." He muses, not taking his eyes off me.

I squirm in my seat. I am unsettled by the way he is looking at me. I know the king said no one knew he gave me to Killian. But I'm worried that might not be true.

"What brings you this way, Victor?" Jace asks, trying to bring Victor's attention back to him.

"Ah, I have a meeting with some of the recently burned-down business owners. The king has tasked the council to find the best way to help them." He explains. He lifts his arm to look at his watch. "I must be going. It was good to see you, Prince Jace. Nice to meet you, Aria." He bows again to Jace and takes off.

I let out the breath I'd been holding. "So that's Nova's father. They seem nothing alike." Even though I got a strange feeling from him, he seemed nice.

"No, they aren't." Jace agrees. "Nova is power hungry, whereas Victor has always seemed content with where he is at."

I don't tell Jace about the strange feeling I got from him. I figure it's just me being paranoid.

"Come on. We have one more stop to make." Jace says after we have finished our hot chocolates. He stands and takes me by the hand, leading me back to the SUV.

Chapter Thirty-Five

S tan drives for about ten minutes before stopping at a nondescript building.

"What's in here?" I ask as we get out of the SUV.

"You'll see," Jace says, amusement coating his voice. He takes me by the hand again and leads me inside.

The inside is painted cream with warm wood floors and a staircase leading up to the top levels. There are four unmarked doors on the opposite side of the stairs.

Jace passes the doors and leads me up to the top level.

He stops at the only door and pushes it open, stepping aside for me to enter first.

I gasp as I take a step inside. It's a greenhouse. I couldn't see the top floor of the building when we pulled up since it was almost dark. But the entire top floor is a glass dome.

Inside the greenhouse, there are plants and flowers everywhere. I can't begin naming all the different types. They fill every inch possible. Only leaving a narrow walkway and a little free space in the center of the room. The room smells of roses, violets, lilies, hibiscus, and many more flowers.

Hundreds of tiny candles are placed throughout, making it romantic. A small table and chairs are set for dinner in the center of the room.

I twirl around to look at Jace, who is still standing in the doorway. His posture is rigid. "This is incredible." I breathe.

Jace visibly relaxes. I realize now that he was nervous. "I'm glad you like it." He finally steps into the greenhouse, pulling me close when he reaches me. I love that he always needs to be touching me. "I know we can't do a normal date right now, but I was hoping you would still like this."

"It's perfect." I kiss him, trying to convey my gratitude.

"Come," Jace says once we break apart.

He helps me remove my jacket and pulls out my chair for me.

Once I'm seated, Jace goes back to the door and speaks with someone on the other side.

Jace comes back over and pours each of us a drink of sparkling champagne before taking his seat.

A few moments later, a servant walks in with two domed dishes. He places them on the table, bowing at Jace, and quickly excuses himself.

I smile as I lift the lid off the dishes. "How did you know this is my favorite?" A gourmet burger and fries sit on the plate.

"I called Killian." Jace grins.

"Really?" I can't believe how much thought he put into our date.

"Of course. I wanted tonight to be special."

"Thank you. No one has ever done anything like this for me." My throat is tight with emotion.

Jace reaches across the table to hold my hand. "I intend to keep doing this kind of stuff for you. Aria, you deserve so much more than life has given you. I can't change what has happened in the past, but I promise you I will make our future good. You will always have me by your side. Your battles are mine now. I will fight beside you and protect you the best I can."

It hits me all at once that I love Jace. I don't know when it happened, but I know without a doubt that I am madly in love with him. He makes me feel whole, something I never expected to happen. I never realized, before meeting Jace, how lonely I was. Living a life full of fear and constantly trying to stay hidden. Don't get me wrong, Killian became the father I never had, but his top priority was to keep me safe. But Jace makes me laugh and smile, something I didn't do much before. He makes me feel cherished, cared for, *loved*. He is what brought light back into my world of darkness.

"Are you okay?"

I looked up to see Jace's face full of concern. I'd been sitting here, not saying anything, not touching my food, for too long.

"Yeah, perfect." I smile at him. I'm not ready to tell him how I feel, worried that he doesn't feel the same way yet.

Jace smiles back and squeezes my hand before letting go.

Jace and I dig into our meals. It is one of the best burgers I've ever had.

"They should add this to the menu at the academy." I joke when we are finished.

Jace laughs. "I don't think I can add it to the menu. But I can bring you to the restaurant that makes them whenever you want."

"I'd like that."

Jace stands and fiddles with something off to the side. Quiet music starts playing through the greenhouse. He turns and extends his hand toward me. "Would you like to dance?"

I groan. "I should have known you'd still make me practice tonight."

"No practice tonight." He chuckles. "Just for fun."

"Okay." I accept his outstretched hand.

Jace wraps my arms around his neck and places his on my waist, holding me close. We sway to the melody, getting lost in the movement.

After a song, I rest my head on Jace's chest. "This has been the perfect first date, thank you."

"I'd do anything to see you smile the way you did today." Jace kisses the top of my head.

"I don't want to hide our relationship anymore," I whisper. I had been thinking about it for a while. It has only been a few weeks, but I am tired of pretending Jace doesn't matter to me. Tired of constantly trying not to show too much affection in public.

Jace pulls away so he can see my face. "Are you sure?"

I nod my head.

Jace blows out a nervous breath. "I don't want to hide it either. I am proud that you are my mate." He gives my waist a gentle squeeze. "I only suggested we keep it a secret to keep you safe."

"I know. But I can take care of myself."

"Oh, I know." Jace's grin is mischievous. Since we became mates, we started sparring more in class. A few times, I've been able to take him down with ease. "I will agree to announce our mate status on two conditions."

"What are your conditions, Your Highness?" I tease.

Jace's eyes darken, going to a deep gold shade. "I love it when you call me that." He nips at my nose. I bat him away, giggling.

"The first being we wait until the winter solstice to announce it." I pout at that. Jace kisses my pout away before continuing. "It is only three weeks away. I want to do it right, and the winter solstice ball would be the best place. The second is that you always have a knife, sword, or dagger on you."

I raise my eyebrow at the second condition. "You want me to carry a weapon? Why?" This is only the second time I have left the academy walls.

"The demons have become bolder in the last two months. I also don't trust that whoever kidnapped you won't return for you. I don't want you to be caught unaware, and I know you are good with a blade. I know you have magic, strong magic at that, but sometimes that is not enough."

"Okay, that seems fair. I accept your terms."

Jace laughs deeply at the seriousness in my tone.

"Will you accompany me to the castle for winter break? I know you were planning on going home. But I have cleared it with my father, and he said that you and Killian are more than welcome to stay with us."

My lips part in surprise. "Really?"

"Yeah. I knew you would want to spend time with Killian. So, I thought he could come here. The winter break starts with the winter solstice ball. After that, we will have three weeks together before classes start again."

"Of course, I will stay with you."

"So, does that mean you will be my date to the winter solstice?" He says teasingly.

"Yes."

Excitement rushes through me. In three weeks, Jace will publicly claim me as his mate.

Chapter Thirty-Six

"Are you ready to go yet?" Theon whines three weeks later. The academy had finals for the last week, and I am ready for a much-needed break.

I aced all my magic finals with no problem and worked hard to get high marks in all my other classes.

Since our date, Jace and I have barely spent any time together. Between studying, practicing magic, and writing our finals, we only got an hour together at night before we collapsed from exhaustion. It didn't help Jace kept getting called away most days to deal with the rising demon attacks.

I don't understand how, but the attacks have gotten even worse. King Baston ordered the city on a complete lockdown from sundown to sunrise. Not even the soldiers line the streets overnight anymore. Baston isn't willing to risk anyone's life. He even ordered soldiers to guard the academy. The grounds are now crawling with soldiers.

I know Jace is stressed about it and needs a break, too. I wish I could help. The first time he tried to bring me with him, the queen stopped me before I could walk into the war room at the castle. Jace tried to argue with his mother, but she pointed out that I didn't know anything about this and would only be in the way. We didn't push further because Baston stepped in and said that next time, I could come, and they would explain everything. He at least seemed to feel bad, but I never went back. Jace and I knew it would be a fight every time and decided now was not the time. Maybe after we announce our mate status tonight, Camila won't fight me being there anymore.

"Coming," I call back.

I walk into the living area with my bag on my shoulder. Jace, Theon, the twins, and Nox were all waiting for me.

"Finally." Theon sighs.

My cheeks heat. It looks like they have been waiting for me for a while. "Sorry, I didn't know what to pack."

"Don't apologize. Theon is just being grumpy." Jace says, coming up beside me and kissing me on the head.

"Let's go." Chase bounces on his feet. The guys are all eager to get home.

Jace and I told the others our plan to announce our mate status at the ball tonight. They all supported our decision, saying it was time.

I laugh at Chase's excitement.

Jace takes my bag from me, grabs his own, and leads us to the cars.

King Baston sent two SUVs to pick us up and two extra SUVs filled with soldiers to escort us to the castle. Even in the daylight, when the attacks don't happen as much, he didn't trust the demons not to attack us on the short drive.

"Your Highness, good to see you again." Conrad dips into a bow when we get to the front entrance of the academy.

Conrad, Stan, and four other soldiers line the entryway.

I notice that when more soldiers are present, Conrad tends to be more formal toward Jace.

"You too, Conrad," Jace says.

"Move out," Conrad instructs, in full commander mode.

Conrad and Stan box in Jace and me as we make our way to the cars.

We make our way outside, where it looks like a winter wonderland. It is no longer just a dusting of snow covering the ground. There are piles of it everywhere.

Jace, Nox, and I share one SUV. While Theon, Chase, and Carter share the one behind us.

As we pull up to the castle, I see even more soldiers than last time. They line every empty space along the walls, walkways, and balconies.

"We always increase security for the winter solstice wall," Jace explains. He must have picked up where my thoughts went. "But since the demons have gotten bolder, Father thought it would be best to have extra soldiers stationed here."

"Why not cancel the ball if he is worried something might happen?" I ask as we walk up the steps.

Jace shakes his head. "I asked the same thing. He said it is best to continue to have the ball. He feels bad enough having the city on lockdown. He doesn't want to take away this too. The citizens look forward to it each year."

Jace explained that the ball was not only for nobility, but everyone was welcome to attend. I appreciated that the working class was not excluded from the festivities.

"There you are!" Queen Camila cries as we walk through the doors.

"Sorry, Mother, one of my finals ran late." Jace lies. He is covering up for the fact we are late because I had a hard time figuring out what to pack. I squeeze his arm in a silent thanks.

"No matter. Aria, you need to come with me to get ready. Boys, you head upstairs to your rooms to get ready. We only have two hours before the ball starts." Camila rushes over to us.

"I thought I was getting ready with Jace." I look at Jace in confusion.

Camila shakes her head, a frown covering her features. "Oh, no. You need a professional to do your hair and makeup."

"Aria is really good at doing her hair and makeup. She doesn't need a professional to do it." Jace tries to argue.

"Jace, don't push me on this. She is coming with me." Camila says sternly.

Jace sighs. *I'm sorry.*

Don't be. It's not your fault. I'll go with her.

"I have a few dress options for you to try on as well," Camila adds.

"Aria has a dress." Jace requested to have a dress made for me when I agreed to attend the ball. He won't tell me anything about it. But I know I will love it if it is anything like the last dress he had made for me.

"I will still have the dresses brought in. You might like something higher quality than the one you got off the rack."

I flinch. Camila has a way of making me feel inferior. I know the queen is all about image. But it still stings that Camila didn't think the dress would be good enough if I had picked it out.

The slight movement doesn't go unnoticed by Jace.

"Mother, stop." Jace growls at her. "I had a dress made for Aria. It's in our room."

"Oh, well, okay then." She turns to leave. "Come along, Aria. We have lots to do."

Jace pulls me into him. Only the other guys, Conrad and Stan, are in the entryway at this point.

"I am sorry for this. I promise to make it up to you." Jace whispers to me. He kisses me long and hard. I melt into him, enjoying his body pressed against mine.

The guys cat-call and whistle at us.

I pull back, blushing. "You are forgiven."

"Aria!" Camila snaps, clearly getting annoyed at being kept waiting.

I step out of the warmth of Jace's arms, take my bag from him, and run to where his mother is waiting for me at the foot of the stairs.

Disapproval lines her face as I run. I guess it's unladylike to run around. Or she disapproves of my outfit. Considering I am wearing skinny jeans, I'm going to go with a combination of both. The few times I have seen her, she is always in a dress.

"We have the best makeup and hair artists on hand for tonight's ball," Camila tells me as we walk up the stairs. "I want you to shower when I show you to the room where you will be getting ready. We won't have time for you to wash your hair."

I look down at my hair. It is still clean from the morning. "I washed my hair already today."

Camila ignores my comment. "It is a shame you didn't take any etiquette lessons."

I clench my jaw. I do not like the queen. I don't understand how someone as kind and caring as Jace could come from someone as conceited as her.

The queen continues to ramble about my shortcomings as she leads us into a lavish dressing room.

The room has cream walls, black and white tiles, and a large picture window on one wall. In the left corner there is a soft green couch, with a low table in front of it. Off to the side there's a large vanity with a matching green chair. One door leads to the bathroom, and the other to a walk-in closet.

I can see some of the dresses Camila wanted me to wear from here. They are atrocious things. They are massive dresses made from the worst colors that look impossible to walk in. Most are pale colors that would wash me out and make me look sickly. I am even more grateful now that Jace had a dress made for me.

"Go take a shower. The hair and makeup artists will be here when you get out." Camila points to the door on the left.

I hurry into the bathroom. I know trying to argue is pointless.

The room screams wealth, just like the rest of the castle. The floors are white marble, with the double vanity matching. The shower is all glass, and the free-standing tub looks like it could fit several people in it at once. All the fixtures are gold. I don't doubt that they are real gold, either.

I quickly shower, dry off, and wrap myself in my silk robe.

I pad out of the bathroom to find two females whispering to the queen.

"Good, you are clean." The queen says when she sees me. "Take a seat at the vanity. Candice and Holly will get started on you."

I look through the mirror at the two females behind me. They both have curvy figures, deep brown hair, and pale green eyes. I would have to guess they are twins.

"I want you to straighten her hair and slick it back. Make sure her curls are gone; they are too wild to be elegant. Do whatever you can with her makeup to make her look presentable. Nothing that will draw attention to her eyes, though. I don't want people to notice the ugly color." With the comment, the queen leaves the room.

My shoulders drop. I have to fight back the tears that form from Camila's words. I like how I look. I like that my waves are a little wild and my eyes are different.

When I first met Camila, she had at least been somewhat veiled with her insults. Now, it doesn't seem like she cares if I know she doesn't like me. She seems like she is going to do everything she can to make me feel small.

Why are you upset? Jace shoots down the bond.

I'm fine.

Bullshit. I can hear the snarl through the bond. I *can tell someone hurt you. What's wrong, sweetheart?* His voice softens.

I don't want to tell him that his mother insulted me, but I know he won't leave me alone if I don't.

Your mother commented about my waves not being elegant enough and said my eye color is ugly. It's fine.

I try to play it off like it's not a big deal.

Of course, that doesn't work. Jace's rage pours through the bond. My breath catches from the intensity of it.

She said what?

It's fine, Jace. Nothing I haven't heard before.

It's not fine. You should never hear that from anyone, especially from my mother. I'll deal with her.

Jace, really, it's fine. I'm okay. I try to reason with him.

Sweetheart, it is not fine. She hurt you, and I will not accept that. I won't say anything tonight because I don't want to ruin our night. But in the morning, I will speak with her. Please, let me do this.

Okay. I know I can't fight him on it. I am glad that he isn't going to say anything now.

I'm sorry she said that. You know none of that is true, though, right? You are gorgeous.

Thank you, Jace. And I know, I like how I look. But it still stings to hear someone say that.

I know it does. You tell the females working on you to do what you want to your hair and makeup. They'll listen. I'll see you soon.

Okay. See you soon.

I cut the connection and focus back on the two females behind me. "I don't look good with my hair slicked back."

With both my hair and skin so fair, I look bald with my hair slicked back. It's not particularly the look I want for my first royal ball.

The female on the right nods her head. "I would have suggested defining your curls and twisting it half up."

"And for your makeup, we should keep it light and feminine. Maybe winged eyeliner to accentuate the color of your eyes." The other one adds.

I didn't even have to ask them to go against the queen's instructions.

"That sounds perfect. Thank you."

The two females get to work.

Chapter Thirty-Seven

I'm nervous as I stand in the hall leading to the ballroom, waiting for Jace.

The dress he had made for me is perfect. It's an A-line style with fluttery cap sleeves and a slit up the right side, stopping mid-thigh, made from black iridescent tulle. The sleeves and shoulders of the dress are sheer tulle, with the neckline dropping into a deep V. The back of the dress is also open. I love that it is not over the top but still stands out.

"You look stunning."

I spin around to find Jace standing a few feet behind me. My pulse flutters at the sight of him. He is striking in a close-fitting tux with a black bow tie. He wears the same crown he wore to the ball at the academy.

"Thank you." I walk closer to him. "You look handsome."

I straighten his bow tie when I get closer to him. "Thank you again for the dress. I love it."

Jace rakes his gaze up and down my body. "It looks perfect on you." He pulls me flush to him. "Do you have your dagger on you?"

I give him a devilish grin. I slide my leg, not exposed by the slit, up to rest on his hip. Strapped to my thigh is a dagger. "Yes."

Jace's grip tightens on me. He can feel the holster of the dagger against his hip. "Thank you." His voice comes out rough.

I can tell he is itching to kiss me. I want nothing more than to pull his face down and devour his lips.

Jace clears his throat. His pupils are still blown wide. But he tries to bring the conversation back on track. I follow his lead and let my leg drop. "Are you ready for this?"

"I am with you by my side." I smile softly at him.

Jace lets go of me to move to stand beside me. I place my hand in the crook of his outstretched arm.

"I am sorry Killian couldn't make it tonight," Jace says as we walk towards the doors to the ballroom.

"Me too," Killian called me this morning to apologize that he would be late and miss the ball. A unit of soldiers showed up a few days earlier than they were supposed to. So, Killian had to stay and sort out what had happened. He said he would try to portal here if he got things sorted out in time. I'm sad he won't make it, but I also understand that he can't do anything about it.

My mouth pops open as we reach the open doors. Nox hadn't been kidding when he said the ballroom at the castle was even grander than the one at the academy.

The room is huge, possibly bigger than the whole first floor of the academy. The floors are made from white marble, veined with gold. The stairs and the pillars, set throughout the room, are also gold. Two walls are glass doors leading outside to the gardens, and the wall opposite the stairs has a massive fireplace.

The ballroom is set up so the tables line the outer perimeter, leaving the center for dancing. There is a long table set along the back wall in front of the fireplace, where the royal family and the council members will sit. The room has spruce trees in every corner, decorated for the winter solstice. Tiny lights are stringed along the top of the ceiling. Lastly, a large orchestra is set up in the far-left corner, playing a soft melody.

"His Royal Highness, Prince Jace Blackwell, accompanied by Miss Aria Umbra." A herald to the right of the stairs announces our entrance.

All heads turn to us as we descend the steps together. Everyone bows deeply to Jace. Once they finish their bow, they turn their eyes toward me. I tried not to fidget under their stares.

Ignore them. They are just curious as to who you are. I have never brought anyone as my date before. Jace says through our bond.

Really?

I don't know why it surprises me. Jace isn't really social if he doesn't have to be. I just figured his mother would have made him bring someone before.

I have never wanted to bring anyone with me until you.

I flush at Jace's words.

"Your Highness." A male steps into our path once we reach the bottom. He has a thin build, close-cropped golden blonde hair, and soft blue eyes.

"Councilman Felix, good to see you again," Jace replies. Felix's eyes fall on me. "This is Aria Umbra, sir. Aria, this is Chase and Carter's father."

"It's nice to meet you, sir." I dip my head in respect.

"You as well, my dear." He smiles kindly at me.

I instantly like him. He gives off the same warm, comforting feeling that the twins do.

"I am sorry, Felix, but we must be making our rounds," Jace says.

Felix nods in understanding and moves on.

Jace leads me around the ballroom, introducing me to people as we go.

I meet Theon's father and mother- Maximus and Lilly, and Nox's father- Dax.

We stop close to the head table to talk to Theon, Nox, and the twins.

"His Royal Majesty, King Baston Blackwell, and her Royal Majesty, Camila Blackwell." The herald announces.

The king and queen descend the stairs. The king is handsome, with his hair styled back, a black tux, and a gold crown with stars made from diamonds sitting on his head. The queen, on the other hand, is beautiful but severe. Her dress is a snow-white long-sleeved ballgown. She has a more feminine version of the king's crown on. Her hair is pulled back in a tight, low bun. The overall look makes her look cold.

I bow deeply along with everyone else.

Baston and Camila make their way over to where we are standing.

"Aria, you look beautiful tonight." Baston compliments.

"Thank you, Your Majesty." I dip into a curtsy. I am very proud of myself when I don't wobble.

"She would have looked better if she had followed instructions," Camila argues. "As is, she is hardly presentable."

"Mother." Jace growls.

"Camila." Baston snaps at the same time.

Both males do not look pleased with her right now.

My cheeks heat with Camila's disapproval. I had hoped that she wouldn't say anything about how I look since we were in public. Boy, was I wrong.

"Aria looks perfect the way she does." Jace places a hand on my waist, drawing me close.

"Fine, I won't make a scene, but she is not sitting with us at the head table," Camila tells Jace. She doesn't bother to look at me again.

"Why not?" Jace says through clenched teeth.

"There is no room. She can sit with your friends." She says with no emotion.

"I told you three weeks ago that Aria would accompany me as my date. She should have a place at the table."

"Well, she doesn't." Camila walks off before any of us can say more.

"I am sorry, Jace, I didn't know Aria doesn't have a place at our table." Baston apologizes.

Jace rolls his shoulders, trying to relieve the tension in them. "It's not your fault."

"Aria, will you be okay with sitting with your friends?" Baston asks me.

"Yes, sir." I am not happy that I won't be sitting with Jace, but I also don't want to make a fuss over it.

Baston nods and walks over to where Camila is talking with some guests.

"I am so sorry." Jace turns to me.

"It's okay." I try not to let Jace know how upset I am. It's not his fault. From the look on his face, I am failing.

"It's not." He sighs. Jace lifts his hands like he wants to run it through his hair before remembering he can't. He blows out a frustrated breath instead. "I promise I will make this up to you."

The king and queen take their seats. The council members join their lead.

"I need to go sit." Jace sighs again. I can tell he doesn't want to leave me.

The others, who I had forgotten were even there, must have been able to tell, too.

"We have her," Carter tells Jace.

Jace nods and gives my arm a light squeeze before turning to take his seat beside the king.

"Don't worry, we will have more fun at our table anyway." Nox winks at me.

I laugh, not doubting they will make this fun.

I start to follow Nox to the table when Nova steps in our path.

"What is she doing here?" She narrows her eyes in my direction.

Nova looks gorgeous in a forest green strapless ballgown. The low-cut sweetheart neckline has tiny gems sewn heavily along the top and disperse as it trails down the dress. Her long golden hair is pulled up into an elaborate updo. It is the most amount of clothing I have seen her wear.

"The prince invited me as his date," I respond.

Nova's nostrils flare. "Is that so?"

"Yes, now, if you will excuse us, we need to take our seats. Dinner is about to begin." Chase says.

As I go to pass her, Nova stanches my arm, holding it tight. She pulls me close, whispering in my ear so no one else can hear. "I warned you to stay away from the prince, but you didn't listen. Now, you will pay the consequences."

I tilt my head so that I can look Nova in the eye. "And I told you, the prince makes his own decisions."

I tug on my arm, pulling it loose from Nova's grip. I won't let Nova intimidate me.

"What was that about?" Carter asks as we take our seats.

"Just Nova being jealous."

Before the guys can respond, Nova joins us at the table, taking the empty seat beside Nox. "Looks like I am sharing a table with you guys again." She smiles seductively at the guys.

None of them respond to her.

The king stands from his seat. "Welcome everyone to another winter solstice." Everyone applauds. "I won't waste everyone's time with a fancy speech. I know the real reason you are all here tonight, and it is not just for my good looks." That earns a few chuckles from the crowd. "Let dinner be served."

Hordes of servants come rushing out of doors hidden beside the stairs.

The bowl they place in front of me for the first course looks to be a butternut squash soup. I take the biggest spoon and take a dainty sip of my soup. Butternut squash and maple flavors burst into my mouth. It is delicious.

"Oh, look, Aria knows how to use the correct spoon." Nova coos.

We all ignore her.

Once we finish our soups, the servants clear the bowls away and bring out the next course. This time, it is roast chicken with carrots, whipped potatoes, and gravy. It is just as delicious as the soup.

I opt out of dessert when the servants clear away the second course. I am too full.

The orchestra, which had been playing softly up until this point, started playing a louder melody.

I look up to see the king and queen gliding to the dance floor. Guests follow their lead and start towards the dance floor.

"May I have this dance?" Jace's voice floats behind me.

I turn in my seat to find a dazzling smile on his face and an outstretched hand.

I stand from my seat and accept his hand. "I would be honored."

He pulls me in close, once on the dance floor, wrapping one hand around mine and the other on my waist. I place my second hand on his shoulder.

Jace begins to waltz me around the dance floor. I am grateful for all the nights he spent teaching me how to dance properly. I don't falter once during our dance.

"Do you have to dance with other females tonight?" I ask halfway through our second dance. The idea of another female's hands on Jace makes me see red.

Jace's eyes narrow. He pulls me closer, our chests touching. "I only want to dance with you."

"That doesn't mean your mother won't make you dance with others." I don't know why, but I feel the queen will do anything to separate Jace and me.

"She can try." Jace growls. "Besides, we will be making our announcement soon."

I am excited and nervous to announce that we are mates. We didn't tell the king and queen that we planned to announce it during the ball. Jace thought if we did, his mother would try to find a way to stop it.

"Excuse me, Your Highness." Conrad interrupts our dance. His face is lined with concern.

"What's the matter, Conrad?" Jace, not letting go of me, turns to look at him.

"It's the demons, sir. There is an army of them throughout the city." Conrad whispers to us. "The king and queen requested you join them and the council members in the war room to strategize a plan."

My blood turns cold.

"How does the city fair?" He asks Conrad. Anger is rolling off him in waves.

"We don't know yet." Conrad's face looks grim. I wonder if he knows, but can't say with this many people around.

Jace nods his head in understanding. "Let's go." Jace starts to walk off the dance floor, still holding onto me.

"Sir, the queen requested only you come," Conrad says sheepishly.

Jace stops in his tracks. "Aria is coming with me. She is my mate and future queen. She deserves to be a part of this, too."

I smile softly. I guess that is one way of telling people.

Conrad looks between us, a smile slowly creeping across his face. "I knew it. Congratulations, you two."

"Thank you," Jace says, keeping me close. He starts walking again.

"She is not coming with us." Camila's voice is cold as we make our way off the dance floor. "She will only be in the way."

"Mother, stop. She is my mate and deserves to be by my side." Jace grips my waist tighter.

"Jace, enough. We are wasting time when there is an important issue. Come, now." Her tone brokers no room for argument.

Jace opens his mouth like he's going to argue more, but I place a hand on his chest before he can say anything. "It's okay, Jace. Just go."

Jace turns to me, looking defeated. "I'm sorry."

"Go. I will be here when you get back."

Jace reluctantly lets go of me and follows the queen out of the ballroom.

Chapter Thirty-Eight

I'm worried. Jace has been gone for almost an hour now.

After he left, more guards came into the ballroom. The other guests didn't seem to notice that their hosts and the council had left, too busy enjoying themselves.

I want to use our mind link to check in and see how things are going, but I also don't want to disturb him. So, for the last hour, I have been trying to distract myself by talking, dancing, and playing games with Theon, Carter, Chase, and Nox.

I know the guys are in the loop about what was going on from the way they are on high alert. They scan the room every few minutes and pull out their phones for updates.

"If you need to go, I understand." I tried to say earlier.

Nox had waved me off. "I would much rather be in here with you and having fun than in a stuffy war room."

"We have the rest of our lives to do that." Theon agreed.

That put the argument to rest. I appreciate they are willing to stay with me, either on their own accord or at Jace's request.

"I need to use the washroom," I say after another twenty minutes pass.

"I'll go with you." Nox offers.

I shake my head. "I'll be okay. There are guards everywhere." I rise from my chair.

"Look, Jace will kill us if we let you go anywhere alone right now. Please let one of us go with you." He argues.

I sigh. I know Nox is right. "Fine. But I am going in alone."

Nox laughs. "No worries there."

Nox and I exit the ballroom and head down the hall to the bathroom. We only pass one guard on the way.

"I'll be right here," Nox says. He takes up a spot beside the room.

I nod my head and step inside. I quickly do my business and wash up.

I hear a shout from the hall just before I leave the bathroom.

"Nox!" I scream as I open the bathroom door.

I crouch beside an unconscious and bloody Nox. I turn him slightly to find that he is bleeding from his head. Luckily, it doesn't seem to be bleeding too much. I shake him lightly. He doesn't respond.

"I warned you." Nova's voice comes from behind me.

My hand goes to my dagger. I remove it from the holster before turning around.

I stiffen when I see a demon standing beside her. I've never seen one before; only heard stories about what they look like from Killian.

The demon is utterly terrifying to look at. Standing seven feet tall, he has charcoal skin, long sharp claws, razor-sharp teeth, yellow eyes, and large bat-like wings.

My breathing quickens. I am good with a blade, but I have never faced an opponent whose weapon is their body.

"W-what?" My voice comes out wobbly.

"You didn't listen when I said to stay away from the prince. Now, you will face the consequences." Nova smiles darkly at me. "I suggest you run."

I turn my gaze back to the demon. I jump to my feet and run at the look in his eyes. I know I won't be able to defend myself against him. My best bet is to get away.

I only make it halfway down the hall before the demon collides with me. I hit the floor hard, screaming in pain, as the demon drags his claws down my back. It feels like he digs all the way to my spine. Too weak to move, I don't fight as the demon hauls me up by my hair, so I stand on my knees. He scoffs as he sees the dagger still firmly in my hand. Without hesitation, he rips it from me. I can't hold onto it. It goes flying, clattering a few feet away.

Aria? Jace asks through our bond. He must have felt my pain.

"My, my, what a predicament you have yourself in, dear Aria."

I look up to see Victor standing beside his daughter. Confusion weaves through me. What is Victor doing here?

"Look at that face, Nova! Such confusion! Should we explain to her what is going on?" Victor says with a smug look on his face. Gone is the male I met that day by the rink. In his place is the true Victor, just as wicked as his daughter.

"I think that is a good idea, Daddy," Nova says sweetly.

"See, Aria, you are my ticket to the crown," Victor says, with a glint of malice in his eye.

"No." I don't understand what he means, but I won't help with anything.

"You know, you look nothing like your parents." He says, abruptly changing the topic.

I stiffen, the movement causing the wounds in my back to pull. I have to bite my tongue to keep myself from screaming again.

"Excuse me?" I finally say.

Victor smiles. "I always found that curious. See, your mother, Annabella Huxley, had golden blonde hair and deep green eyes, and your father, Lance Huxley, had dark chestnut hair and blue eyes."

It takes everything in me to now show emotion. "I think you have me mistaken for someone else. I am an Umbra, not a Huxley."

"An Umbra by adoption, not birth." Victor corrects. "You see, I have been looking for you for twelve years. I would know you anywhere."

He's been looking for me for twelve years? I can't focus on that right now. I need to get out of here.

"I won't help you." I struggle against the demon's hold.

Jace? I need help. I shoot down the bond.

"You will. I killed your parents. I am not above killing others you love."

I stop moving, stop breathing with those words.

It's him. He is the one who killed my parents. He is the one who kid-napped me. It makes sense to me now why he said he has been looking for me for twelve years. I somehow escaped him when I was five.

Tears stream down my face, not from the pain in my back but from the pain his words cause.

"Why?" I choke out.

"Because they were in the way. I needed you. I needed your power. They wouldn't give it to me, so I got rid of them." He shrugs.

"They were on the council with you!" I shout.

"Oh, they were more than just fellow council members." He chuckles darkly. "Annabella was my sister."

I stare at him, wide-eyed with shock. "You killed your sister?" I can only whisper.

"I will kill many more to get what I want."

Aria, what's the matter? Jace's response finally comes through. His worry for me is evident in his voice.

I thrash against the demon holding me, smashing my head off his face. He roars in pain, losing his grip on me.

I run as soon as he lets go, heading in the opposite direction. I push through the pain in my back.

Jace, help. I am in... Is all that I can get out before the demon slams into me from behind again.

This time, when the demon tackles me to the floor, he smashes my head against it. Warmth trickles down the side of my face. The demon stands, hauling me up with him. He drags me back over to where Victor and Nova stand.

It's then that I notice the guard that we passed earlier. He's slumped to the ground, with a massive hole in the center of his chest, where his heart used to be. Bile rises up at the sight.

"You shouldn't have done that." Victor nods to the demon holding me.

The demon pulls my left arm in the wrong direction, dislocating my shoulder.

I scream in agony. I sag against his hold, no longer able to hold myself up.

ARIA! Jace roars in my mind.

"Any disobedience will be met with punishment. You would be wise to remember that." Victor has a sick look in his eyes, like he wants me to disobey so he can punish me.

"I will never do what you want." I spit at his feet. His eyes darken in disgust.

The demon, still holding me, twists the arm he dislocated, snapping the bone. He doesn't stop there. Next, he turns me roughly and punches me in the ribs multiple times. Bones snap with each hit. White hot pain courses through me.

No one can hear my screams, not with the orchestra playing.

"See, the thing is, you say that you won't do what I want now. But you will." Victor brings my attention back to him.

"*She who is born with lavender eyes will bring forth darkness and command armies to raid the land. She will sit upon the throne and bring forth a new era.*" Victor's voice takes on an eerie tune as he recites the prophecy.

My blood turns cold.

"See, you have unique abilities that are locked away. I just have to find a way to unlock them, and then you will be mine to command." Victor says. I can hear the excitement in his voice.

I don't know what the prophecy means or what Victor is talking about when he says I have locked powers. But I do know that I won't help him. Even if it kills me.

Jace... I try to say more, but I am having a hard time focusing now.

Aria, where are you? Jace sounds panicked.

"Grab her, and let's get out of here before someone notices she is missing," Victor says to the demon.

Before the demon can move, I try to reach for my magic. I will my hands to fill with fire, but only a little flame dances across my knuckles. I am too weak to use my magic.

The demon ignores my pathetic attempt to use my magic and picks me up, throwing me over his shoulder and jostling my broken bones in the process. I whimper in pain.

Aria, Sweetheart, please answer me. Jace pleads with me.

I am being taken by Victor. He is the one who took me when I was little. It's hard, but I manage to tell him that.

I'm going to kill him. Jace vows. *Where are you? I am coming.*

A blast of cold air hits me as Jace asks. I lift my head enough to see us pass through a side gate of the castle. There are two dead guards, holes where their hearts used to be, lying beside it.

It's too late. We are already outside the side gate. I'm sorry, Jace.

No, I am almost there.

I know Jace isn't going to make it in time.

I suddenly remember Nox lying unconscious in the hall.

Jace, someone needs to find Nox. He is hurt.

We'll find him.

"Put her in the trunk," Victor instructs the demon once we reach what must be their getaway car.

I am almost there. Just hold on a little longer. Jace's voice is a broken rasp.

I kick at the demon as he throws me in the trunk, trying to buy Jace time to get here.

"Knock her out. We don't have time for this," Victor growls. "And put the magic binding cuffs on her in case she wakes up before we arrive." He gets into the driver's seat. Nova slides into the car, too.

The demon punches me in the head. It feels like someone threw bricks at me; his hit is that hard. I fall back into the trunk. The demon punches me a second time for good measure. Black spots coat my vision. Before closing the trunk, he removes the vile cuffs from his pocket. He slaps one on each wrist. I can feel my magic drain out of me as soon as they are on. Somehow, the cuffs don't block my connection to Jace. I can still feel him.

Between the broken bones, the claw marks, and head punches, I will lose the battle of holding onto consciousness soon.

Jace, I am sorry we didn't get more time together. Just know you are the best thing that has ever happened to me. Thank you for bringing light back into my life.

Aria, just hold on, please. I am outside the castle now. I'll be there in minutes. He pleads with me. I can feel his desperation through our bond. I don't have the heart to tell him it's too late, that the car is already moving.

So instead, I tell him the words I should have said weeks ago.

I love you.

No, Sweetheart, you hold on and tell me that in person.

I can't hold onto consciousness any longer.

ARIA! Jace's broken cry of my name is the last thing I hear before everything goes dark.

Epilogue

Jace

I was still in the war room when Aria's fear and pain slammed into me, alerting me that something was wrong. I tried to take off instantly, but Mother stopped me. She wanted to know what was going on.

"My mate is in trouble," I yelled at her. I could hear gasps from the other council members in the background. "Move out of my way."

"Let him go, Camila." My father told her. "Conrad, Stan, go with him."

So, now, I am sprinting through the castle, with Conrad and Stan on my heels, trying to get to Aria.

Unfortunately, the war room is two floors up and on the opposite side of the castle. So, it is taking me longer than I want to get to her.

I curse at the fact that I can't portal inside the castle.

I'm being taken by Victor. He is the one who took me when I was little. Aria's response comes through.

Rage, like I have never felt before, rushes through me. It eats away at my soul.

I'm going to kill him. I vow. *Where are you?*

I finally reach the ballroom. Fae dance around, oblivious to the dangers outside.

When we got word about the demons being in the city, the soldiers were able to gather up those who did not attend the ball and bring them inside the castle walls. Luckily, no one got hurt.

Now, the demons are sitting at the castle gates, not attacking. They seem to be waiting for something.

I finally find Chase, Theon, and Carter.

"Where is she?" I grab Chase by the shoulders to get him to face me.

He must see the panic on my face because he doesn't comment on how hard I am holding him. "Aria went to the bathroom. Nox took her."

"How long ago?" I ask. I turn to leave the ballroom to find her. Chase, Carter, and Theon follow me.

"It's only been ten minutes, maybe fifteen," Theon says.

It's too late. We are already outside the side gate. I'm sorry, Jace.

The side gate. I turn down the hall leading in that direction. I run faster than I ever have. There is a sense of urgency, one I can't ignore.

No, I am almost there. I tell her.

Jace, someone needs to find Nox. He is hurt.

We'll find him.

As I say the words, a dead guard and an unconscious Nox come into view.

"Theon, stay with Nox. Aria said he is hurt."

I don't stop. I can't stop. It kills me not to know if Nox is okay. But I have to find Aria.

I am almost there. Just hold on a little longer. I beg her.

Jace, I am sorry we didn't get more time together. Just know you are the best thing that has ever happened to me. Thank you for bringing light back into my life.

It's a goodbye. I know it but refuse to accept it. I can't. I rush through the door leading to the outside. The outer gate is only feet away.

Aria, just hold on, please. I am outside the castle now. I'll be there in minutes.

I love you. She tells me.

I stagger, almost falling to the ground from her words. Words that I was going to say to her tonight, but never had the chance.

I don't tell them to her now, though. I can't.

No, Sweetheart, you hold on and tell me in person.

Aria doesn't respond.

I rush out of the outer gate to find no sign of Aria, no car, no Victor, nothing.

My body gives out, and I drop to my knees. I don't feel the impact of my knees on the hard gravel. The tight leash I had on my magic snaps. The sky clouds over, and rain starts pouring down. Thunder and lightning accompany it. I throw my head back and roar. The sound that comes out of me is nothing short of primal.

ARIA!

She doesn't respond again.

She's gone.

Aria is gone.

Acknowledgements

First off, I'd like to thank my amazing husband. Thank you for the support you've shown me during this journey. Thank you for telling me to go for my dreams and to write this book. Thank you for helping me talk through plot lines, even when you didn't understand what I was saying. I couldn't have done any of this without you.

I'd also like to say a huge thank you to Tabitha Chandler for the incredible editing job. Your work made my book to be the best version it could be. Thank you for helping me achieve my dream.

Lastly, I'd like to thank the readers. Thank you for taking a chance on my book and for your support.

Made in the USA
Las Vegas, NV
18 June 2024

91208703R00164